CANDLELIGHT
Ecstasy Supreme

"WHAT IS IT ABOUT YOU, KATRINA, THAT WON'T LET ANYONE GET CLOSE?"

"And what is it about you," she shot back, "that you're not content to let the situation be? We've had a good time together, so don't push it."

Blair smiled knowingly. "That's your way of keeping your distance from people, isn't it? A sharp tongue, your money, your looks, and whammo—you've got the toughest woman in Texas. I think you enjoy it all, but you're smart enough to know something's missing. I think you're looking for someone to love."

"And I think you don't know what you're talking about. What if I said I was perfectly content with my life?"

"Then I'd say I didn't believe you, and that I'm just the man to change all that."

CANDLELIGHT ECSTASY SUPREMES

Published by
Dell Publishing Co., Inc.
1 Dag Hammarskjold Plaza
New York, New York 10017

Dell ® TM 681510, Dell Publishing Co., Inc.

Candlelight Ecstasy Supreme is a trademark of
Dell Publishing Co., Inc.

Candlelight Ecstasy Romance®, 1,203,540, is a
registered trademark of Dell Publishing Co., Inc.

ISBN: 0-440-15031-0

Printed in the United States of America

First printing—March 1985

LOVESTRUCK

Paula Hamilton

A CANDLELIGHT ECSTASY SUPREME

*This Book Is Dedicated to My Mother
and Father*

To Our Readers:

Candlelight Ecstasy is delighted to announce the start of a brand-new series—Ecstasy Supremes! Now you can enjoy a romance series unlike all the others—longer and more exciting, filled with more passion, adventure, and intrigue—the stories you've been waiting for.

In months to come we look forward to presenting books by many of your favorite authors and the very finest work from new authors of romantic fiction as well. As always, we are striving to present the unique, absorbing love stories that you enjoy most—the very best love has to offer.

Breathtaking and unforgettable, Ecstasy Supremes will follow in the great romantic tradition you've come to expect *only* from Candlelight Ecstasy.

Your suggestions and comments are always welcome. Please let us hear from you.

Sincerely,

The Editors
Candlelight Romances
1 Dag Hammarskjold Plaza
New York, New York 10017

CHAPTER ONE

Katrina Longoria McAllister tried to ignore the ceaseless drone of the Lear's engines. No matter how soundproofed they'd promised to make it, her pilots couldn't block out the insistent noise of restrained power.

Restless, she unlatched her seat belt and walked toward the back of the plane. The colors weren't too bad, she decided. A touch of bold purple on the seats and a lavender and cream wallpaper had improved the once-dreary look of the plane's interior. Katrina was glad it had all been paid for in advance. If the decorator she'd hired to refresh the looks of her airplane were to demand his money now, she thought, he'd be up the proverbial creek without a paddle.

She stopped at the feet of Andy Anderson, her dearest friend. "Andy, I'm still thinking about that old night watchman we've got working out at well thirteen."

Andy pushed back his black Stetson hat, the one he'd insisted on wearing to New York. "I knew it, Katrina. I knew we wouldn't get fifty miles out of Houston before you'd be bothering me about those damned wells again."

He looked out the window and then back at her, tucking one finger into the invisible space between his neck and high-collared shirt. "I'm getting too old for all of this, I'm telling you." He stretched his neck upward and unfastened his starched collar. "I never should of told you about him. It'll be okay," he added with exasperation.

"Not if he's sleeping on the job," she argued, perching herself on the edge of his seat. "And you're not getting too old." Katrina looked down at his crag-lined face and smiled. Right now Andy was the only bright light in her life, she thought—she wouldn't let him get old.

"It won't happen again," Andy said. "I've sent two of your best men around this week to check all forty wells." Andy's face grew red with exertion as he yanked hard at one hand-sewn lizard boot before expertly kicking it off with his other foot. "And if you ask me, you'd be spending your time a lot more wisely if you were thinking about how you're going to ask this Blair Warren fellow for eleven million greenback dollars."

Katrina reached down and helped him remove the other boot, then laughed to herself. If the people who read the Houston society columns and the magazines about the rich and famous could see her now, she mused, they wouldn't believe she was the same woman who traipsed so stylishly across the pages.

Turning serious again, she said, "We can't keep people on the payroll who can't do their jobs. The KLM Oil Company is not running a giveaway program." She swallowed hard. "That's almost a joke."

Their eyes met: the old man's gray, glinty; the young woman's fathomless, dark.

"Why not give the watchman another chance?" Andy said. "Isn't it enough that you've fired thirteen people in the last three months, and that you've got everybody else quaking in their boots waiting for your next fit? Come on, Katrina, you've made your share of enemies and it's not doing you a bit of good."

"Do you want a drink?" she asked, her voice husky with emotion. She turned away from him, frustration pounding at her, her mind filled with the purpose of their trip.

"Since we'll be doing business with this young computer wizard in less than five hours, I'll pass," Andy replied. He took out a can of chewing tobacco, opened it, and stuck in two fingers, pulling out a wad of fresh tobacco.

"That's the only thing I'd like to change about you, Andy."

Katrina poured herself a cup of coffee from the bar, shaking her head as she watched him ball the tobacco up and tuck it into one corner of his jaw. She wondered if he'd done that same thing the day she was born. Probably, she mused. At the ripe old age of sixty-eight, Andy Anderson was as loyal to his creature comforts as he was to her.

As her godfather and her father's best friend, he'd promised on the day she was born, thirty-two years ago, to protect and care for her. He'd never once let her down, though Katrina knew she was headstrong, wildly independent, and too bold for her own good. Often she wondered how he could put up with her.

When her parents had died, leaving her sole owner of one of the largest independent oil companies in Texas, there had been no one she could turn to or trust but Andy, and now here he was, once again by her side—when she was on the brink of losing the entire company.

After her parents had died, Andy suffered a massive heart attack. Unable to turn to him, Katrina had made a monumental error by allowing her distant step-uncle, Albert Barnes, to wheedle his way into her confidence. Before she'd realized what a crook he was, she'd allowed him to help her run the oil company.

Now, two years later, he was suing her, claiming she'd made an oral agreement to make him a partner in KLM in return for his help. He'd even had one of his henchmen swear he had been a witness to the agreement. And now all hell was breaking loose around her.

Katrina had closed her eyes. Andy spoke to her as he neatly stacked his boots next to his leather chair.

"Just because you're famous all around the country as a high and mighty rich gal from Texas don't mean I have to be anything but myself, missy. I ain't the one who goes around getting my picture in the papers and every fortune-hunting man in the world trying to get me to look their way."

Ignoring Andy's wheedling, Katrina looked down at her diamond-faced gold Rolex, wondering if they'd make good time to New York. It had been a long while since she'd been there.

"Did you hear me, missy?" Andy teased. "I read just the other day that you went to some Houston charity ball looking svelte." He laughed. "I'm going to find out

14

what that means if it's the last thing I do. Anyway, your picture's always in those cussed newspapers."

"It's not like I ask for it, Andy."

"No, I guess not," he said with uncharacteristic tenderness. Andy looked over at the strikingly petite young woman who'd rocked Houston on its heels with her absorbing looks, brash manners, and commanding way of doing business.

"There's a lot of things that have come to you that you didn't ask for," he said, "some of 'em real good, like your daddy and your mama. Some of 'em . . ." His voice trailed away to silence.

Katrina felt a burning inside her stomach as she resisted once again the urge to feel sorry for herself. But she knew she didn't have to pretend with Andy. To him, she was still little Katrina, not some hard-edged oil woman or some glamorous prize to be sought after.

"You know, Katrina, your daddy would turn over in his grave if he could see the terrible situation you're in now." Andy slapped his Stetson against the cabin wall and jumped up. "He'd be madder than hell at me for letting this happen to you."

Katrina sighed in frustration, wrapped her arms around him, and nestled her face against his barrel chest. He smelled like bar soap and tobacco, a comfortably familiar smell that she knew she'd always associate with him.

"Andy, you had nothing to do with what's happening right now." She could feel his body begin to loosen up. "Nothing at all. I've made some mistakes that I shouldn't have made, the first one years ago, when I should have been working with my daddy in the business instead of running off to every spot in Europe I could find, trying to entertain myself."

There was no nostalgia in her husky voice, only a hint of regret for what might have been. "And right now," she went on, "I just happen to have my biggest oil rig down, two others mysteriously losing oil after it's piped up out of the ground, and a son of a gun for a step-uncle who's trying to keep my businesses tied up in court until I cave in and give him part of KLM Oil."

She stood back, brushing her long coal-black hair away from her cheek, a steely gleam in her dark brown eyes. "The only problem is that my dear step-uncle doesn't know me very well. I'll go broke and blow it all to hell before I'll let him near KLM Oil."

Andy walked to the bar. "I changed my mind. Just thinking about that jackass Albert makes me thirsty." He quickly poured himself a stiff shot of bourbon and swallowed it, noting that her face was alight with the prospect of stopping her opponent. "No, my beauty," he said, "I don't think he has any idea what kind of little wildcat he's tangling with."

"If things go my way, he'll know soon enough," she proclaimed.

"Miss McAllister, there's a telephone call for you," the young steward said as he stepped out of the pilot's area.

"Who is it?" She watched as the steward hurried to refill her cold coffee cup.

"It's your office."

Katrina took two quick strides to the newly designed corner sofa and turned on the overhead reading light. She smoothed down her white wool slacks and sat down,

16

making herself comfortable as she picked up *Forbes* magazine.

"Andy, why don't you talk to them? If I do, I'm going to tell them to fire that night watchman for sleeping on the job." With a nod she dismissed the steward, and watched Andy open a wall cabinet and pull out the lavender telephone.

"Yeah." Andy's gruff voice rang out as he shot her a dark glare.

With one newly manicured finger Katrina skimmed the magazine's pages until she came to a section marked with a paper clip. Blocking out the sound of Andy talking in his normally loud tone, she studied the picture of a handsome man silhouetted against a giant computer. The article was about Blair Warren, and she read it with immense interest.

With a face that denies his thirty-five years Blair Warren, the newest computer king in America, seems easily approachable. But those who know him say he's a tough negotiator despite his gentle manner. And from one look at his profit sheets it's no wonder he's been described as the shrewdest of the new faces in American business today.

"Pretty impressive," Katrina murmured aloud, and read on about his modest background, his discovery of a microchip which was revolutionizing the computer industry, and his anticipated one-hundred-million dollar profit within the next year and a half.

From his background and the article's reference to his lack of interest in becoming a celebrity, Katrina couldn't help but believe she could handle Blair Warren easily. After all, she thought, she'd handled some of the roughest men around—oil men. A man still reeling from his newfound fame and fortune could hardly be too difficult.

She smiled to herself when she finished reading the article, conjuring up a mental image of the man she was about to meet. It was common knowledge that he was looking to diversify, and if the rumors were true that he might be interested in the high-stakes oil business, she wanted to be the one to introduce him to it. Reluctantly, she closed the magazine and listened to Andy.

"That was Ted on the phone. He says Old Baldy is in bad shape."

"Of course it is. Otherwise the rig wouldn't have broken down."

Old Baldy was the most important well Katrina owned, and the thought of it being shut down gave her nightmares. She hadn't calculated the precise loss, but knew that each day the well was down cost her about ten thousand dollars.

"He wants our permission to call for a new part for the big crankshaft," Andy said.

"Well, why in the hell does he have to ask our permission? Tell him to get it fixed." She raised her voice in unbridled frustration.

"Have you forgotten that every purchase over fifty thousand has to have your approval?" Andy replied just as quickly.

Momentarily taken aback, she stared at him. In a low voice she said, "Give him the okay."

"I already did."

Katrina leaned her head back on the cabin wall, feeling the throb of the engines vibrate against her. "You're right, Andy. My daddy would be terribly unhappy if he could see what kind of a mess I've gotten his company into right now."

Andy started to say something, then stopped himself. He frowned, then spoke softly. "I've seen your daddy in messes almost as bad as this, Katrina. It's that damned step-uncle of yours trying to get your company. Plain and simple. With all your assets frozen while the court takes a look at things, you're in a pickle, that's all." He walked over and sat down next to her.

"But I never should have spread myself so thin," she replied. "If I had more cash on hand it wouldn't be quite so bad, and if I'd spent more time working at KLM when my father was alive and less time partying, I'd have known better." She sighed, staring down at the magazine cover.

A wide smile broke across the old man's face, and he scratched at the few white hairs left on his head. "I don't know if it's the Longoria or the McAllister in you, but it seems fitting somehow. You're the kind of woman who's destined to take chances. And that's a fact."

Hearing his words of praise caused Katrina to reflect back for a moment, back to a time when Andy was a constant visitor to her parents' mansion in the heart of River Oaks, the most exclusive subdivision in Houston. For a long time Katrina hadn't understood why Andy was practically the only visitor to her parents' house. It took a schoolmate to explain the facts to her, facts she'd come to know well.

Working as a wildcatter with a well he'd won in a

poker game, Katrina's father Karl had discovered one of the most productive oil pools in the state in 1941. Overnight he went from a hardscrabble gambler to an oil baron. Suddenly, though he hadn't been born to be listed in the social register, he was Houston's most celebrated citizen; he was somebody.

But when his wife died and left him childless, Karl McAllister married his wife's Mexican maid, leaving the city shocked with scandal. It didn't matter that Beatrice San Miguel Longoria came from a family that could boast of being related to the aristocracy of Mexico before the turn of the century. Nothing mattered except that Karl McAllister had shamed Houston society so deeply that he was never to be forgiven. When Beatrice gave birth to a daughter, the town turned its back.

Katrina remembered running home from school to tell her mother the terrible names she'd been called by her classmates, and her mother taking her into her arms, telling her stories about her great-grandfather fighting in Mexico for independence, soothing her with love and a deep sense of security that could not be shattered. Until she was much older, Katrina never knew why her father had arranged to place her in a private school outside Houston. . . .

Katrina brought herself back to the present. Now, after being raised all her life with such devotion, she vowed there was absolutely no way she was going to lose KLM. She would do what was necessary, she told herself, to hold on to what she'd been so lovingly given. No sacrifice would be too great.

"What should I wear to a business meeting with the newest rich man on the block, Andy?" Still thinking about her parents, she smiled over at him with eyes that were a little too bright.

Scrutinizing her, Andy let his voice become teasing again. "If I looked like you, I'd wear something cut real low and slinky, something to make the fella's mouth water. Now's the time to pull out all the plugs, Katrina." He cleared his scratchy throat. After a few seconds he said, "We're going to have to do whatever it takes to get him to say yes. The man's your last hope."

"How long before we land?" she asked, already thinking ahead.

"About an hour."

"Good. That's just enough time for me to get ready." She began to unbutton the sleeves of her white silk blouse.

"Just pull out some of those real expensive things you're having fitted all the time by those little men with the fancy names." Andy yawned and shook his head. "No wonder everybody makes such a fuss over you. You're a regular clotheshorse." He made no attempt to conceal his pride. "Of course, it's turned out to be a good thing that you are. This way you can tell anybody who's nosey enough to ask why you're in New York that you're here to do that photography session with your friend for *Town and Country* magazine." He winked.

"That's right, Andy, and be reasonable—if I'm going to entice the poor fellow with all my feminine charms, I have to look my best, now don't I?"

"For you it won't be hard."

She walked to the back of the plane, where she'd left her suit hanging, and pulled the curtain. "Call the steward," she said, "and tell him we'll have lunch in ten minutes, Andy. I'll bet you're starving."

"I'd about given up on you. I like to eat at six, twelve, and six again, regular as clockwork," he answered, punching the button for the steward and stretching out on the new sofa Katrina had insisted upon having installed.

"On second thought, Andy, I'm not hungry, so why don't you eat mine and yours too."

He rubbed his growing paunch playfully. "I'd be happy to."

While Andy ate, Katrina took her time changing. She'd carefully chosen what she would bring to New York, and especially concentrated on selecting the suit she'd wear to the initial meeting with Mr. Warren.

Without benefit of shoes Katrina stood barely five feet two inches tall, but she carried herself in such a manner that everyone assumed her to be much taller. Full of enormous energy and stamina, she wore couture clothes with the same self-assured flair she exhibited in everything she did.

With the triple combination of her unique looks, sharp mind, and tough business temperament, Katrina was well known as a formidable businesswoman. In the short time he had worked with her, Katrina's father had trained her to be tough in business, and her mother had emphasized that to think yourself something was to be it.

In addition, Katrina always came prepared. Now, she knew the impression she intended to create for Blair Warren was about to be achieved. She'd applied shiny red lipstick lavishly with a lipbrush, the color emphasizing the striking contour of pearl-white teeth with the olive shade of her baby-smooth complexion. Her hair had been pulled up into a dignified chignon, a few wisps of curl whispering around her face wherever they came loose.

Slipping into the lightweight black wool suit with red piping around the edges of the jacket, Katrina looked at herself once more in the mirror. The slightly raised shoulders of the suit added height, as did the short cut of the jacket. The fitted skirt tapered down to just below the swell of the knee and ended with one deep slit in the front. The bright-red suit lining was exposed with each step Katrina took as she practiced walking in front of the mirror, satisfied with her appearance.

Following her plan, she stepped into red lizard pumps and took out a matching handbag from her suitcase. She wanted Blair Warren to see her as a conflict of personalities. And that was what she was—two people. One was cold, cutthroat, businesslike; the other feminine, all woman. After putting on her two-carat diamond-stud earrings, Katrina returned to the main part of the cabin.

"Whooee," Andy whistled. "You sure as hell don't look like a woman on the edge of financial disaster."

She smiled and sat down in the chair across from him. "Thank you, kind sir."

A deep rumble of laughter came from Andy. "You did good, missy. Real good. He won't know what hit him when you walk in the room."

"Well," she began, "if I look all that good, why don't I just ask him for the thirty million I really need?" She smiled, and her animated face took on a lively air.

"Whooah now, Katrina. Start at eleven. If he's

23

interested, he'll get you the thirty. If he isn't interested at eleven, thirty sure as hell won't do."

"Okay, I just thought I'd make it worth my while."

"Katrina." Andy's voice turned serious. "This ain't no game. This is the most important meeting of our lives."

She stared at her old friend, thinking of all he'd been through with her. When her troubles first began, Katrina had considered pulling a board of directors together. Instead, she'd decided that soliciting the financial support of one individual was more expedient and practical: When the crisis was over she could rid herself of one man more easily than a group.

Andy had agreed, assigning two of her top counselors to study dossiers of the thirty richest people in the world. It took them three days to compile the information. After studying their findings Andy had insisted that, given their conditions, Blair Warren was the best choice. Now she hoped he was right.

She found herself growing edgier by the minute, but tried to hide her concern with humor. "That's why you insisted upon wearing that hat of yours to New York?" she teased, eyeing his wide-brimmed Stetson.

"Hellfire, missy, that's what you call my identity. Besides all that, it's my best hat."

The pilot's phone line was flashing. Katrina deftly opened the hidden cabinet and picked up the receiver.

"Miss McAllister," the pilot said, "we're trying to land at La Guardia and we've been told they have no room for private planes due to a back-up in the commercial lanes. We're being sent to a neighboring airport."

Katrina held the telephone in her hand and looked out the window of the airplane at the pale white foam of clouds. "Hank, I'm not interested in landing at any other airport. My limousine is waiting at La Guardia and I plan to land at La Guardia. Now, if you can't take care of it, I will." Her voice crackled with intolerance. "Understood?" She dropped the receiver back into its cradle before the pilot had time to reply.

In another minute the overhead light went on, signaling them to fasten their seat belts. Andy moved from the couch back to his chair and picked up his boots, putting them on as he spoke. "Now, Katrina, I hope you won't be too . . . Well now, I think you could put this fellow inside the palm of your little hand with a dab of sweet talk. You know what I mean?"

Katrina couldn't see Andy's eyes, but she knew what he was trying to say. He'd often tried to warn her about coming on too strong when she was doing business. Now after listening to his hint, she remained silent. Meanwhile, she was planning how she'd deal with Blair Warren.

"Katrina!" Andy's voice bellowed out as the plane began its descent. "There's more than one way to grease a polecat. If your daddy was here he'd tell you that in his day he didn't always use enough diplomacy."

The air currents caught the plane and lifted it before dropping it down again. Then the wheels landed with a thud and they felt the pressure of the plane breaking to a gradual halt.

"Are you listening to me, missy?"

"Loud and clear," she called out above the shriek of the engine, though she was thinking about something else.

With the federal and state government regulating the

oil industry, she thought, it wasn't easy keeping what one had. On top of worrying about that, Katrina felt guilty about not spending more of her time studying the family business. If she hadn't been such a socialite, she mused, maybe she wouldn't be paying so dearly for her mistakes now. But she intended to live up to her recently earned reputation for being tough-minded, no matter what anyone said—even Andy.

Impatiently, she unlatched her belt and waited for the plane to taxi forward. Out the window she could see the waiting limousine. The pilot stepped out of the cockpit, letting his co-pilot taxi them in.

"I hope you enjoyed your trip, Miss McAllister," he said, helping Katrina up from her seat.

"If we're at La Guardia, I did," she replied quickly.

The pilot looked uneasily down at his boss, not sure whether he should laugh or remain serious.

He nodded. "Yes, ma'am, we're definitely at La Guardia."

"Then I had an enjoyable trip." She let her slow smile overtake him before adding, "There's one more thing. I want you to call back to the office and tell them we've arrived and are on schedule. Then tell them that my orders are to fire the night watchman on well thirteen . . . today."

With her head high Katrina stepped off the plane and into the limousine, ignoring the chortling noises Andy made as he stomped along behind her. She waited until he was seated in the rented limousine, then motioned for the driver to retrieve the luggage, instructing him to deliver it to the hotel after he took them to Blair Warren's office.

They rode to Manhattan in silence, Katrina choosing to ignore Andy's fuming anger, instead turning her full attention to the excitement of the city. New York was a special place to be, she thought.

"Katrina," Andy said, "I'm going to bust in two if I don't get to say what's on my mind."

Katrina pulled her attention away from the sights and sounds out the window. "Of course, Andy, anything."

"You're probably not going to listen. You almost never do, but I just want to warn you not to let yourself get too hard. It's not good."

She let her eyes travel over his wrinkled face and then she looked away. Maybe even Andy didn't understand how desperate she'd been lately, she thought. This was no mere company she was on the verge of losing. This was her family legacy, delivered into her hands with love and faith.

"There's a difference, Katrina, between being a tough businesswoman and being a hard-nosed son of a gun. It's a fine line you have to walk. Be careful that you don't fall off on the wrong side."

His words stung. She didn't like it when Andy criticized her. But he didn't understand how important this was, she thought. No one did.

"I'll try to remember that, Andy." She kept her voice noncommittal, and looked out the window as the driver slowed down then came to a full stop.

Katrina picked up her purse, waiting for the door to be opened. She caught the eye of the chauffeur as he opened the heavy Cadillac door and reached inside to help her out. He'd waited a minisecond, staring at her exposed legs where her skirt had ridden up above her knees.

She glared at him irritably, but it didn't seem to bother him one bit. He let his eyes travel appreciatively up her torso.

"If you manage to keep yourself this absorbed in all your clients I'm sure your business does well," she taunted him.

The chauffeur smiled flirtatiously. "I only keep them on the clients who are the most deserving, miss."

"Well, from now on," she countered haughtily, "you'd best keep your eyes straight ahead." She watched to see if her words had affected him, and was rewarded with a formal nod as he closed the door behind her.

She told herself she should be used to this. Even in New York, home of the most glamorous women in the world, she drew more than her share of attention.

Katrina walked toward Blair Warren's office, aware of the passersby on the street as they turned to glance at her a second time, wondering if she might be a movie star. She carried herself regally, her head proudly lifted in such a way that everyone knew she meant business. She intended to be intimidating, never intimidated. It was all part of the game, she thought.

CHAPTER TWO

The Warren offices were located on the eighth floor of one of New York's most prestigious skyscrapers. Katrina felt her blood pressure rising as they stepped into the steel-encased elevator. Once inside, she resisted the urge to allow herself the luxury of nervousness. Instead, she gave all of her attention to making amends with Andy.

He was scowling at her so hard she wanted to laugh. He had the tendency to carry a grudge forever, she thought, and by his refusal to say anything Katrina could tell he was still cross with her for firing the night watchman.

She smiled beguilingly at him, giving him the same look that had been winning him over since she was a little girl. "Wish us luck," she coaxed when the elevator stopped and they got out.

"Good luck to us," Andy said as they stepped through the wide oak doors of the Warren offices.

The receptionist nodded when they entered. Using his most ingratiating Texas charm, Andy introduced himself. Expecting to be ushered right in, Katrina stood impatiently near the door she assumed led to Blair Warren's private office. But the receptionist asked them to be seated, offering them coffee before going back to her business.

Katrina, unaccustomed to that kind of treatment, ignored Andy's motioning her to be seated. "Do you know what time it is, Andy?" she fumed.

"Yep," he said, pulling out his pocket watch and double-checking the time.

"I don't like to be kept waiting."

Andy put the antique watch back into his pocket and absentmindedly began to twirl his Stetson around his hand. "I know."

"Well, it's rude." Katrina began to pace back and forth in front of Andy.

"Maybe the man is tied up on the telephone, or maybe he's got someone in there he can't get rid of. It's possible, you know."

"I've come thousands of miles to this meeting. If I can be on time, I think the least he can do is give me the same courtesy."

"Now you know how it feels, Katrina." Andy kept twirling his hat.

She stopped her pacing. "What do you mean?"

"Have you ever taken a look outside your office?" Andy wore a lopsided grin. "I don't think you've ever been on time before in your life."

Katrina knew better than to try and deny it. "That's beside the point. The man shouldn't be doing this now."

"Just stay cool."

Katrina sat down in the steel-and-chrome chair next to Andy. "I know how to play this game, Andy. I've had winning poker hands before," she reminded him as she took out her compact and began to study herself in the mirror.

"I'm counting on you, missy. Just play those cards close to your chest. We don't want this Warren fellow knowing any more than he has to. So far nobody knows how bad things are for us. Let's keep it that way as long as possible."

Katrina opened her mouth to remind Andy that he wasn't telling her anything she didn't know, but then it dawned on her: He was nervous. That was why he rattled on about things they'd been over time and time again.

Just when Katrina was considering whether to leave, the receptionist walked over to them. Katrina watched her break into a broad grin as she gave Andy's finely polished boots and his huge hat a quick study.

"Mr. Warren asked me to invite you into his office. Follow me, please," she said, making eye contact with Andy.

With her head raised, Katrina followed the receptionist into a cavernous room filled with computers and unidentifiable machines clicking and whirring noisily. Then they entered a side door and stepped into an office as quiet as the other one had been loud. Tall windows ran along one wall and abstract paintings covered the remaining three walls with ultra-bright colors. In the center of the room sat a rectangular glass table on brass legs, the table flanked by four modern chairs.

The room looked as if it were never used, Katrina

thought, and her reaction was was swift and unfavorable: It was far too impersonal for her taste.

"Mr. Warren will be right with you. Please have a seat," the receptionist said, and then left.

Blair Warren entered the office just as the receptionist was leaving. For a moment he stood at the threshold, eager to catch his first glimpse of Katrina Longoria McAllister, a woman whose image had virtually become burned in his mind since he'd begun his detailed investigation of her a few weeks earlier.

Silhouetted by the light from the window, he saw her as a small woman in a very expensive, very sophisticated two-piece suit. Her hair was piled high on her head, black and shining, catching the light in flickering glimmers from the overhead chandeliers and the outside sun. Her figure was full, and her skin coppery—as if her ancestors and the sun had been dear old friends, he thought. She had the hollowed cheeks of a model and curved red lips.

Her dark eyes widened when she spoke his name. It made the hair stand up on the back of his neck. He took a deep breath, knowing better than to try and fight the primal instincts so suddenly aroused in him. Katrina Longoria McAllister was spectacular, he realized.

"Yes, Miss McAllister," he replied, and walked directly over to her, taking her small hand into his. "I apologize for keeping the two of you waiting." He nodded to the man with her, hesitant to let go of the soft hand. But he did, offering it to her companion, who took it and began pumping.

"Mr. Warren, I'm Andy Anderson. It's good to meet you, boy."

Katrina watched Blair Warren's smile deepen in response to Andy, and she took the opportunity to study him while the two men talked. He stood a little taller than average, although she knew she was a poor judge of height. To her, practically everyone seemed tall.

His face was much stronger-looking than the picture in the magazine had shown. His hair was not blond and not brown, but sandy-colored, giving the impression that it might lighten easily in the sun. His hazel eyes were deeply set above prominent cheekbones, his profile lean. There was a pleasant ruggedness to his face and a provocative quality to his eyes. Blair Warren looked much more commanding, Katrina thought, than she'd expected.

"Won't the two of you sit down?" he asked, motioning them around the table. He slid Katrina's chair back for her and watched the old gentleman casually seat himself next to her.

Blair had been prepared for Andy Anderson. He was exactly what Blair had pictured—a shrewd old Texas roughneck, wholeheartedly loyal to the young woman at his side. But Blair was a bit surprised about Katrina McAllister. He knew from numerous pictures he'd seen that she was a petite woman, a beauty, but now that he'd met her he had a hard time believing that all the dark rumors he'd heard about her could be true.

Time and again he'd been warned about her, yet now he was confused. Why had he spent an entire week planning an offensive strategy to force her to accept his offer? he wondered. She didn't look at all formidable. Deep in thought, he started to shake his head, then stopped himself. His informants had warned him that dealing with her would be like taking on four Texas-sized rattlesnakes poised to strike, but this diminutive woman looked more like a disarmingly genteel southern belle.

He smiled again. "Would the two of you like some coffee? Have you had lunch?" he asked.

"Well . . ." Andy began.

"We're fine, Mr. Warren. Maybe later. After we've finished our talk." Katrina gave Blair Warren her most beguiling smile.

Remembering that Andy wished she'd go easy, Katrina could feel him twitching in his chair. But despite Blair Warren's courtesy, she hadn't forgotten that he'd left them cooling their heels in his reception area and she wanted to make sure he understood with whom he was dealing.

Since taking over KLM Oil Katrina had continually been forced to proved herself. The oil business was a man's world, a world that scoffed at the idea that a woman—especially a woman who looked like Katrina—could have a place in the business. Sometimes she wondered if it would have helped if she were eight feet tall and ugly, but she knew it wouldn't have mattered. She decided that the only way she could make an impression was to be as tough as the men who dominated the business, and she'd worked hard at it.

"I propose we get right down to business, Mr. Warren," she said, reaching down to pull out two sheets of paper from the attaché case Andy had brought with him. She handed him the papers containing reports of her profits the last two years and a projection for the next two years.

Blair listened, keenly aware of Katrina's huskily melodic voice. Once again he felt the hairs on the back of his neck tingle. She spoke with such a rich quality, he thought, she could have been a singer. He was captivated just listening to her speak. The fact that behind the lulling vibrations there seemed to be a hint of steel didn't alarm him at all.

"You don't believe in wasting any time, do you, Miss McAllister?" he said. "I had hoped to take the two of you on a tour of my offices. We have a working office here, as you probably saw in the outer room, all the latest computers and a bank of talent trying to improve them." Blair looked at Andy, who seemed interested, and Katrina, who sat with both arms on the table, her body leaning forward, not even attempting to conceal her spirited impatience.

"Again, maybe later, Mr. Warren," she insisted. His laid-back style troubled her. She supposed it was merely his personality, but his casualness was distracting. Right now she had no time or interest for anything but her business, she told herself.

"Please, call me Blair."

"All right, Blair." She leaned away from him as he sat down in the chair across from her and put his hands on the table without touching the papers. She wondered if the intense way he had of looking directly at the person to whom he spoke was a negotiating ploy or an integral part of him. She noticed that the faint laugh lines around his hazel eyes deepened when he talked, and that his nose narrowed nicely above a slightly crooked mouth.

"Now then, can we get on with our business?" She

was growing more and more impatient, eager to hear what he'd say when she made her proposal. "I've come to offer you a chance of a lifetime, an opportunity which is so special, so unique, that it's difficult to comprehend. No one outside of my family has ever had the chance to invest money in the most productive independent oil company in the country. I've come to talk to you about an opportunity which each and every one of the big seven oil companies would give their eyeteeth to have, an opportunity which is being offered solely to you."

He kept his eyes riveted on her as she spoke, taking note of the expressive way her eyes flashed and danced, and the way her entire body seemed to vibrate with intensity. He couldn't define what made her so compelling. He'd find out soon, he thought.

"I see," he said, glancing over at Andy, wondering if the two of them thought he had been stupid enough not to have thoroughly investigated KLM Oil.

"If you'd look at the sheet"—she turned one page around so that he could see it—"I'll explain my offer."

"Fine, Katrina, that's fine."

For fifteen minutes she talked non-stop, presenting her case for investing in KLM Oil. He didn't interrupt. He kept his attention focused totally on her, absorbed as much in the woman herself as the skewed facts she was presenting.

Once, he almost let his glance wander. She was moving her hands, caught up in the fervor of her speech, and he wanted nothing more than to take the time to watch the way her small, delicate fingers moved through the air. But Blair kept his eyes on her face. And once, as she spoke in her sultry Texas drawl, he listened to an inner voice reminding him to keep his thoughts impersonal: This was strictly business.

When Katrina began, she exercised total control, expressing herself precisely as she'd planned. But the longer she talked, the more her convictions swelled to the surface. She let her voice dip and sway, and felt like a spinning top gathering speed as she heard her convincing words reverberate throughout the room.

Before she realized it, Katrina was summing up. ". . . and so we hope that you'll join us. I can virtually guarantee you won't ever regret it." She stopped, then turned to Andy. "Do you have anything to add?"

"No, missy, I don't," he said with a shake of his head. "Let's hear from Blair, here."

Blair stood up and began to walk around the room. "Your proposal sounds very interesting," he said.

A warning knell sounded in the back of Katrina's head, and her heart sank. She didn't want interesting, she wanted a definite yes.

"What are your bottom-line terms?" Blair spoke from across the room, where he was looking out at the Manhattan skyline.

"I just gave you my terms," Katrina replied, trying to keep her voice unemotional. Andy was looking at her with a question in his eyes. What was Blair driving at?

"You wouldn't consider an offer, a compromise?"

"Take it or leave it," she insisted, her pulse quickening.

"Very well. I'll tell you what. Why don't I take the two of you to dinner and I'll let you know tomorrow morning? How's that?" Blair walked back to the table and stood looking down at her.

Katrina leaned back in her chair, confident she could win him over. "I had hoped we could settle this today."

His hazel eyes darkened to amber. "I'd like to have a little time to think it over."

"Now, Blair, don't you know how we women are?" She gave him her most feminine smile. "We can't bear suspense." She put one hand daintily on his arm and stared up at him. "I do think it would be best for all of us if you were to let us know today."

Realizing she was obliquely managing to push him into some kind of commitment with her flirtatious charm, Blair let his eyes trail from the point where her hand rested on his arm to her sparkling eyes. "If you insist, Katrina," he said pointedly, "then I'm afraid I'd have to say no to your offer."

Automatically, she stood up. "Why?" she asked crossly. "I don't understand."

"Because you leave me no room for negotiation."

Immediately she realized that the expression on his face, the one she'd thought to be gentle, had become hard and intractable. How much, she wondered, had she misjudged this man? He wasn't going to be nearly as easy as she'd thought, she realized, and a quick glance at Andy told her to step lightly.

"All right," she said with a wave of her hand, "you tell me what you're interested in."

"You'll negotiate?" Blair asked, acting as if he might sit down again.

Katrina gave a short laugh. "Mr. Warren, no matter what anyone says, everything's negotiable." She raised one arched brow and waited for him to make what he would of her words. "Tell me what you want," she added softly.

He pulled out his chair, but instead of sitting he walked toward the outer office and left the room. Katrina looked at Andy.

"Just keep smiling, missy," he said. "Let's see what he's up to. If he makes an offer anywhere close to what you want, tell him we'll go to dinner with him and think about it. This boy's already taken with you, I can tell."

"Oh, really?" Katrina laughed. "That's funny. I'm beginning to think he's about as warm as his computers." She sat back in her chair.

"Now, Katrina, you weren't looking for a pushover, were you?" Andy started to chuckle but stopped himself when Blair returned and sat down across from them, laying a thick manila folder on the table.

"I want to be made a partner," he said. "To do that I'm willing to bring to KLM Oil a total of thirty million dollars, rather than the eleven you're asking for." He watched Katrina's face.

She answered coolly, taking no time to think it over. "That's impossible. We're oil people—one hundred percent family-owned and independent. I intend to see that it stays that way."

"Then you must understand my position. There's no chance that I'd be interested in anything less."

He couldn't help but admire the way she behaved, sitting coolly erect and speaking in slow, measured phrases. He could see she was a woman who was very sure of herself, and he hated that they were about to clash in corporate combat.

Katrina put her hand out, picked up the sheets of paper she'd laid on the desk, and matter-of-factly tucked them back into the attaché case. "There's nothing more to be said, Mr. Warren."

He shrugged his shoulders and squared his jaw. "Not as long as you're willing to risk losing KLM. I had the impression you were devoted to your company."

"I am. Of course I am," she bristled.

"Then I think you'd better talk to me. My sources tell me I'm your last hope."

"Mr. Warren, I can assure you that there are many people out there who'd like to invest in KLM Oil. In fact," she said icily, "you should consider yourself lucky it was offered to you at all."

Blair reached over and opened the manila folder, spreading the sheets of paper inside it around the tabletop. The way she handled herself reminded him of his friends' earnest warnings about her. "The true facts are all here, Katrina. Not the embellished ones you gave me earlier. See, I know the truth."

Her eyes flashed with brilliant color. "I don't know what you're talking about." It was like dealing with Jekyll and Hyde, she thought. He was a completely different man from the one she'd been introduced to.

"I'm talking about the true conditions of KLM. I'm talking about how your largest oil well is down and losing you big money, and as of eight o'clock this morning you haven't even approved the repair order on it. I'm talking about how many storage tanks you've got that are somehow losing the oil before it can be shipped off. I'm talking about how you've tied up your cash so that you can't begin to help yourself, and how you've let your step-uncle get you into court so he can see your records and maybe take your company away from you. I'm talking, Katrina"—his voice became low and threatening—"about how you've managed to screw up one of the finest independent oil companies in the world in less time than it takes a farmer to raise a good cotton crop."

The entire time Blair talked, Katrina felt Andy watching her carefully. Bit by bit Blair hit upon her confidential problems, leaving her stripped and isolated. Feeling her face flush and her throat tighten, she wondered if Andy could sense her shame.

She'd come here at Andy's request, she thought, to see if this cold, calculating man she'd fancied could save her dream as well as her business. Instead, he'd gone for the jugular. She didn't think she could bear the indignity of it.

"I've been told you're a clever woman, Katrina, but not a fool. I think my offer is very reasonable. You need someone to help—"

"My dear Mr. Warren," she cut in, "you can take your offer and stuff it into your computer terminal."

Grabbing her purse, Katrina pushed back her chair and stormed out. Andy could take care of himself, she thought. He knew where the hotel was. And as for Blair Warren, she didn't give a damn what he did.

Angered far beyond rational thinking, Katrina swung the heavy glass door of the building open and charged out into the New York crowd. She heard the hired chauffeur call out to her, but she ignored him and instead plunged ahead, passing people like a jogger in a footrace.

She knew she'd made a terrible mistake—a costly one. She misjudged Blair Warren and instead of altering her plan, proceeded full steam ahead. Now she realized that Blair was the sort of man—with the looks, style, and demeanor—who was totally confident and sure. Game playing, conniving ploys—all the things she'd been forced to do in business—would go against his nature. She'd obviously underestimated him.

Katrina ignored a stoplight and felt a hand on her shoulder as someone from out of the crowd grabbed her and pulled her back to the curb before she was hit by a car. Turning around to thank the stranger, she happened to glance back down the street in the direction she'd come. Stunned, she saw Blair loping toward her, his sandy hair blown back from his face, his jaw set with determination.

Wanting not to be caught by him, she began to run, weaving her way in and out of the cars. After she'd made one long block, Katrina took a quick left down a side street and hailed a passing cab.

"Take me to the Palace Hotel, and hurry," she huffed, jumping in and slamming the door behind her.

The taxi driver stopped working his crossword puzzle to gaze indifferently at her through the rearview mirror. Then he resumed what he was doing.

Still gasping, Katrina looked back in the direction she'd come. If Blair was still after her she couldn't see him in the sea of faces. "Please hurry!"

"Lady, I'm not moving. Didn't you see my off-duty

sign? That means I'm not moving." The driver turned back to stare at her.

"Now I remember why I always hire a limo," Katrina muttered. "Look, this is important."

"So is my break. I can't take you."

Infuriated, she looked back just in time to see Blair running down the street. "I've got to get to the hotel!" she yelled.

The driver shrugged his heavy shoulders and lifted up his hand. "Then you'd better get out. It's union rules. I can't go nowhere for fifteen minutes."

"I'll pay you double your usual price." Accustomed to deferential treatment, Katrina had forgotten how difficult people could be when they had something she wanted. Today, she realized, was indeed her day for finding out. "Triple. I'll pay triple."

"Get out, lady." The driver swung his door open, stepped out on the street, and yelled at her inside the cab. "This is *my* cab and I'm telling you to get out."

"And it's a beautiful day for a walk," Blair said, opening the door nearest Katrina and pulling her out. "Come on. I want to show you some of the city."

Silently, Katrina allowed him to help her out of the cab, aware of the bystanders watching them. Once out on the street, she glowered at the taxi driver, who got back inside his cab and locked all four doors.

Blair held her arm, afraid if he let go she'd stomp away. "Do you start fights with everyone you meet?"

"Do you follow people around just to prove how annoying you can be?" she replied haughtily, trying to wrench her arm away from him without making a further spectacle of herself.

"No, not really." He let go. "Good grief, you're awfully strong. No wonder the cabbie locked his doors."

"What happened to Andy?" she asked.

"He said he'd meet you back at the hotel."

She swung around and began walking down the street at a brisk pace, but she could still hear his footsteps directly behind her. At the corner she took a right and was immediately sorry. There weren't very many pedestrians on her side of the street.

Doggedly, he stayed right behind her. When they reached the next corner she waited until he'd caught up to her, then turned stiffly toward him. "I have a low threshold for boredom, Mr. Warren, and you are boring me. Do you understand?"

"I understand, all right." He paused for a moment and stared at her. "But I'm going to have my say, one way or another."

The way he said it, she believed him. She caught the command in his voice and the suggestion of unleashed power. This was the second time today she'd underestimated him, she thought.

She walked across the street and turned back to look at him. He was standing on the corner, hands in the pants pocket of his pin-striped suit, looking not at all as she wanted him to. Blair Warren seemed every bit as sure of himself as she did.

"Say it from where you are and be done with it, please," she called.

"Okay," he agreed with a swift nod, and started walking quickly toward her. When he reached her side he grinned. "I was afraid you wouldn't hear me from over there."

"I am very bored," she replied, tapping her foot and glancing around for something else to look at. Actually, Katrina was trying to figure out why he seemed to be getting the upper hand.

"I'll bet you are," he replied dryly. "And just for the record, I'm not exactly having the time of my life."

"Is that what you wanted to say?" she demanded.

"What I wanted to say is that I'm sorry, Katrina, for the way I acted back there in my office. I mean that most sincerely."

Her throat tightened as she recalled the exact words he'd used. "Good-bye, Mr. Warren."

"Wait." He reached out and took her arm again before she could leave. "I know there's no excuse for my actions. I came on too strong. I have a lot on my mind."

She shook her head. "Don't we all!"

"I know that's no excuse. But for a minute there I nearly forgot I wasn't dealing with a man."

"You don't have to treat me with kid gloves. I spend every day of my life dealing with men," she lectured, feeling unexpectedly defensive, brusquely freeing her arm from his grip.

"No, I was too hard on you." He tried to take her arm again.

"I can handle myself," she countered, pulling her arm away and folding both arms defiantly across her chest.

"Oh, I have no doubt," he answered with a crooked smile whose appeal shocked her. "See, I believe you can handle just about anything."

Feeling an abrupt shift in the tension between them, she retorted, "Now you're being insolent, Mr. Warren."

"Fine. I won't be insolent if you won't play games with me, Katrina."

Grudgingly, she had to admit that she admired the way he stood up to her. Most men either patronized or tried to con her. With Blair Warren she felt on fairly equal footing, even though they seemed to be seesawing back and forth. She was more than a little surprised, and found herself enjoying the feeling.

A smile spread across her face and he held out his hands in an open gesture. "What do you say we start all over?"

She gave him a nod that might have meant anything, and started walking again. Now that he had apologized, Katrina thought of Andy and knew he'd want her to try to win Blair Warren over. Game playing was a big part of the oil business, she mused, a nasty part, but this might be her most important game—a game she had to win.

Blair walked beside her, his pace measured so that the two of them were in step together. Katrina was very much aware of his presence, of his eyes on her—so much so that suddenly she had the overwhelming urge to tell him the truth and get it out in the open.

It had to be his eyes, she thought, that made her think he could look at her, picture the truth inside her, and store it away. It was as if he were focusing only upon her—there was nothing else going on in the world.

"Do you think you and I could spend some time together," he said, "maybe go to dinner and get to know one another—all business aside?"

They stopped in the middle of the sidewalk, ignoring the people who grumbled as they stepped around them.

A bag lady walked by, eyeing Katrina's bright red purse. A breeze dipped down from the sky and blew odds and ends of trash from the streets, swirling it around their feet. He stared at her with intensity, and she realized she felt a twinge of melancholy.

Finally she answered him. "No, I don't think so."

"Why not?"

"Because I didn't come here to make friends. I came strictly for business."

"Where's your sense of humor, Katrina? I would think a woman of your caliber would have a strong sense of humor."

"I left it in my suitcase."

Suddenly they were on a different level altogether. Her breath came uneasily, and she felt as if she might have to come up for air. Slowly, she began to walk again, knowing that somehow they'd crossed the barrier from acquaintances to something more, and it rocked her right down to her toes.

"Which should be in my hotel by now," she said, referring to her suitcase.

"Why don't we just go to your hotel then and pick it up?"

Katrina knew he was making casual conversation, but that there was also a different discussion going on between them. She could sense it so strongly that she imagined she could reach out and touch it.

"Why don't we say good-bye right here?" she said, trying to regain the detachment she'd once had.

"Because I don't think you've completely forgiven me, and I don't want you to leave. It's as simple and as complicated as that."

The street traffic began to pick up, and the early afternoon New York shadows fell across them. The practical side of her wanted nothing more than to go to her hotel room, have a drink with Andy, then take a long hot bath before going out to eat in one of her favorite restaurants, maybe Pearl's. The wild, irresponsible side of her wanted to find out why this exasperating man so intrigued her.

"I know what you're thinking," he said shamelessly. "You're trying to decide if I'm worthy of your interest."

She shook her head and looked straight ahead. "All I'm trying to decide is which direction to go to find the Palace Hotel."

His laugh was a low, rolling sound, full of vibrant life. Once again she felt melancholy.

"Why don't you give it some thought," he said, "and if you'll agree to let me take you to dinner one night before you leave, I'll tell you how to get to the Palace Hotel."

"Is it close by?" she asked.

"Will you let me take you to dinner?"

"A business dinner?" At least when Andy asked she could tell him she'd tried.

"A business dinner." He smiled.

"I'll have to think about it."

He shrugged his shoulders. "You didn't say no. Come on, it's this way." They walked in silence for a few minutes.

"How far are we going?" she asked.

Blair turned, moving his head slightly, his electrifying eyes meeting hers. They stared at one another, neither one willing to break the connection.

"I'm not sure yet," he said. "If we were betting right now, though, I'd say we're going very far."

She'd had a thousand suggestive comments tossed her way, and had held her own with every kind of man imaginable. But when he spoke those words, Katrina felt her blood pound, and suddenly her mouth was dry and parched.

"How far to the hotel, Blair? That's all I'm asking."

As he led her across the street she glanced at him, trying to ignore the troubled sensations inside her body, and then she looked quickly away again. Play your cards close to your chest, she thought. Wasn't that what Andy had said?

But Katrina realized there was a side of her that felt a distinct, almost overwhelming physical attraction to Blair, a feeling she'd never planned on, never even considered. On top of everything else happening to her, it left her feeling defenseless, and she knew she couldn't afford the uneasiness.

She saw the hotel down the side street and walked faster, telling her tired feet to stop their complaining. "Thanks for the directions," she said, and sauntered toward the side entrance without looking at him again. Something told her there had already been too much said in the silent looks they'd shared, and that her poker hand was at best shaky right now. She'd better stay away from him, she thought, if she wanted to make the deal.

"I'll call you tomorrow morning," Blair said, watching her walk majestically away.

He stood there a long time, staring at her and then at the hotel doors she'd passed through, then shook his head vigorously and turned to hail a cab.

CHAPTER THREE

"What are you going to say when he calls, Katrina?"
Andy was sipping his first early morning cup of black
coffee, ordered from room service.

They were sitting in the living room of her hotel
suite. Outside, New York commuters were scurrying to
work, the street noise bombarding them through the
windows.

"I don't know," Katrina replied. "I guess I'll play it
by ear." She knew her feeble answer wouldn't satisfy
Andy for long. "He may not even call," she added
teasingly.

"He'll call all right, missy. I saw the look on his face
when you stomped out yesterday. Besides, after what
you told me about his following you, I'm sure of it."

Andy sat across the small table from her, wearing a
different pair of handmade boots and a western-cut tan
suit, ready for his morning appointment with a very
important Chase Manhattan banker. Back in Houston
he and Katrina had agreed they'd make the most of
their East Coast trip, contacting people they might

need if things became so desperate that Katrina was forced to consider declaring bankruptcy.

Dressed in a pale blue Christian Dior peignoir, Katrina sat sipping her coffee. On and off during the night she'd tried to sort out her impressions of Blair Warren. Normally she paid close attention to people and was a good judge of character. But after she'd so badly underestimated Blair the day before, she didn't quite trust herself to figure him out.

"Katrina, that man is ready to loan you the money," Andy said. "If he wasn't, he'd have let you walk out of his office yesterday without another glance. Now the first thing you've got to do when you talk to him today is find out how he got his information. Do what you have to do, but find out his source."

Stabbing a fresh croissant with her fork, Katrina lost what little appetite she'd had. The mounting stress was getting to her. "I was afraid to push him too hard about it yesterday."

"I know, but we've got to find out. The court has issued a standing order that your assets and liabilities are to be disclosed in a certified financial statement, and the statement's due in five days. At this point we thought no one else knew about your being dangerously short of cash." Andy shook his head in regret. "But somebody told Blair, and if he tells anyone else, all hell's going to bust loose for us. We can't hold out past the day we file your financial statement."

She nodded, pushing her plate away. Everything, it seemed, was coming down on her at once.

Andy was talking hard business facts and her mind was full of Blair. One minute she was telling herself

51

there was nothing wrong with mixing business with pleasure, just as long as the pleasure didn't get in the way of business; the next minute she was reminding herself of the high stakes involved.

Andy looked down at his watch, and stood up. "Two things you've got to do when you talk to this Warren fellow. First, find out who in our organization leaked information, and second, convince him that he needs to invest in KLM." Andy grinned. "That's a tall order, I know, but you can do it, missy." He reached over and chucked her playfully under the chin.

The telephone rang. Andy went to answer it while Katrina stepped into her dressing room. Her photography session for *Town and Country* magazine was less than an hour away, and although there would be a make-up artist at the studio, she wanted to do her own hair because she was never satisfied with the way other people styled it.

"Katrina, it's for you," Andy informed her.

"Okay." She walked back across the room, took the phone, listened for a few minutes, then gave a tight-lipped order and hung up.

"When it rains it pours. Isn't that what you always say?" Katrina asked Andy.

"What's up?"

"They can't get the replacement part for Old Baldy right away. There's going to be a ten-day delay."

"Why the hell—" Andy barked.

"Who knows? Maybe I'm being a little paranoid, but I'll bet dear Uncle Albert has something to do with it." She shook her head in despair. "And the wells up by Lubbock are still losing oil. One of our men disappeared from the area yesterday. They don't know whether he just walked off the job or whether to suspect foul play. Right now the sheriff says there's no evidence to warrant an investigation."

The telephone rang again.

"I don't want to talk to anyone, Andy. Things can't get much worse, but in case they are I don't want to hear it."

Andy grabbed the phone and caught it on the third ring. "Yeah," he said briskly. Then his voice changed abruptly. "Well, sure. Uh-huh, just a minute and I'll get her."

He put his hand over the mouthpiece. "It's Blair. He wants to talk to you."

Katrina ignored Andy's grin. The prospect of hearing Blair's voice, knowing he was waiting at the other end, made her apprehensive. The complications in her life, she thought, were multiplying by the second. She reached for the phone.

"Pour on the charm, Katrina." Andy's grin spread as he handed her the phone.

"Hello," she said.

"Katrina, this is Blair. How are you this morning?"

His voice sounded as if they might be in the same room. It came to her in a rush of intimacy which only served to intensify her edginess.

"I'm fine," she managed to say. "And you?" Katrina wished Andy wasn't there. She felt her face flush. This was her first experience with reticence and she wasn't handling it very well.

"Hmmm," he said. "I don't know whether to tell you

53

the truth and say I went to sleep dreaming about you last night, or give you the standard 'I'm fine too.'"

Sitting on the edge of his bed, Blair held the telephone in a tight death grip. He was telling the truth. He had thought of her last night. He'd gone to bed with her on his mind and dreamed about her—a seductive dream that had been vivid with unabated passion. When he awoke, he told himself to be cautious. He'd met a beautiful, wild, impetuous woman, but she was not interested in him, only in what he could do for her.

"I'm fine," Katrina answered coolly.

She was trying to concentrate only on getting the necessary information from him, but when she switched the telephone from one hand to the other, she saw faint beads of perspiration building along the creased lines in the heart of her palm. Reacting as if Blair could see them also, she brushed them away.

"Okay," he agreed. "I want to take you to dinner tonight. I'm hoping you'll say yes."

"Tonight?"

"Yes."

Andy had been pacing across the room, watching her as she talked. Now he stopped and bobbed his head up and down.

"I'm sorry, Blair, but I'm already committed," Katrina replied, despite Andy's entreaty.

In the past, Blair's impulsiveness had always worked well for him, taking him from an average middle-class life as the son of a midwestern grocery store manager into the world of computers and megabucks. Now, feeling as impulsive about Katrina as he had since meeting her, Blair impatiently said, "Please cancel your plans."

He added with authority: "I shouldn't have to tell you that this is very important, especially since we have unfinished business."

"Well, if it's business," Katrina replied, "perhaps I should bring Andy along."

She could hardly think, watching Andy waving his hands in frantic appeal, acting like he'd gone mad. Purposefully, she turned her back so she couldn't see any more of his gyrations.

"I think we could get some specific things settled if it were just the two of us," Blair said. "I'll pick you up at your hotel at seven. Good-bye," he concluded, hanging up before she could argue with him.

"I swear, missy, you are going to give me another heart attack," Andy hissed. "What did he say?"

Katrina sat down on the nearest chair, distinctly aware of how glad she was that Blair had ignored her suggestion to bring Andy. "We're going to dinner—just the two of us." She sighed, looking down at the floor.

"That's good. For a minute there I thought you were going to shoot us out of the saddle for good. Now go easy with that man, missy. Go easy."

Pushing back her shoulders and glaring at him, Katrina answered, "There's no way I'm going to mess up this deal, Andy. Believe me, if I act like he's more important to me than I am to him, he's going to think he's definitely got the upper hand." She stood up and put her hands on her hips argumentatively. "I'll handle our new friend Blair in my own way. If I come on too pushy with him he's going to be convinced I'm desperate, and that will never do. Leave him to me."

"All right, missy," Andy agreed. "I don't want to

tangle with you." He picked up his Stetson and walked to the door. "I'm just trying to protect you."

Seeing the tenderness in her old friend's eyes, Katrina longed to go over and embrace him. But like everyone else, she thought, even Andy must be made to understand that Katrina McAllister was, first and foremost, her own boss.

Riding in the limousine to the Manhattan studio to take part in the *Town and Country* photography session, Katrina tried to revive her eagerness to see Lindee Bradley. Lindee was from San Antonio. They had met briefly at a political bash for Lindee, but Katrina had known of the Bradley family since she'd paid her first trip to the state capital. Lindee was brilliant, lovely to look at, and a budding young politician following in her father's footsteps.

Katrina had been pleased when *Town and Country* magazine had contacted her and asked to photograph the two of them together for a layout which would be the first of a series about Texas women. It had sounded like fun—beautiful clothes, terrific photography, good publicity, and an excuse to give anyone who asked why she was in New York. But so much had happened to Katrina lately that her desire for fun had almost disappeared.

Trudging up the long flight of stairs to the studio of Uli Carra, a photographer famous for her pictures of the international ultra-rich, Katrina was reminded of how long it had been since she'd taken part in the glittery social world she'd once been so involved in.

By the time Katrina was nineteen, she had become

Houston society's darling. Houston, being a fickle and young city where money and power had a way of nullifying even the worst of societal blunders, had embraced her as the only heir to KLM Oil and a newspaper-headline personality.

Quickly, Katrina became one of the most sought-after young women in the city. Whether or not her parents approved of local society's change of heart, they gave their daughter every advantage. They opened their home to the very people whose parents had once ignored them, hosted grand parties that people clamored to attend, and provided their child with whatever she might want. And then she'd taken up with the jet set, traveling all over the world on a whim.

Only when her father began to tutor her with a vengeance fueled by his poor health and fear that she would be left alone with something too many wanted, did Katrina begin to unearth the truth about her past. When her parents died in an airplane crash caused by a freak lightning storm, Katrina abruptly found herself besieged by destitute viscounts and oil men who wanted to own KLM. And then her ruthless step-uncle tried to take over.

She hadn't been prepared for the turbulence that occurred, but Katrina was a determined woman. Now, standing in front of the studio door, she put a smile on her face. "Hello," she called out, turning the iron handle of the metal door.

"Come, come," Uli shouted in her clipped European accent.

Lindee stood in the center of the gigantic room, wearing only a white terry-cloth robe draped in casually chic fashion around the smooth curve of her creamy shoulders. She smiled when she saw Katrina, and hurried to embrace her.

"Oh, it's so good to see you," Lindee cried. "I've looked forward to this ever since they asked me to do the layout."

Katrina looked deeply into the young woman's clear brown eyes. Suddenly, the comforting touch of another woman made her want to put her head on Lindee's shoulder and spill out all her troubles, but she knew she wouldn't. Katrina hadn't shown weakness, hadn't cried, hadn't even wanted to, since her parents had died.

"Ladies, ladies, there will be ample time to talk while we dress you. We must try very hard to stay on schedule." Uli clapped her hands and motioned for them to follow her.

Laughing, Lindee said, "She reminds me of Monsieur Dante, an instructor I had for ballet when I was thirteen years old. He was as tough as leather." Lindee wrinkled up her nose, still smiling.

Katrina laughed, watching the photographer. She was always barefoot, dressed in old army fatigues, wore her hair cropped close to her head, enormous dark glasses, and no make-up. Everyone guessed she was in her sixties.

"I must be very strict with my subjects or else they will take forever," Uli insisted. "You must first have your hair washed."

"I've already washed mine." Katrina ran her fingers through her hair.

"Yes, but I have a young man here who will work wonders with the both of you. First your hair."

58

They followed her into a small room, which looked like a miniature beauty shop, and shook hands with a young man standing beside a shampoo bowl, ready to perform.

"Uli," Katrina began, "I have a natural wave in my hair, and it seems to give most people who try to work with it fits."

Absentmindedly, the photographer began to run her fingers through the lush, wavy strands of Katrina's long hair. She looked over at the young man, who shrugged his shoulders indifferently.

"If you think that's bad, try mine." Lindee laughed, tugging at one of the dark curls clustered around her shoulders like a gay bundle of ribbons.

"Ladies." Ula raised her voice, and stared back and forth at the two of them like a schoolmarm. "Let's get this settled once and for all. Here, *I* am the boss. Back in Texas you may run your businesses any way you choose, boss anyone around, do whatever you want." She swung her hand wildly in the air. "I have studied your pictures. I know what I want. I will have it." Mischievously she gave them both a grin, then turned to Katrina. "You," she pointed—"sit down."

Both Katrina and Lindee burst out laughing. Good-naturedly giving in to house rules, Katrina sat where she'd been instructed. The young assistant washed her hair and then Lindee's long tresses, and wrapped fresh white towels around their heads.

Whenever they had the chance, the two women talked. But it wasn't until their hair had been done and they were seated side by side at a small, heavily lighted makeup table, that they had the opportunity for uninterrupted conversation. Uli was busily applying makeup to Katrina while her assistant worked on Lindee.

"Katrina, I've got something to tell you," Lindee said in a secretive voice, looking over at her reflection in the mirror.

Her tone reminded Katrina of teenage slumber parties long ago. "I know it's going to be something good. You look too happy."

Lindee blinked her eyes as Uli's assistant applied a bold line of turquoise eyeshadow to her eyelids. "Can you really tell?"

Katrina nodded. It was obvious, from the shine in her eyes to the natural glow of her cheeks. Something had happened to give Lindee a new radiance.

"Get ready. You're not going to believe this." Lindee waited for a second until the makeup man moved out of her way. "Katrina, I'm getting married. Tomorrow."

Simultaneously the two women reached across their chairs to embrace one another again, ignoring Uli's protests, then Katrina listened eagerly as Lindee described the man of her life, Brooks Griffin. The more Lindee talked, the more introspective Katrina found herself becoming.

"Love," Lindee was saying, "is better than all the politics and all the oil wells in the world. You'll see."

"I'd have to find quite a man to make it that exciting," Katrina said with a dreamy quality to her voice. "Very special. Of course Brooks is a special man." She recalled the night they'd danced together at Lindee's party.

Lindee nodded. "Don't think you won't find one like him. I went out to campaign and win an election, never imagining I'd meet the man of my life at a crowded press conference. And if it could happen to me, it can happen to you too."

"Well, I'm content with my life just as it is," Katrina protested, but her words rang strangely off-key in her head.

"Please be still, my dear Miss McAllister," Uli demanded. "You are beautiful, but I'm going to make you even more so."

Katrina and Lindee went on talking. "It's wonderful, Katrina. Believe me, being in love is the most wonderful thing in the world."

"It is?" she asked, concealing the wistfulness she felt. "Well." She cleared her throat. "The man for me would have to be able to let me be me, and you know how that is. I'm pushy, hardheaded, entirely too aggressive, all the things that men detest in women."

"And you're gorgeous, sophisticated, witty, exciting. Oh, Katrina, you're talking about insecure men. I guarantee there's a man for you. Is there a man in your life right now?"

Immediately, thoughts of Blair's hard yet gentle grip on her arm occurred to her. She could almost smell his distinct manly scent, and recalled how she'd felt the powerful pull of attraction. "No." She shook her head from side to side. "No one."

When their make-up was finished, the two of them went to the clothes rack where their first session's clothes were hung. Lindee put her hand on Katrina's arm to stop her. "Who knows, your man may be here in the big city right now."

Her speculation was momentarily unnerving to Katrina.

"Are you into reading tea leaves, or strictly guessing?" she asked.

"Guessing. You seem so preoccupied, it must be a man."

Katrina wanted to laugh. If Lindee knew the black cloud that was hanging over her right now, she thought, she wouldn't believe it. There was no time for a man, even one who'd appealed to her as Blair did.

"Shame, shame, shame, ladies." Uli swept toward them. "Both of you have been transformed and you don't even bother to notice, you are so busy with your little chitchat of men and love." She grabbed each of them by the wrist and dramatically turned them around toward the mirror. "Look."

Katrina took a close look at herself and drew a deep breath. It was true. She'd been so absorbed in her conversation with Lindee that she'd failed to notice the way Uli had used makeup to create a different look for her.

Katrina's face now seemed even thinner, her cheekbones far more prominent, and her eyes like enormous dark orbs with golden lights dancing about. Retaining the rich red color Katrina normally used on her lips, Uli had made them look even bolder, more seductive than usual. Her hair was pulled high atop her head with a cluster of dark curls gathered there, and just as Katrina often did, Uli had allowed tiny tendrils of hair to escape and drape enticingly around Katrina's face, giving the impression of a translucent shadow of vapor around her head.

Next to her, Lindee had been magically transformed too. Where Katrina's natural olive complexion had been accented, Lindee's had been made even creamier, and her brown hair had shining copper highlights added to it so that she seemed aflame with color.

"Yes, I think you did make me more beautiful," Katrina finally answered.

Lindee began to laugh with delight. Then, as soon as they had slipped into their gowns, Uli clapped her hands and waved them to their positions near a Louis XV gold-tapestry chair situated in front of a completely white background.

"Katrina, you are to stand up, slightly to the side of Lindee," Uli commanded with a trace of her usual impatience. "That is why you are in the beaded gown, my dear."

"I was wondering why you were the one who got to show all the cleavage," Lindee teased, looking down at her own high-necked Yves St. Laurent design of kelly green.

"I still don't understand." Katrina waited until Lindee was seated and then posed herself next to her. Katrina's strapless gown was made to mold itself to her body, created with thousands of sparkling gold sequins. In order to make it fit exactly right, the designer had sent an apprentice to try the gown on Katrina six different times.

The gown was tight, but Katrina was ready when Uli began taking rapid-fire shots. Abruptly, she stopped and then called loudly for her assistant to bring the jewels. When he approached with an open black box which looked as if it came from a safety deposit vault, Uli began to extract large velvet boxes, searching intently for something, ignoring the armed guard who appeared out of Uli's office and watched the movement of the box.

"Here we are," she yelled excitedly.

A grin broke across Katrina's face. She recognized Uli's spurts of excitement. It had happened often enough to Katrina when she'd become utterly absorbed in her work.

"Here, here, Lindee, you must wear these." Uli placed a large stone necklace around Lindee's neck and handed her two matching dangle earrings. "Sixty-five carats of emeralds, nineteen carats of diamonds. Lovely."

"Has he been here all this time?" Lindee inquired, her eyes following the cautious guard.

"He came with the jewelry," Uli acknowledged before turning to Katrina. "Now you."

"What have you chosen for me?"

"For you, all diamonds." Uli placed a simple strand of diamonds the size of small seed pearls around Katrina's neck and a diamond tiara just at the peak of her curls. "Spectacular. Absolutely spectacular. You are made for the diamonds. I knew. I knew."

In less than thirty minutes Uli took five rolls of film of the two of them in varying poses with the sparkling jewelry. Katrina teased Uli once about the jewels but Uli was absorbed in her work and suggested offhandedly that the two Texas heiresses might buy the expensive pieces. While Lindee happily explained that neither of them wore such ostentatious jewelry, Katrina couldn't help but take it as a reminder of her own dire financial straits. But she quickly shook off her glum mood and regained her lighthearted attitude of playing dress-up with a friend.

Then, after Uli returned the jewelry to the metal box and dismissed the guard, Katrina and Lindee drank iced Perrier and changed for their second session. This time Lindee was dressed in a two-piece yellow and white Bill Blass suit of fine linen, and Katrina wore a bright red Oscar de la Renta short dress. Uli added a flattering red straw hat and high red heels for Katrina, and black flats for Lindee. Satisfied, she took another three rolls of film, snapping out commands like a drill sergeant, sending her assistant scurrying to brush invisible pieces of lint from the clothes or to add lipstick to already shining lips.

Thinking they were finished, the two of them hurried back to change clothes, but Uli stopped them before they could take off the suits. "I brought along something I want you to try on. It was a spur of the moment idea and I hope you'll go along with me. I want you two dressed as contemporary Texans."

Surprise registered on their faces. Uli went on, "Normally, we try to photograph our people in their own locales. That's why I'm trying to set up dates with your secretaries for times I might come to Texas and get some more shots of the two of you. But for now, humor me." She handed each of them an outrageous-looking cowboy hat with feathers in a snakeskin band, silk blouses, and leather pants. "Here," she added, handing a pair of brightly colored ornate boots to each of the women.

"I don't know your ballet instructor, Lindee, but I'm sure the marines could use Uli," Katrina said good-naturedly as she took the accessories from Uli for the final shoot.

When they'd finally finished, fatigued but grateful to have completed the session, Katrina realized she had enjoyed a temporary reprieve from her own problems. She had her chauffeur drive them to Kennedy airport, where Lindee was flying to Jamaica to marry Brooks Griffin the next day. They made two brief stops. One to Lindee's hotel to pick up her luggage, the other stop when Katrina sent her chauffeur into a store to buy a magnum of Mumm's champagne and two glasses for congratulatory drinks. After promising they'd meet again soon and wishing Lindee her heartfelt best for the impending marriage, Katrina saw her off with a laugh and a hug.

All the way back to the Palace Hotel Katrina mulled over Lindee's parting words: "I hope you find my same magic." They reverberated in her head. Lindee was nobody's fool, she thought, yet she had been talking about the magic of love.

Later, as Katrina dressed for her evening with Blair, her thoughts returned once more to the touching conversation she'd shared with Lindee. What was it that she hungered for? she asked herself. More than anything she wanted to save KLM and see it prosper, but there was something else she wanted, too. She wanted to taste all of what life had to offer, she thought. In fact, she longed to find a man who would love her. Not just any man, she amended, but a man who'd be as thrilled by her challenging ways and as impressed with her mind as her looks or her money. She wanted to be loved, unequivocably, irrevocably.

Was that wanting too much? she wondered. At this point in her life she couldn't be certain.

CHAPTER FOUR

Blair knocked at her hotel door and brushed a stray strand of hair off his forehead. He'd worn his black tuxedo, knowing from the way she'd dressed yesterday that Katrina would wear something elegant and stylish for the evening.

When she opened the door and he saw her once again, she took his breath away. It struck him then that there had been no sense in asking out a seductively beautiful woman who was interested not in him but in using his fortune. In fact, he thought, it was downright self-destructive.

"You look stunning," he announced, following her inside the suite. Then, seeing the jacket she was slipping into, he began to laugh. "I don't know of any other woman," he said, "who could pull that off and look so dynamic."

With a mocking smile Katrina turned toward him. "You seemed worried about my sense of humor yesterday. I thought I'd prove to you that I indeed have one."

Katrina wore a medium-blue Oscar de la Renta satin

jacket over a teal satin sleeveless dress. On the back of the jacket was a sequined flower in a profusion of gay colors and appliquéd so the tops of the petals overlapped onto the shoulder and could be seen in front.

Shrewdly, she looked over at him, curious about his reaction. His mouth was twisted into an affable grin that made his stare unintimidating. She wished she knew what he was really thinking. It would make things so much easier, she thought. But at least this time, she mused, she knew more than before: she knew better than to underestimate him.

"I knew it was important for us to be together again," Blair said with a brief nod and a wide grin that was both knowing and secretive.

"Well, we'll see, won't we? I'll let you know what I think when the evening's over."

Laughing heartily, in the rich way she now recognized as his, Blair led her out of the hotel. All the way to the restaurant they sat in the darkened limousine, catching glimpses of one another then averting their eyes as they carried on simple conversation. Once, Blair instructed his driver to drop off a business document, explaining to Katrina that it was the most expedient thing for him to do.

When he helped her step from the limousine, Blair noticed the commanding way she accepted his outstretched hand and emerged with her shoulders set square and straight. He thought he'd never seen such dignity captured in one small package and the urge to possess her came suddenly upon him. Instead of being put off by her power he was fascinated by it.

She allowed him to take her arm and he could feel

the swell of energy contained within her. Katrina McAllister had quality, he thought. It virtually oozed from her, stirring to life the powerful emotion inside him, one that he didn't think would soon pass.

They ate at the Four Seasons. Blair found himself trying to reevaluate his position as he ordered a dry wine from the wine steward. He was acting like a man with a fever, and he knew he'd better start backtracking fast. It wouldn't do, he thought, to show any vulnerability with this woman.

"I'm curious about you and your life-style," he said. "I've never been to Texas." Blair was hoping idle conversation would keep things neutral.

"Most people unfamiliar with Texas want to know if our families are like J.R. Ewing's." She smiled easily at him, being proficient at social conversation and feeling on safe ground.

With a sympathetic nod, he asked, "And how do you answer?"

"I tell people that except for the accent there are families like J.R.'s everywhere." Again she smiled, her dark eyes full of amusement.

"Have you always lived in Houston?" Finding it hard to take his eyes off her, Blair watched the way her mouth softened whenever she smiled.

Meanwhile, Katrina's natural gift for chitchat allowed her to watch him closely as she talked. "Yes, I was born there and I've never felt the urge to leave. I have a ranch about two hours from the city and from time to time I've toyed with the idea of leasing an apartment in New York. But I'm never away from Houston for very long."

She decided she definitely liked the way his eyes seemed to see through her, admired his charged directness. She also found herself admiring his crooked smile and his calmness.

As they talked, she was becoming more and more aware that this wasn't mere idle conversation with him. Blair actually seemed interested.

"Besides oil, what are your other interests?" He waited while a waiter poured more wine.

Suddenly, the waiter spilled some of the wine on Blair, staining his crisply starched white shirt as well as his coat. Taking it all in stride, Blair allowed the waiter to wipe away the liquid and dismissed the maître d' who had rushed over.

She was impressed as she watched the smooth way Blair handled the situation, and then remembered how he'd stopped to have a document delivered on the way to the restaurant. Once again, she thought, he was proving himself altogether capable with a most pronounced efficiency. Was there anything the man couldn't handle? she wondered.

She supposed that trait was what made him such a computer wizard—the ability to neutrally analyze any given situation. Would he ever rant and rave the way she sometimes did? she mused. She recalled that even when he'd been attacking her the day before in his office, he'd used his words like a surgeon's scalpel—quickly and to the point.

After the waiter left, she said, "I'd ask you something about computers but I'm not even sure I could ask an intelligent question."

Blair grinned, unruffled by the red stain on his clothes.

"There are a lot of people like yourself, but I've always been fascinated by them. I built one when I was twelve years old. Of course, it didn't work."

She began eating the Caesar salad that had been brought by a different waiter. "You definitely have the mind for it, I'd bet. You seem to be all logic and practicality."

"Tell that to my mother." Blair laughed and his eyes flushed with several hues of color. "She'll be delighted to hear what you have to say."

"Am I wrong?"

"Only slightly, I guess. I think the reason I like computers is that I enjoy intricate kinds of things. The more intricate the better."

He stared openly at her for an instant and Katrina looked away, feeling a twinge of unaccountable nervousness. She could never have just a mild flirtation with a man like this, she realized. There wouldn't be anything mild about it. His eyes told her as much.

Katrina said, "Now . . . now that we're getting along so well, I feel I have to ask you a question. Actually, it's a business question, but it's a quick one." Maybe getting her mind back on what she'd come for, she thought, would crush her romantic feelings.

He sat back in his chair, relaxed, regarding her. "Not too complicated, I hope. It's much too early in the evening and I'm at my best after I've eaten."

"Not complicated at all," Katrina said, thinking of Andy's last-minute coaching and her own internal pressures. "All I want to know is how you got your information about KLM. If I seem to be pushing you about it, I hope you'll understand it's because the infor-

71

mation is bizarrely inaccurate, and for that reason potentially quite harmful."

He looked at his wineglass for a moment and then at her, and when he did Katrina felt like the heavens had opened up and released the iciest of rain. Again, it was if he could see through her, only now his eyes said he didn't like what he saw.

"Funny, Katrina. I thought you were concerned because if I could find out about the truth, so could your competitors."

Warily, she said, "That's ridiculous."

"I won't make things any worse for you," he said with a shrug. Now, he purposefully kept his eyes averted. "You can relax. One of my very nice secretaries has an equally nice cousin who works for you. The cousin, by the way, wouldn't confide in anyone else like that. She was worried about you."

Katrina fumed, but maintained her cool facade. "Thank you for telling me."

"You know," he said, his impenetrable gaze focusing on her, "if you were as open with me as I am with you, we'd be well on our way."

She decided to use flattery. She'd changed her mind about allowing herself the luxury of enjoying the man, but that didn't mean she couldn't remain female. "Where are we going?"

He watched the way she lowered her dark, sooty lashes and then opened her eyes solely to him. "That I haven't quite decided yet," he said.

"Well, I've always liked unpredictability."

Thoughtfully, he replied, "Sooner or later, all of us become predictable, Katrina."

Her heart danced as she realized her ploy wasn't working. He was taking her words and using them to suit his purpose, and her flattery wasn't doing anything except making her feel like stepping back from this absorbing man.

"I don't intend to be."

He licked the edge of his wineglass. "We all prove predictable. It just takes understanding to figure out what motivates a person."

She didn't answer him.

Throughout the rest of the meal, as they made small talk, Katrina continued to study him. She found she alternated between being comfortable and uneasy with him; uneasy when she thought about negotiating with him.

He was polite, engaging, self-assured, and interesting— far different from the men whom she usually dated. But she'd recognized an icy core in him whenever the subject of KLM came up, and it made her feel she'd probably be better off simply telling him the truth. But, of course, she thought, that would be impossible.

As they were finishing their meal, a reporter walked up to them. "Miss McAllister, I just heard you were in town. Is the rumor true about your being in New York to buy our basketball team? Are you taking them back to Texas with you?"

"Well, I really don't want to confirm or deny your rumor," she replied. "I'd prefer to say I was in New York to meet an old friend, and to take care of a few commitments." She gave the man a polished smile and encouraged him to leave.

"Why did you do that?" Blair asked as soon as the man had disappeared.

"You mean be gracious to him?"

"No," he replied impatiently. "I mean why did you leave him with the impression that you were thinking about buying the basketball team?"

"In my business there's always an image to be maintained. Why not let people think I might buy a basketball team? It doesn't hurt."

"It doesn't strike you funny that the truth could be just as effective?" He found his voice rising in judgment.

"Look, Blair, I think it's time we quit entertaining one another and get down to brass tacks. It's obvious you don't understand the oil business or how it works. It's unlike any other business. There's no comparison I can think of, except maybe politics." She moved forward in her chair, directing all her attention to him. "In my business the vultures are out there waiting for you. The slightest sign of weakness and they'll pick your bones clean. That's why it doesn't hurt to let people think I might be here to buy a twenty-million-dollar basketball franchise."

"You make it sound more like the old frontier days of cattle rustlers and range thieves," he joked, but his accusation was just below the surface of his smile.

Damn, he was naive, she thought—not in the same way she'd thought of him before, but in his simplistic attitude about the oil business. "Don't laugh," she replied. "It's not too far removed from cattle rustling."

He shook his head in disbelief. Quietly, he drained his coffee cup and set it down beside him on the linen-covered table.

"You don't believe me, do you?"

"It's hard to believe."

"I'm telling you that the oil business is a squalid world all its own. These people feed on their own greed, and there's nothing they won't do to make money. Even the most honest ones eventually become tainted." Absentmindedly, Katrina pressed her lips together in a tense line, thinking of what she wanted to say next.

Meanwhile, Blair was thinking about what she'd said. The oil world sounded exciting and interesting, and he wanted to be a part of it. He'd met the challenge of the computer business and made his fortune, but now there were other heights to climb. He could almost taste his excitement.

"Sometime when you're ready to listen, I'll tell you about the oil-field trash. That's people, not paper. Then I'll tell you some of the fine arts of thievery, about slant oil riggings, missing oil, and missing employees." She took a deep breath.

It wouldn't do any good to argue with her, Blair decided. "I think I can help you, Katrina," he said. "Besides my money, I think my background with computers will help you."

She began to laugh, slowly at first and then so hard there were tears in her eyes. "You think a computer can help?" she spat. "Oh, you're too much. I'm telling you that it's a tough world out there. Computers aren't the solution to the problem."

"Your attitude," he replied, "is precisely what keeps me from jumping into your business right this moment. That and the fact that you deliberately lied to me about KLM. I don't like subterfuge, and at this point in my career my reputation is impeccable. I want it to stay that way."

"Are you suggesting I might somehow tarnish your image?" she charged vehemently.

"I'm only suggesting that I intend to proceed with caution, with some checks and balances of my own."

She held herself back, choking down the rage she felt, yet remembering that she desperately needed him. "I think we've talked enough for the time being. You obviously don't understand what I'm trying to convey."

She shoved back her chair and Blair hurried over to help her. It wasn't until they were inside the limousine that he spoke again. He didn't know what he was going to say, only that he intended to say something that would make up for his bluntness.

"Katrina, I'm not very skilled at the type of negotiations you're accustomed to. I guess that's why, ever since we met, I've been saying and doing all the wrong things at the wrong time. With computers I deal strictly with the machine and its parts and I sell them on that basis. I guess you can tell I've never had much practice at the manipulative game playing you have to engage in. They say it's an art, and I'm beginning to see why."

She felt a knot in her stomach and wished he hadn't been so candid. His candor touched and intrigued her, reminding her of how she wanted to be. All her life Katrina's basic nature had been to tell the truth, but in the last few years she'd learned how to battle for what she wanted. It wasn't easy, and often it wasn't pleasant, but she'd managed to win so far, and that was what was important, she told herself.

Like her, Blair said what he thought and did what he wanted; but unlike her, his attitude was far more trusting. He didn't need to be anything but himself. She envied him that.

"Forget it," she said, ignoring his eyes. She turned toward the window.

"No, I don't want to forget it. I want us to try and understand one another."

She turned to look at him, wondering about his statement. He was the strangest man she'd ever met, she thought—too sincere or too honest for his own good. Then she felt shaky, conscious of the force of will behind his eyes. They were a powerful match for her own.

"I don't know if we can or not," she said softly.

"Good, then that means there's a possibility that you're as confused as I am." He wouldn't take his eyes away from hers.

I can stop this anytime, Katrina assured herself. *I control my emotions. They don't control me.*

She told her heart to slow down. She told her eyes to stop watching the way his mouth smiled crookedly at her. Suddenly, the two of them were smiling together.

Casually, he draped his arm around the back of the seat and let his fingers idly trace an outline around the flower on her jacket. Katrina imagined she could feel the soft flesh of his fingers caress her bare skin, and suddenly her body began to tingle.

He brought his fingers closer to her throat. Katrina's breasts began to ache and she longed to take a deep breath. What was wrong with her? she wondered. How could his almost innocently casual touch sensitize her entire body? Her mind fought hard to stop her turbulent emotions.

Blair saw her eyes droop almost shut and then lift, opening wider and wider to him, and he felt as if he might drown in them. His chest tightened and he felt his ardor rise.

Courage, bravado, intellect, and beauty. She was the most unabashedly sexual woman he'd ever met. Sweat broke out along his forehead as he let his fingers slowly move toward the provocative swell of her lips. She tilted her head back slightly, looking even more enticing than before.

In that instant he knew he wanted to possess her, to claim her, if only for a flickering moment in time. With the same sudden intensity as before, he felt his desire swell.

She was unique, he thought, and he felt as if she could give him a particle of her uniqueness if he could somehow capture her spirit and touch it with his.

He moved forward and brought his mouth down on hers, holding her tender face with his hand, losing himself to the sweet moisture of her lips. Then he stopped thinking and gave himself up to the feelings their kiss was evoking, sliding his tongue softly, shamelessly into her lovely mouth in passionate exploration, overwhelmed by the knowledge that she hadn't resisted.

Blair tried to hold himself firmly in control, afraid to let go, to unleash the demands he felt marauding inside his tense body. Gently, his mouth played against hers, his tongue persuasive, playful, smooth.

All the while he was longing to let his hands touch the tender body next to him. His mind spun with the explosive thought of feeling her pressed against him as they made love. He wanted this woman, he thought. God, how he wanted her.

Every part of him burned with unquenched need.

His body was aflame, his mind clamped down like a trap, and his heart open.

When she pulled away from him, he made a feeble attempt at a joke, still too thunderstruck by what was happening between them. "This is a relatively new experience for me."

She waited, still thinking about the tenderness of his kiss, staring at the reflected glimmer in his hazel eyes. "Explain yourself."

"I've never kissed a woman in a limousine, or, for that matter, in a taxi. Not like this."

They laughed and she felt the vibrations of warmth and attraction play between them. She hated to have the evening end, but at the same time she realized she needed to hold her emotions in check.

Seconds ticked by as she tried to pull her thoughts away from him, and then she felt his finger graze gently against the fullness of her cheek and move slowly downward to slip across her lower lip. She knew better, but despite herself, Katrina slightly parted her lips and took his finger into her mouth, tasting it with her tongue before abruptly moving her head away.

"We didn't get around to business like we'd anticipated," she said, feeling as if all the air had spun away from her. "But I'm going to bring it up only to say that I can guarantee you that if you'll loan me that eleven million, you'll have your money plus much more back in six months or less."

"You'd have to be more specific," he whispered, struggling with himself. "I couldn't consider anything that didn't promise me I'd be with you, running the company, giving me the time and freedom I'd need to involve myself in KLM. The basic question still remains: Are you willing to negotiate?"

He could hardly think of eleven million dollars right now, not when he was like a crazed man looking for a fix. He smiled, wondering how she'd look when she woke up in the morning.

"I'm leaving for Houston tomorrow."

"I thought we were going to negotiate."

Blair pulled her to him again and she came willingly, bringing her arm around his neck, sending shock waves of desire rippling along each delicate spot she touched. Impulsively, he let his hand race across her waist and hips before coming to rest in the curve of her back, where he held her close, not wanting the kiss to end.

And when he felt his body burning with the passion of their embrace, Katrina let her tongue move commandingly on his until she was exploring every part of his open mouth with a tense insistence that made him flinch with mounting excitement. As the limo slowed she used her tongue to make lazy swirling circles around his lips, and he groaned aloud. She moved back and stared at him, this time giving him the kind of intense look he normally gave her.

"Are you always this way?" Blair asked in a choked voice. "I'm asking because I think about making love to you and how it might be between us."

Katrina made no effort to answer. Instead, she studied him as if she were making up her mind about something very important. The blood pounded at her temples and she felt her head whir at his suggestion of intimacy. But as appealing as it sounded, she reminded herself that she was here on business and decided it was inopportune. She found herself enjoying his company as well as his compliments.

When they pulled up to the hotel, Blair started to get out with her, but she pushed him gently back. "It's been fun, Blair," she said in a husky voice. "Let me know when you make up your mind abut KLM Oil. Until then, good night."

Not looking back at him was difficult for her, but she knew that right now she needed to put some distance between them. To let herself continue their intimacies, she thought, to acknowledge any sort of interest in Blair, would be devastating. They were of two worlds, their lives intricately woven of different fabric. A part of her cried out for the man. But something else, equally strong, denied her need for him.

He'd never understand her way of life, she told herself. In her universe no one told the truth about business. Instead, they kept the details secret for fear of losing what they had.

Blair was vastly different from the kind of man she knew. He represented a clean, fresh look at the world, and as odd as it seemed, Katrina was overwhelmed with the sudden knowledge that she desired a man like him. He made her feel like white balmy clouds floating through a turquoise sky, gentle waves washing up on a solitary shore, and bright summer days with the crisp odor of fresh clover permeating the air.

Even as she indulged her thoughts, she knew they wouldn't stand up to any test of rationality. Nevertheless, she knew she'd never known such feelings existed, even if they were feelings that couldn't be encouraged or nurtured.

* * *

An hour later, as Katrina was about to change for bed, her telephone rang. She answered on the third ring.

"Meet me in exactly fifteen minutes outside your hotel," Blair said matter-of-factly. "I'll tell you what I've decided about your business proposition. This is my final offer, Katrina, so if you're interested in hearing what I have to say, be there."

She held the receiver in her hand and looked at it for a minute before replacing it. Blair had sounded disturbed, almost hostile, and she had no idea why. Quickly, she stepped into a pair of white raw-silk slacks, a long-sleeved matching pullover, and a peach-colored full cloak.

By the time she stepped out of the hotel, she saw Blair standing on the corner, leaning against a streetlight, looking both handsome and mysterious under the garish light. His tux was unbuttoned, as was his shirt, and he had a white muffler thrown casually around his neck. The chilling night breeze ruffled his hair.

Katrina noticed all of this as she strode purposefully toward him, reminding herself with each step that she mustn't succumb to her feelings of attraction. They were here for business.

"Thank you for coming," Blair said, longing to reach for her.

"It sounded frightfully important." Katrina had taken down her hair, and the breeze caught it up in billowing waves and set it back down again.

Blair watched her raven-colored hair glistening from the overhead streetlight, then looked past her. He cleared his throat once, then again.

"I have two conditions to offer, Katrina. I want you to listen carefully to my offer, because I'll not make another."

"My, my, we sound very serious," she teased. But she could tell he wasn't in a playful mood. "All right, I'm listening," she stated, wondering what had happened in the brief period since they'd been apart.

"These are the conditions." Again he cleared his throat. "I want only two things, Katrina. First I want to be made a fifty-fifty partner in KLM Oil for a period of six months, or until the time comes when I can be assured of getting my money back plus an additional ten million dollars for each six-month period my money is invested in KLM. At that point we will negotiate further arrangements. I am willing to bring thirty million dollars into KLM as part of the agreement to my full partnership, as a decision-making partner. Secondly, I want to spend one night with you."

"What on earth are you saying?"

"If you want," he spoke calmly, "I'll repeat it again."

"No." She thrust out her hand as if to push him away. "That won't be necessary."

She glanced up into his eyes for the last time, reeling with disbelief, calling all her inner resources together to keep herself under control. Finally, she gathered her cloak around her and walked away, her regal head held high, her shoulders straight and square.

CHAPTER FIVE

"Why him?" Katrina protested aloud to the still, dark room in the early morning hours. Her words filtered across the thin air and fell back on her, making the humiliation of the evening before seem even more unbearable. "Why?" She shook her head stiffly but nothing she did would relieve the pain.

A rolling fury was radiating through her with unbelievable force, and Katrina found herself completely unable to come to grips with the hurt and disappointment she was feeling. Where was the honorable, honest man she'd mistakenly thought she'd met?

It seemed Blair Warren wanted more than his pound of flesh. He wanted to be an equal partner in what her family had made solely hers, and to strip her of her self-esteem. He was no better than her step-uncle Albert, she thought. They were two of a kind.

The desire she'd felt when he'd kissed her was now irrelevant, and the smattering of hope her subconscious had raised was dashed as surely as if Blair had thrown a piece of priceless Baccarat crystal to the pavement. She was mortified not only because of what he'd demanded of her, but because of the way her heart had secretly begun to respond to him.

Now she had some idea of how a quarterback felt when he'd been decked by a defensive team: Clear thinking was an impossibility. At least she had left Blair with no clear-cut answer. Right now he had to be as confused as she was.

All the time she'd spent telling herself that she'd never succumb to Blair's impossible offer, there remained the niggling thought in the back of her mind that if nothing else were to work out she would be forced to do anything she had to do to keep KLM afloat.

When the first light of day came in her window, Katrina picked up the hotel telephone and dialed Andy's room, "Good morning," she said with false spiritedness. "I know I didn't wake you up. It's well past five."

"When I'm eighty I'm going to start sleeping late in the mornings," Andy rasped. "Until then it's a waste of time."

"Have you had your breakfast?" Again Katrina kept her voice light.

"Not yet. I was waiting to hear from you. How'd it go?"

Pulling herself up to her full height, Katrina stood and gazed at her reflection in the bedroom mirror. "Things are going as planned," she answered, telling herself that there was still hope that she could think of some other way out of her desperate situation. All she needed was a plan.

"So?"

She should have known Andy was too clever a fellow to accept a neutral comment. "So let's get in the plane and go back to Houston. He's going to let us know."

"Do we have him or not, Katrina?" Andy's voice became apprehensive.

"We're still negotiating, Andy, but he asked for time to talk to his lawyers. I think that's fair, don't you?" She didn't want to give him a chance to ask any more questions. "I didn't want Blair to think I was going to anxiously wait around, so I said we were going back to Houston."

"Well, goll darn it, missy, I want to know if you think you've got him!"

Her mirrored reflection cast back worried eyes. Katrina bit her lip, then said, "I don't think we have a problem."

"I'll call for the plane then. Wouldn't you rather have breakfast in Houston?"

"I'm ready," she said, and hung up, hoping she'd done the right thing in keeping Blair's demands from a man who was like her second father. Andy might be an old Texas roughneck, but his sense of gentlemanly chivalry would have created too much havoc if she'd told him. Katrina knew that the ordeal with Blair was far from finished. If she couldn't come up with an alternative plan, she might have to resort to actions which Andy would be better off not knowing about, given the strain it might put on his heart.

All the way to the airport, and after her jet took off for Houston, Katrina waited for Andy to quiz her further about Blair Warren. But Andy seemed satisfied with what she'd told him, and instead, was absorbed in his own thoughts. He was talking about the good old days and her father Karl, and Katrina tried to give him her full attention.

They were sitting on the corner sofa, sipping hot coffee, and the nearer they were to Houston the better things appeared. She told herself that she could worry about Blair's offer later, and that somehow everything would be all right. But with her conflicting thoughts of Blair, a general feeling of unease permeated her spirit. Listlessly, she reached over and poured more coffee for Andy.

"I've told you this story a hundred times," Andy said, "but I got up thinking about your daddy this morning. You think old Karl would be disappointed in you because you've gone and got yourself in a heap of hot water, but he wouldn't do any such thing. He'd say you were a chip off the old block." Andy's eyes gleamed with pleasure.

"You really think so?" she managed, her thoughts snapping back to the demands Blair had so blatantly presented.

"Yep. It's like the first time your daddy made it big. He was damned sure close to losing it all." Andy laughed at the memory, shaking his head.

"Tell me again. I love to hear it as much as you love to tell it." Katrina smiled, pouring more coffee for them both from a silver coffee pot on the nearby table.

"Back in the days before World War Two, me and your daddy used to scramble our brains out hustling up money for a poor-boy oil rig. There were still plenty of farmers then who were eager to lease the mineral rights to their land." Andy leaned back and swung one leg up over the other one, caught up in the telling of his story.

"Your daddy and I couldn't come up with enough to buy a drilling outfit, so we started buying scrap pieces and used parts and then putting them all together. We had to work like dogs, but one night when we just about had the rig finished, your daddy got into a poker game with a guy who'd come down from Amarillo selling pipe. The old boy looked like he didn't have any more than we did and Karl was on a real winning streak. They played for six hours, until they were both bleary-eyed, and when it was all over, the old boy owed Karl six hundred dollars, enough money to lease several drilling spots." Andy started to laugh once again. "Lord knows what would have happened if Karl had lost. He didn't have twenty dollars to his name.

"Sure enough the old boy couldn't pay up, but he offered Karl a signed lease to a plot of farmland between Houston and San Antonio. Karl knew there was no way to squeeze blood out of a turnip, so he took the lease and three days later I was helping him set up our drilling rig on his new lease. Because the rig was ours and the lease was his, we agreed that I'd get twenty percent of anything we drilled."

Andy shook his head slowly. "Your daddy started sinking that well and I told him he was an absolute fool. I didn't think there was a dime's worth of oil anywhere near the spot. But Karl was the stubbornest cuss I ever knew and he went right on with his drilling. He even went over to the farmer's house the next day and offered to buy the hundred acres of land around that well. The farmer thought he was crazy and I did, too, but he wasn't listening to nobody. He just paid the last cent he had with a promise of more and went back to that well and kept on working."

Katrina was listening intently, her coffee cup untouched. Andy spoke with such animated fervor she nearly imagined she'd been there with them.

"The next day I took off for the nearby town we'd passed through. I was tired and still convinced that your daddy had lost his mind. Three days later he hit crude. He'd only drilled down five thousand feet, but what he found wasn't any shallow pool. Old Karl found himself a real deep one. I went tearing back out to the site, and sure enough, that beautiful black gold was gushing up out of the ground. Karl was drenched in it, and right then and there, with the two of us screaming and yelling, he named it Old Baldy after the bald-headed guy he'd won the lease from." Andy stopped for breath, his story nearly finished. "I still wish he'd named it Ace High," he said with a touch of regret.

The two of them shared an appreciative laugh, and Katrina felt her flagging spirit fire back to life. *This is my bloodline*, she thought with renewed commitment to finding a way to save KLM.

Gratefully, she reached over, took Andy's rough hand, and held it until they heard the pilot announce their imminent arrival in the hazy city of Houston. At the same time a plan began to form in her mind, a plan which, if successful, would mean she'd never have to deal with Blair again.

Her chauffeur was waiting for them when the plane landed, and he greeted the two of them with a wide grin. Like the rest of Katrina's staff, James was untrained in the ways of his trade, but he'd needed a job and had come to the KLM offices on the advice of a cousin who was a gardener for Katrina and her parents for many years.

"I'm glad the two of you have come," James said as Andy gave him a friendly slap across the back.

"Not any more than we are." Katrina watched the two men shake hands and waited as the luggage was brought from the plane.

She'd never forgotten James's look of surprise when she'd asked him how well he could drive, nor his disappointment when he found out how little she actually needed his services. Katrina had always liked to drive herself around Houston, but James stubbornly persisted and she'd given in. Quickly, he'd proven himself eager and loyal, two traits Katrina demanded of her employees, and so he now served as a combination chauffeur and butler.

"Katrina, I hope you're not gonna need me for a while. I want to go back to the ranch," Andy said as they were getting into the white limousine.

Andy owned a small ranch outside of Houston and since his heart attack he'd spent more and more time there. Named the Lazy A, the ranch was a favorite place for Katrina too.

"James, after you take me home I'd like you to take Mr. Anderson out to his ranch. You wouldn't mind doing that, would you?" Katrina smiled over at Andy and then into the rearview mirror.

"No, Miss McAllister, I sure wouldn't," the ageless chauffeur beamed.

"And after you drop me off at home, James, I won't need you anymore today," she said purposefully.

"Yes ma'am," he said, driving a little faster through the airport gates.

Katrina knew that Andy and James played poker whenever they had the chance. Many nights Andy stayed at Katrina's when he was in Houston, and far into the morning a light could be seen through the crack beneath the door of the bedroom which had been solely his since the house had been built.

The maids complained that the entire second floor reeked of cigar smoke and the smell of bourbon on the days following their long games, but Katrina liked the idea of the two men getting together for a little fun. Whenever she could she encouraged their friendship, while reminding Andy of his doctor's orders. Now she looked over at her dear friend.

Andy was worrying again, drumming his fingers on his knees. "You call me when you hear from Blair, you hear? I can be here in forty-five minutes. Don't commit to anything," he lectured.

"I won't." She gave a promising nod.

"Our lawyers can handle the details. Just hook him."

"Andy, why don't you just stop your worrying. You remind me of a man in need of a good card game to relax himself." Katrina winked into the rearview mirror at James. "Besides, the way Blair talked, it may be a day or two before I hear from him."

"In a way I'm glad, although that puts us mighty close to our deadline," Andy said thoughtfully. Then he yawned. "I'm bone tired. Maybe I'll have a little time for fishing out at the tank." He closed his eyes, then opened them wide. "After that little poker game you recommended."

Laughing, Katrina pictured how Andy would look at his ranch, dressed in faded western jeans, an old cowboy shirt that would barely stretch across his paunch, and his favorite scarred brown-leather boots. Andy would stretch out under an oak tree near the water tank he kept stocked with fresh fish and dangle his pole out into the water, alternately worrying and napping. Now that she had a new plan, she hoped he'd stay put for at least a day or two, giving her time to put it into action.

When they drove up the circular drive to her home, Katrina said a hurried good-bye to Andy and James, who then happily left for Andy's ranch. She gave little notice to her stucco mansion with its heavy red-tile roof, the house she had lived in since the day she was born. The majestic home harked back to a day of opulent wealth, but in the River Oaks area the mansion was unremarkable. Every home nearby was the same—a reflection of money and power.

It was her past Katrina was thinking of as she stepped inside the arched entry. She was greeted by one of the household staff, then moved toward the library adjoining the downstairs den. Passing a vase of fresh white garden flowers, and without breaking her stride, she withdrew one with a tinge of brown around its edge and dropped it on a side table with a pointed glance back in the maid's direction.

"I have some business to take care of," she commented, and closed the walnut doors behind her with a flourish.

With shaking fingers Katrina picked up the telephone to dial the long-distance operator. Realizing how near panic she was, she hung up and put her head in her hands. What if it didn't work? she wondered. How could she ever agree to Blair's two conditions? The mere thought of acceding to his wishes blinded her with fresh anger and a sense of helpless doom.

But a few minutes later, Katrina lifted her head and looked around the room. The library was wood-paneled, had floor to ceiling French-paned windows and a massive brass chandelier. Handwoven Oriental rugs had been artfully placed throughout the room, and a marble fireplace and bookshelves filled one wall. There was a painting of Katrina's father over the fireplace, and she stared at it now, hoping to capture some strength from the benign-looking face looking down upon her.

With effort Katrina calmed herself, and opened her private notebook. She looked through it until she found the name Miguel Carasco, and again dialed the long-distance operator, but this time her hand was firm and steady.

"The number I want is in Venezuela," she began, and then recited the phone number and name of a man she'd come to know well over the last year or so. "I see," she said when the operator had made the connection. "Very well, ask them where we can locate Mr. Carasco."

She ran one hand up and down the telephone cord as she waited impatiently for an answer. The connection was poor. She could hear static in the background as the operator tried to get information for her.

"Mexico?" she asked incredulously. "Okay, don't let her hang up," Katrina demanded. "Find out where in Mexico. I want to know the town and the hotel." She took a pen from the drawer and pulled out a pad of paper with her monogram stamped in gold. "All right," she said with a grimace. "I'll talk to his secretary. I have one more question."

"I'm sorry, ma'am, but our call has been disconnected," the operator replied.

"Naturally," Katrina said with disgust. "Very well, I want you to call the Maria Isabella Hotel in Mexico City."

Within five hours Katrina was in Mexico City, registering at the Maria Isabella's ornately carved front desk. Back in Houston she'd made a few more phone calls, had one of the maids repack her suitcase, and left strict instructions that no information was to be given out to anyone about her leaving.

She hoped Andy had been describing his condition accurately when he'd said he was bone tired. She didn't want him to call her home and find her gone. For now, she wanted no one to know where she was, or why.

The gracious hospitality of the Mexican people was something Katrina had temporarily forgotten. The three smiling, uniformed men who greeted her in the open-air hotel lobby were an abrupt reminder. They escorted her to her room with a profusion of compliments. Katrina smiled superficially in response, being absorbed in thoughts about finding Miguel Carasco.

The young men led her into a plush suite overlooking the brightly tiled courtyard in the center of the hotel. But Katrina paid scant attention to her surroundings. After giving them a generous tip, she went immediately to the telephone and dialed the hotel operator.

A few minutes later she breathed a sigh of relief upon hearing Miguel's rich baritone on the telephone. Miguel was a Venezuelan whom she had met at a Houston charity dinner party given by one of the vice-presidents of Texaco. At the time, Miguel was serving as an OPEC representative, and Katrina had made it a point to get to know him.

To her surprise she'd found the darkly handsome man likable, and the two of them became friends. Katrina believed Miguel to be trustworthy, and what she was about to ask him to do required complete discretion on his part.

After Katrina told him she needed to see him, she waited on the line while he changed his plans for the evening and agreed to meet her in her room. As soon as she hung up, she ordered a chilled lobster dinner for two to be sent up at nine o'clock, then unpacked. She had barely enough time for a quick shower and a change of clothes before she heard the expected knock.

"Miguel," she said, opening the door to her suite. "Thank you for coming." After brushing her lips to his cheek, she softly closed the door behind them.

"For you to come so far I knew it must be urgent," Miguel Carasco said.

Katrina felt her body tense up. Urgent was too light a word.

"You're right." She nodded and led him into the part of the suite where she'd carefully laid out the documents she wanted to show him.

"As always, Katrina, you take a man's breath away." Miguel remained standing while she sat down on the sofa next to her open attaché case. "You're a very beautiful woman."

Katrina smiled up at him, the first real smile she'd

been able to manage since the night before. One thing about Miguel, she thought, he always made her feel exceptionally feminine. And yet, while he made no attempt to conceal his admiration for her, he never made any overt move to change their platonic friendship. For that she was grateful. She needed him to be her friend.

"Thank you, Miguel. Your kinds words come at a very good time." She smoothed down one long sleeve of the flowing white-silk Halston caftan she wore, conscious of the way he was staring at her hair. "I've ordered dinner for us later. Would you care for a drink? I can have something sent up."

"No." He shook his head. "I can see that you want to spend little time on anything but business right now." A smile crossed his face. "Please, what can I do for you?"

For one harrowing instant she felt desperation clog her mind and was afraid she might crumble. She could feel Miguel's eyes boring into her but pictured Blair's face.

If Miguel couldn't help her, she thought, she would have to say yes to Blair. She would be forced to take him into her business, and into her bed. If she let that happen, she would never be the same again.

In an attempt to hide her discomfort, Katrina picked up a piece of paper and handed it to Miguel. "This is what I want," she began. "I want you to find an investor for me, Miguel. Someone from one of the OPEC nations . . . someone who will be willing to loan me the money I need to keep KLM going."

Regaining her composure she began to describe in

greater detail what she needed. Then it was time for him to question her.

"Do I look surprised?" he asked.

"Maybe a little."

"Here is the woman who told me the first night we met that she was all independence and her oil company could not be touched. You wouldn't do this, especially go outside of the country for help, without a very good reason, Katrina."

She nodded. "That's true, but my step-uncle has me over a barrel right now. The court has declared all my assets frozen and I need the cash. I bid and won a state lease on an offshore drilling site which is going to cost me big money. I've got a well or two down." Briefly she let her sad eyes meet his, then she spread out her hands. "I'm in real trouble."

Their conversation continued over dinner and on into the night. Miguel studied her reports closely and promised he would make his contacts within twenty-four hours and then call her in Houston.

The next morning she flew back home and Miguel left for Venezuela, cutting short his vacation to help out his friend. At no time had he given her anything but the vaguest of hopes for his chances, but his sincere promise to try was encouragement enough for a disheartened woman.

Katrina thought the security of her own home would be enough to make her feel less uptight, but when she arrived in Houston, exhausted and worried, she still felt like an unsteady tightrope walker. She knew that until she heard from Miguel, she couldn't rest, so she slipped on her bathing suit and went out to the heated indoor pool where she swam laps until she thought her lungs might burst.

Crawling out of the pool and throwing a robe over her shoulders, Katrina sank down in a cushioned chaise longue, too tired to stop her mind from wandering along its own persistent course. She closed her eyes, listening to the sporadic sounds of the stirred-up pool water gradually becoming still.

When Katrina opened her eyes again, the sun was going down and she remembered sleeping on and off as her thoughts passed in and out of lucidity. A soreness in her neck was her reward, along with a twofold aware-ness of the truth about herself.

The most obvious truth was that she hated Blair for the predicament he'd placed her in. It would break her heart, she thought, to be forced into taking a partner into KLM, a business formed by her father's own bra-vado and blood, a business handed down to her with love, a business meant to be solely her own. But she hated Blair equally as much for the way he'd demeaned her.

The second truth, more shadowy and elusive than the first, was that her hate was harbored in an inner grief and wonder that she'd let herself respond to Blair on a level far different from what she'd intended. She'd experienced an undeniable, immediate desire for him that went far beyond the physical. She'd let her heart lead her actions, she thought, and that was a humilia-tion she couldn't handle.

Katrina skipped dinner and went to bed, trying to compartmentalize her emotions in order to fall asleep.

Tomorrow would come soon enough, she told herself, and the verdict would be known. Then she'd do what she had to do. But one thing she knew: Katrina Longoria McAllister would retain KLM Oil. One way or another she'd keep what was rightfully hers, no matter how painful the price.

She'd left specific orders with the servants that she was not to be disturbed unless the call was Miguel's, and at ten o'clock the next morning, when she picked up the telephone, her palms were perspiring and her head filled with a thudding anxiety. "Hello, my friend," she said with forced calmness.

"Katrina, I want you to know I tried every contact we discussed. I'm afraid—" He stopped.

"Go on."

"I'm afraid it is impossible. The three men we originally discussed . . . each told me it sounded interesting, but clearly, my lovely Katrina, you must understand, their cultures do not place women on the same level as men."

She said nothing, wanting to rail out against the injustices women faced all over the world. But now was not the time.

"They are afraid to deal with a woman, especially a woman in trouble."

"I see," she said, fighting back tears whose sudden arrival surprised her.

"One thing, Katrina—these people have a great deal of information about the oil business in the United States. They have their ways of finding out things, and all of them knew of your court suit. Perhaps when the

99

suit is resolved, if you will contact me, perhaps I can do something more then."

"Miguel, I can't thank you enough. I know you've done everything you could to help me, and I'm indebted to you." She brushed a tear away from her cheek.

"I am sorry. There is one more man I thought of this morning. I would rather not speak his name over the long distance wires. I'm sure you understand."

Katrina could only guess at the number of contacts Miguel had made on her behalf already. Secrecy was as important in diplomacy for Miguel as it was for her transactions right now. "Certainly," she replied solemnly.

"If there is a chance for me to see this man personally, I will. At this time I do not think it is wise to send my request through a messenger. And I must tell you I am doubtful he will see things differently from the rest. I cannot give you false hope."

His kindness touched her. "I will repay the favor someday, Miguel."

"Between you and me there are no debts owed. I am honored to have been offered the opportunity and saddened because I could not do more. Take care, my Katrina."

He hung up the telephone, and she listened for a moment to the humming and buzzings on the line. After hanging up, she rubbed her eyes and walked over to the bedroom windows.

Outside, the day was bright and springlike and life went on as usual. Two gardeners worked in the morning sun, clipping a hedge to manicured perfection, talking among themselves.

As she watched, her heart and mind heavy with sorrow, Katrina told herself she could give all this up. The luxurious surroundings, the material wealth, all of it had been something like a gift, one she knew she could manage without. Her father had started with nothing, as had her mother, and their only daughter had inherited their determination. But what she wasn't sure she could live without was her self-respect, and now it looked as if it was in jeopardy.

Yet Katrina had also inherited a fighting instinct, and after a few more minutes of reflection, she pulled herself together and called Andy. Her desperation was propelling her into one last ditch effort at saving herself.

"Hi there," she said tenderly. "How are you feeling? Rested?"

"A little," Andy drawled. "Did you hear something from our computer boy?"

She had known that would be his first question. "No, not yet. I wanted to see if you'd drive in for lunch. James could come for you."

"Sure could. And I just might stay around for the afternoon, missy. We've got to see what your lawyers have done on that financial statement of yours."

A bolt of pain shot through her forehead and wedged itself in to stay. Katrina gently rubbed her temples. She needed an aspirin in the worst way, she thought.

"Katrina, if you don't hear from Blair by the middle of the afternoon, I want you to call him. Do you realize this is Friday, and Monday is the day you're supposed to present your financial statement to the court?"

The pain tightened its grip and wrapped itself around her head. She closed her eyes. "Oh, yes, Andy, I know the day, all right." She blinked her eyes open. "Shall I send James?"

"Yeah, send him," Andy said, and hung up.

Judging the time it would take James to return with Andy, Katrina sat outside at a patio table on the edge of the garden. When Andy did arrive, she suddenly felt heartsick at his appearance. He looked drawn and tired with worry. Had she done this to him? she wondered with remorse. Had she indulged herself in sharing the weight of her misery and ignored what it was doing to him?

She ground her teeth together until they hurt, then she stepped forward to greet him. "Thanks for coming, you old darling," she murmured, wrapping her arms around his stooped shoulders

"I was coming, anyway," he replied. "You just didn't know it. Think I could have let the day go by without pestering you?" He beamed and held onto her arm as they walked across the flagstone terrace to the patio table. "Iced tea?" he complained, seeing the glass she'd poured for him.

"Yes." Katrina nodded and pulled her chair closer to his. "It's tea or milk. That's all you're being offered." She motioned to the crystal tea goblets on the Irish linen tablecloth.

"Humph," he mumbled. "I'll take the tea."

"I knew you would."

"I suppose we're having rabbit food for lunch?"

Katrina laughed. "No, sir. I ordered a small chopped steak for us and a fresh spinach salad."

She eyed him with a smile on her lips and the brittle

taste of fear in her mouth. She couldn't bring him any more of her problems, she thought.

"Let's eat," he said, and she motioned for the maid to serve them.

As they ate, the sun gently shining down on them in lacy patterns through the tall trees and the smell of new mown grass wafting around them, Katrina told herself she'd have to involve Andy once more. She had to know if there was any way she could find an investor other than Blair, and right now only Andy could tell her for certain.

Discussing the current price of gold, the stocks Andy had traded recently, and general economic conditions, Katrina unobtrusively led Andy toward the conversation that would yield the information she needed. She took her time, listening with interest to his comments, waiting for the right moment, and when it did she was ready.

"We've been so busy over the last two weeks, I never had the chance to ask you the specifics on Blair's being our investor choice," she said. "Are you absolutely sure there were no other individuals who could come close to his qualifications?"

"Yep." Andy shook his head and ate his last bite of steak.

A sinking feeling came over her, but containing her disappointment, she tried again. "I'd like to see the list sometime."

"I've got it right here, missy." He reached into his shirt pocket and pulled out a piece of bond stationery, opening it with a single wave of his hand.

"My, aren't we efficient," Katrina said jauntily, intent upon concealing her purpose.

"Yep. When you get right down to it, the next three people weren't even a close match. It was this computer wizard all the way." He ran his finger down the short list, commenting on each name, explaining away each possibility.

"You carry around more information in your head than the man you call the computer wizard, Andy."

A wide grin broke across the old man's lined face. "When your daddy and I got started, we did all our figuring in our heads. We thought we were pretty smart in those days."

"You still are," she said.

He looked over at her for a second. "You look tired, missy."

Katrina turned her head away.

"Probably too much socializing again. Where'd you go yesterday? Some all-day tea party?"

She frowned. "Go?"

Andy leaned forward in his chair after the maid had taken his plate away. "Yeah. When James picked me up today he said you'd been gone when he got back from my ranch day before yesterday."

She shook her head, feigning gaiety. "Oh, you know me. I can't resist a good time. After New York I needed a break."

"Humph," he spat. "If you were as worried about yourself as I am about you, there ain't no way you could be gallivanting around like that."

Looking at the old man, Katrina felt her resolve harden. She was the only one who could take care of her problems now, she thought. It was all up to her. Andy was paying too great a price

"Why don't you get some sleep yourself, Andy?" she said. "I've got a few phone calls to make, and a nap would be good for you. I'll wake you up in an hour or so." She stood up.

"I don't need a nap," he replied.

Katrina took a step, then turned back to look at him, forcing a weak smile. "Then maybe an hour of poker. But if I catch you and James smoking or drinking, I'm going to fire him. Hear me?"

"What about chewing?"

"Not funny," she answered quickly, and then went to him, planting a kiss on the top of his head.

"I think I'll call the office then," Andy said.

She was halfway up the brick terrace steps when she heard him call her name softly. She turned around once more.

"You know, missy, I've been thinking about when we get all this settled," he murmured in a low, thoughtful voice. He leaned back in his chair and watched her. "I would consider it a real favor to me if you'd start looking for a husband. Before I die I'd like to see Karl and Beatrice's grandkids. That would make me real happy."

Katrina stood mutely staring down at him, the soft spring breeze playing with her hair, her eyes bright with pain and determination. Steeling herself, she left him, intent upon making her call to New York.

CHAPTER SIX

Katrina sat at her desk in the library for a long time, her mind wandering, avoiding the inevitable. She heard James's voice and Andy's rumbling laugh as they passed the locked library doors. She also heard muted household noises: the vacuum cleaner being run somewhere, the kitchen telephone ringing, even the off-key voice of someone singing. Meanwhile, Katrina fought to control her turbulent emotions.

"This is for you, KLM," she said to herself as she picked up the telephone and dialed Blair's office. "And you, Andy, and . . ." Her faintly whispered words faded away.

Hearing a secretary's voice, Katrina snapped out of her moody self-pity and assumed an icy control. "Mr. Warren, please. Katrina Longoria McAllister calling."

She felt a rush of exhilaration flood her body and her mind begin to clear. All right, she told herself. I'll give in to his demands. There's no other choice. But she was determined to do it in her own way.

A wisp of a smile came to Katrina's red lips, and she

used her free hand to sweep a thick wave of hair up off the back of her neck in a flamboyant and spirited gesture. By the time she finished with Blair, she thought, he'd be a different man. Temporarily, he might have the upper hand, but this was to be a long race, and in the end, Katrina vowed, she'd prove he was no match for her.

She abruptly stood up, holding the receiver to her ear, letting her smile widen as she threw back her head. Aloud she said, "I'll show him yet."

When Blair answered the telephone she was still smiling. "Hello, Blair, this is Katrina."

His secretary had told him who was on the line, but Blair could still hardly believe it. He'd been convinced he'd pushed her too far, but here she was, sounding every bit as spellbinding as the last time she'd spoken to him. Her deep, throaty voice filled him with renewed hope

He held his breath, then spoke. "After hearing it the first time, I'd know that voice anywhere."

"That is a compliment, isn't it?" she chided.

"Indeed it is," Blair replied, still filled with awe.

Katrina laughed, and this time he heard her husky voice dip and sway like a perfectly pitched musical instrument. His picture of the way she'd looked when he first saw her brought a jolting pang of desire.

"Blair, after having time to think it over, I've made up my mind. I'll be waiting for you. Your terms. You name the time and place."

Electrified with surprise, he remained silent, trying to think. She sounded as calm and self-assured as if she were buying a rare painting she was certain would skyrocket in value.

He'd been prepared for two things. The first possibility had been that his demands had been too overwhelming and she would never speak to him again, the second that she would try to strike a different deal, one more in keeping with her own terms. He hadn't imagined her accepting his conditions with what sounded like pleasure.

"You can't imagine how glad I am to hear you say that, Katrina."

"Of course I can. The opportunity to be a part of KLM is a little like involving yourself in another part of history. Texas history, at least."

Her confidence was unbelievable. If he didn't know better, he'd swear the phone shook with it.

"You're saying you agree to all the conditions I established that night?" he asked. In the back of his mind the first stirrings of wariness arose.

"Yes."

"All of them?" He had to know if she intended to carry out her part of the bargain.

"Shall I review them for you, Blair?" Her voice was a trifle cold, even to her own ears, so she lowered it in order to sound more convincing.

"I—"

"Let's see," she interrupted. "You are going to become an equal partner in KLM Oil for a period of six months. In return, I will receive a one sum payment of thirty million dollars. At the end of the six months, if there are sufficient funds in the company, the sum of thirty million will be repaid with an additional ten million profit. If I am unable to come up with the money at that time, you will remain an equal partner until such a time as the money is available. If at any time before the six months time period is up, I am able to pay you forty million dollars, then you relinquish all rights and privileges of the partnership." She took a deep breath, then laughed. "There, I think that's it."

"Well said." There was admiration in his words.

Katrina held the telephone a little distance away from her, knowing what was to come. She'd wait Blair out, force him to ask about the second part of their agreement. Why not, she thought—it was his idea, anyway.

Meanwhile, she'd make sure she was getting exactly what she wanted. "All right, then. I have only one stipulation to add. The thirty million dollars must be transferred to KLM before ten A.M. Monday morning." She paused. "Agreed?"

"There won't be a problem," Blair said, looking down at his watch, calculating if he could take care of it before the banks closed for the day. He frowned. "Except, Katrina, I would naturally want to have all contracts signed by both of us before there is any actual transfer of funds."

She laughed then, and Blair felt as if she'd won and he'd lost. His wariness grew. She was saying all the right things, he thought, but something definitely wasn't right.

"Of course you would. I'm available. You name the time and place. Just as long as I have your assurance of receiving the thirty million before ten A.M. Texas time Monday morning, I'm at your beck and call."

For one wild, giddy second, Blair thought there was a chance that Katrina felt some sense of the same attraction to him as he had for her. Abruptly, he shoved the idea away, thinking it crazy. He'd been warned repeatedly about Katrina's crafty way of getting what she wanted in business, and the wily game she was playing now was just that, he told himself—a game.

She listened to the silence and smiled stiffly. This time he was the one caught off guard, and she the one who was prepared. This time, she thought, he would know that Katrina Longoria McAllister was getting what she wanted, what she had to have. KLM would be saved.

"Let me see, Katrina. It will take me the rest of the afternoon to arrange for the transfer of the money, and my lawyers will have to finish the final legal preparations with your people in Texas." He stalled, trying to decide how best he'd phrase his final question to her. "And I've already made plans for the evening. How about tomorrow?"

"Where?"

"Why don't I come to Houston? I've never been there, and now's as good a time as any. I could fly in sometime tomorrow, have a messenger deliver the final contract and give you an opportunity to read it. You and I could meet tomorrow night."

Wanting to make things as difficult as possible for him, Katrina said sweetly, "We'd meet and sign the contract?"

"Yes."

"That sounds perfectly agreeable to me," she answered pleasantly, wanting him to be confused by her attitude.

"There's one more—"

"I'll see you tomorrow, Blair. Until then—"

"Wait!" he called out. "There's one more thing."

"Oh, what's that?" she asked as innocently as she could.

Blair swallowed. Could he go through with it? he wondered. "There was a second part to my conditions."

"A second part?"

"Katrina," he said more firmly, "I asked for one night with you. Remember?"

Silently she counted to thirty, then in a distant voice she answered him. "Oh, that's right. You did."

Blair held his breath. He couldn't begin to predict what this woman would say next.

"I remember now," she went on. And then her voice dipped into a husky breathlessness. "Then shall we say tomorrow evening both stipulations will be resolved?"

A wave of desolation washed over him. The reasons behind it were so complex, he couldn't analyze them. She'd made it sound as if they were about to exchange formal handshakes, he thought. Yet, listening to the sensual quiver in her voice, his mouth went dry with excitement.

Again she waited for his reply, but this time her heart was singing. She was calling his bluff.

"Katrina, I want to explain something to you," Blair began, then stopped himself. It was not time yet. He had to wait until she'd signed the contract, then see if she intended to carry out her part of the bargain. Speaking up now would destroy his advantage. "I, uh, I'm looking forward to tomorrow night. We'll talk then."

As pleased as she was with the way she was handling herself in this game of one-upmanship, Katrina couldn't resist the question that had preoccupied her since the last time they were together. She'd never forgive herself for asking, she thought, yet she was aware that she'd never forgive herself if she didn't. "One question, Blair. I'm curious."

"What's that?" He waited, expecting anything.

"Why am I a part of this deal?"

Sitting alone in his office, feeling as if he'd been wrung through an emotional wringer, Blair shook his head. He should have known, he thought, that she'd confront him. How could he have assumed she wouldn't demand an explanation?

Yet how could he tell her? he wondered. Certainly not over the telephone. Not now. Tomorrow night when they were face to face, if things worked out the way he hoped, he'd try to explain. Not before.

"There's an old saying, Katrina, which goes something like this: 'There is a pleasure in being mad which none but madmen know.' For now, let's leave it at that. We'll talk tomorrow evening."

She waved her hand in dismissal, as if he could see her. But she was glad he couldn't, because she could feel a tinge of heat on her cheeks as humiliation swam through her. She should have known better than to ask for an explanation, she thought. It had been a mistake, a weak move. "Make certain I have the money by Monday morning, Blair."

"Good-bye, Katrina, until tomorrow." But she'd hung up before he finished

After Blair made the necessary phone calls to begin marshaling his millions, he left the office. His secretary's raised eyebrows acknowledged his unusual behavior, since Blair's normal work schedule was an uninterrupted fifteen-hour day.

But he felt he couldn't stay there any longer. His legs and arms stung, and he wanted to do something physical to relieve the feeling that every nerve in his body was on emergency alert. Whether it was from the convuluted twists of Katrina's way of talking to him, or from some inner reaction of his own, Blair couldn't say.

He ran toward his Trump Tower apartment vaguely aware of the stares of passersby, uncaring, knowing only that he had to find release and that the pain in his feet and chest from the running were replacing the unfamiliar feelings he'd experienced earlier.

The next day, in the airplane flying to Houston for his rendezvous with Katrina, Blair sat lost in thought once again. He wasn't at all prepared for a woman like Katrina, he thought. All his life he'd been a loner of sorts, absorbed in a world of unemotional machines. Until now he'd liked that sort of life, thinking of himself as a man who wasn't anti-social, only reserved in public. Now, however, he wished he'd spent more time around people—especially different types of women. Maybe if he had done things differently, he mused, he'd know how to handle Katrina. As it was, he felt helpless, as if he were on a collision course with a runaway train.

The night before, he'd taken a date out to dinner, a woman whom he'd been seeing for the past two months. He enjoyed her company, found her attractive and witty, all the things he thought he wanted. But when she opened her apartment door and began to talk, Blair realized he wouldn't go out with her again. Upon reflection he knew it wasn't anything she'd said or done—it actually had nothing to do with her. It was Katrina. How could he find anyone exciting after being with her? he thought. And so, he'd ended the evening early, using the age-old excuse of a headache, saying good-bye as gently as he could.

He was reminded again of Katrina's power when he dialed her number from his hotel room at five o'clock that afternoon. He'd sent the contract to her by messenger when he'd arrived, and waited a few hours before calling her, giving her time to read it.

"Katrina," he said when she answered. "I hope you've had time to read the contract. I'm afraid it was a little long."

She listened to Blair's voice, aware of the practicality of his words, wondering why he didn't seem to be feeling the same rush of tension she felt. "I've read it," she replied. "Andy's studying it right now, along with my lawyers."

"I'm sure they'll find everything just as you and I agreed, but if you like, I can call back later when your people have finished going over it, or you could call me back. Then we'll set a time for our meeting this evening."

His politeness was lost on her. "They'll be finished within the next hour or so. Have you arranged for the money?"

Blair bit his lip. She was interested in only one thing. He could hear it in the way she spoke and feel it in her words. "Yes, Katrina. I have."

"Good," she replied. "Why don't you come to my home this evening. We can sign the contract and take care of our business here." Her voice rose with impact.

It was important to Katrina that the night be spent in her own familiar surroundings. She'd decided that if she were going to be coerced into giving away a part of her self-respect and dignity as well as her business, she wanted the security of her own home.

Again he felt as if he were losing control. "I was thinking of asking you to come here, to my hotel. I have a nice suite of rooms."

"You've never been to Houston, and it would please me very much to have you in my home for the evening, especially since we're about to be partners." The words stung the inside of her mouth. Katrina had never felt as humiliated—it was searing through her like a red-hot poker.

"What time?" he asked, giving in to her wishes.

"I'll send my chauffeur to the hotel to pick you up at ten o'clock. I have a previous engagement and won't be back until then."

There was no such engagement, but when she saw Blair, she intended to dress as if she'd been out for the evening. Since Blair couldn't see her the night before because of plans he'd had, she'd decided to keep him waiting tonight.

"Very well," Blair answered, still uncomfortable with the plan.

She hung up and went to see how Andy and her lawyers were doing. She'd read the contract three times, word for word. The document appeared to be exactly as they'd agreed, but thinking she might have missed something, she was anxious to hear Andy's opinion as well as that of the lawyers.

Katrina walked down the imposing staircase to the library where the group was meeting, but instead of going directly to the library, she walked out to the pool, trying to clear her mind so she could concentrate on the contract. Blair's demand interfered with her concentration, the thought of what she was going to have to do tonight jarring her. Revenge would be her only satisfaction, she thought.

She shook her head, absentmindedly bending down at the pool's edge to run her fingers back and forth through the water. There was still one extremely important factor she couldn't avoid thinking about. Coming hand in hand with her anger, the idea persisted that if Blair had never demanded it, her attraction to him might have willingly sent her into his arms. Instead, she was going as if there were a loaded gun at her head.

It seemed to Katrina that her emotions were being shredded apart, piece by piece. Retracing her steps back toward the library, she remembered how Andy had reacted the night before, when she'd told him about Blair coming to Houston.

She'd gone up to the bedroom she called Andy's, carefully devising a way to tell him about Blair's contractual offer without mentioning the embarrassing details of his personal demand upon her. She'd been nervous and uneasy, aware of her need to hide information from Andy, worried that he'd tell her she'd made a serious blunder. Andy's approval meant so much to her that she didn't think she could bear it if he was angered by what she'd agreed to give Blair in return for the money.

But she quickly realized she needn't have worried

about her old friend. When she entered his room after a hasty knock, she saw James quickly fanning the air to clear away unmistakably strong cigar fumes. Meanwhile, Andy was popping a mint into his mouth. Neither of them could hide what they'd been doing—the guilt on their faces said so.

"I won't comment on what's been going on in here," Katrina teased as she closed the door behind her.

"That's good," Andy told her, "because we're just having a little fun and it's all my fault."

Katrina had laughed. "I'm sure that's the truth." And then she'd told him why she'd come, and James had excused himself, leaving the two of them alone.

As directly as she could, Katrina explained her version of Blair's offer. She told Andy only that Blair had offered the money in exchange for the partnership and the conditions. She deliberately didn't tell Andy about Blair's personal demand.

Andy sat at the poker table for a long time, his hands idly playing with the scattered plastic chips, his mind obviously at work on what she'd told him. When he finally spoke, she felt an enormous relief.

"Well, missy," he'd said, "I think you've done as good as you could do. The man would have been a fool to ask for anything less, and we sure didn't go to New York looking for any fool, now did we?"

She had shaken her head. "No."

"All right, let's put it behind us. You don't want to have to do this, I know, but that's the way things are right now. It seems to me that we're just going to have to use this computer wizard's money to our advantage, pay him back as fast as we can, and shoo him back to New York."

She'd smiled, fighting back the wellspring of emotions threatening to overflow inside her. "Okay," she'd said softly.

Taking her soft hand in his gnarled one, Andy had looked at her for a long time before adding, "Now, then, missy, let's get on with it. Let's put KLM back where she belongs. You can do it."

Now, as she turned the knob to the library door, she took comfort in the confidence Andy had in her, and told herself to harden her heart against Blair and the mistaken feelings she'd allowed herself. She stepped inside, all eyes turning her way.

"What do you think?" she asked

"It's good," her head lawyer exclaimed, raising her hand in salute. "Your money is guaranteed, and there's enough latitude in the wording so that he can't do anything to KLM you don't want done."

Andy nodded, along with the other two top-flight lawyers on the KLM payroll. Katrina trusted them, and the sense of relief she now felt was immense. "So be it," she said.

There was a knock at the door. "Miss McAllister, telephone for you, ma'am. A Mr. Warren," the maid said with a curt nod.

Katrina picked up the telephone, feeling a surge of adrenaline flow through her body. What if he wanted to back out? she asked herself. "Hello."

"Katrina, I've been thinking," Blair said decisively. "I'd like our first night together to be in a place unknown to either of us. I'd like you to come to my hotel suite tonight instead of my coming to your home."

"Our *first!*" she cried out incredulously. Then it struck her that she was surrounded by people who would be interested in the interaction between the about-to-be partners in KLM. Her heart was beating hard and her hands had turned clammy with rage

"Yes," Blair continued. "I think neutral ground is best."

There was no way she could bargain with him. His voice sounded too commanding, and she was caught in a far-from-private conversation. "I'll be there at ten o'clock," she finally answered.

This time Blair was the first to hang up.

Enraged beyond reason, Katrina managed to remain outwardly calm long enough to carry on a brief conversation with her guests, then excused herself. She stalked up the stairs feeling physically sick. She felt a clutching tightness within her, as though a strong metal hand were grabbing at her and then letting go. By the time she reached her bedroom and slammed the door behind her, she was breathless with frustration.

She quickly went to her bathroom, wet a washcloth and wrung it out, then patted it along her cheeks and neck. Her fury felt like an unchecked fire. Blair's insistence that she come to his hotel room was the last straw. She'd been pushed to the edge.

She didn't know how long it took her to pull herself together, but at some point her heated rage began to cool, allowing her to think more clearly. She had to have revenge, she decided, determined to show Blair which one of them was in control.

Purposefully, she stepped across the room to a wicker table, took out a pen and stationery from the drawer, and began to write.

> Dear Blair,
>
> I have no doubt you have enjoyed the evening. Now that you have accomplished what you set out to do, I think it would be best for you to go back to New York and live your life. Leave the work to those of us who can handle it.
> Please don't kid yourself into believing that spending one night with me gives you any rights and privileges. As far as I am concerned, this night means no more to me than a new hair style—different but unmemorable. Our contractual arrangements have been completed and I believe it is best for you to go back where you belong. Your money will be well taken care of.
>
> > Katrina Longoria McAllister

She completed her signature with a flourishing upswing and waited for the ink to dry. Then she folded the letter, placed it in an envelope, and sealed it.

Reaching for the telephone, she wrote Blair's name on the envelope and dialed a number. "Emerson Messenger Service? I want a messenger sent to pick up an envelope and deliver it to a Mr. Blair Warren at the Remington Hotel at precisely six o'clock tomorrow morning." Completing her business, she hung up, a smug smile on her face.

She was going to have to go through with her part of

the agreement, she thought, but she'd do it on her terms. She'd give Blair a night to remember, be the vamp, entice him to desires he'd never known, and by the time he received his message be safely back home with the contract. She'd get everything she wanted from him, she thought while he'd only receive a taste of what he wanted from her. She began to dress for the evening, the smug smile still on her face.

CHAPTER SEVEN

Standing outside the door to Blair's hotel suite, Katrina experienced an unexpected flash of despair. Slowly, she lowered her raised hand. She couldn't knock on the door, not just yet. Instead, she closed her eyes and took a deep breath. The entire episode was tearing her apart, made her feel degraded. It was not the time to let her defenses down, she thought. Reluctantly, she straightened her tense shoulders and tilted her chin high, calling upon the reserve of inner strength she knew she had, aware that now was the time to use it.

She knocked hard two times and waited. When Blair opened the door Katrina stepped inside, smiling warmly at him as she passed, leaning nonchalantly against the entry wall as he closed the door behind her.

Once more Blair felt unprepared for Katrina as she stepped around him and then turned to look back. "Thank you for coming here, Katrina," he said quickly, locking the door.

The imposing air of hers, and the tantalizing fragrance of her seductive, flowery perfume washed over him in waves. Without warning, Blair's legs went rubbery.

"I'm right on time, aren't I?" she asked in her most beguiling voice, meanwhile reaching out for his arm and lifting his wrist so she could see his watch.

Her touch was like a hot brush of flame, startling him. He yanked his hand away. "Uh, yeah, you are," he stammered, feeling tongue-tied and clumsy.

"Your watch says ten thirty. I swear I thought it was ten o'clock." Katrina reached out for Blair's arm again, letting her long red fingernails slide across the top of his hand before running her fingers lightly around his watchband. Then she raised her eyes to his.

"I, uh, I always keep my watch thirty minutes ahead," he said, intensely aware of the way she was looking at him.

There was a knowing glint in her dark brown eyes that matched the smile on her lips. Each time he saw her, he thought, she was more beautiful than he'd remembered. His eyes lowered to take in the creamy olive smoothness of her shoulders. The seductive way she leaned against the wall made his pulse soar.

"The truth is that my watch doesn't keep very good time, but I've gotten used to it." Overwhelmed, he didn't know what he was even saying.

"With all your money why don't you buy yourself a new watch?"

"Uh, I don't know," he began, looking down at her small hand as it hovered over his. "I just sort of make do. My secretary keeps telling me to buy a new one, but honestly, I like this one. I'm a creature of habit, I guess."

He knew he was talking gibberish, but it didn't matter. What did matter, he thought, was the way his hand tingled in response to her touch.

"Oh, do you have a personal secretary?" Katrina turned and walked into the living area, deliberately keeping her back to him.

On and off for the past twenty-four hours she'd planned her entrance, what she'd wear and how she would look. Right now, she wanted to make sure Blair had the full effect of her clothes. After a great deal of thought, Katrina had chosen a Bob Mackie black-cotton cocktail dress cut particularly low, with color bursts of sequin streamers running gaily across the front. She also wore a red-satin wrap with rows of feminine-looking gathers; she wore it below her shoulders.

She had chosen diamond earrings that dangled down beneath her earlobes, and wore no other jewelry. Her Charles Jourdan shoes were black satin, with a dainty bow tied at the back above soaring high heels. Meticulously, she'd applied extra touches of her current favorite perfume, Giorgio, to every part of her body, and she could smell its provocative scent rise up all around her.

Finally, she turned around and glanced up at Blair. Immobile, he stood where she'd left him. She couldn't discern the look on his face. Dressed in a peach silk shirt and richly colored charcoal slacks, he looked offhandedly handsome

He was staring at her, and while she had his full attention, she let her red-satin wrap fall from around her arms and drop to the sofa. She dropped the red leather envelope in her hand on top of the wrap and smiled. "I asked if you had a personal secretary. Do you?"

He shook his head, and walked toward her.

"Does anyone travel with you?" Katrina glanced around the suite.

"No. I take care of myself," he answered.

"That's something we all have to do, isn't it?" she asked. "One way or another." Her comment was an unsubtle reminder of her dilemma. Resentment seethed inside her, but she fought it down.

Yet even as she was playing the role of seductress, Katrina found herself trying to think of another way to save her company. No matter how many times she'd been reassured by Andy and her lawyers, she still had a gnawing fear that there might be some legal loophole Blair could use to hold onto her company after the contract had ended. She'd never had to share anything before, and hated even the thought of sharing anything with him.

"I ordered champagne for our celebration," he was saying. "I thought we'd open it as soon as we sign the contract." He motioned toward an iced bottle inside a champagne bucket on the coffee table.

Next to it, Katrina saw a dish of caviar, assorted crackers, and an arrangement of fresh white flowers. She took a moment more to glance around the beautifully decorated suite.

"For a man who won't buy himself a new watch, you certainly know how to travel." She sat down on the plush tapestry sofa.

Blair shook his head and laughed. "I didn't request this room, believe me. My secretary back at the office does all my travel arrangements and she thinks this is the way I should travel."

He laughed again. Katrina watched his hazel eyes change color in the light, noticed his expressive shrug, and was struck by how relaxed he seemed.

"My secretary would have me living like some sultan, spending money like there was no tomorrow, if I let her run my life. I made the mistake of agreeing to let her find me a new apartment in New York when the rental agreement on my old one ran out. I was so involved in one of my computer projects that before I knew it I had signed an agreement for a place in Trump Tower. Can you imagine me in Trump Tower?"

Before she could think, Katrina said "Yes. And it would be very understated, subdued . . . quite masculine."

"Maybe someday you'll come there."

Lowering her eyes, Katrina felt the need to remind herself of her purpose for being here, but every second made it more difficult. Blair was behaving as he had when she'd first met him—all attentive politeness, gently persuasive—and she was reminded of how easily she'd once been attracted to him.

She glanced at him and looked away again. He had the most off-guard grin, she thought—white, even teeth caught between a crooked smile. There was something else she found appealing: his calmness. He never seemed anything but at peace with himself. What right did he have to be calm, she thought abruptly, when he was about to take away what little peace she had of her own?

All business again, Katrina picked up the oversized leather envelope and said, "Here's the contract. My lawyers suggested we sign it with two witnesses present, and so I have two of my lawyers waiting downstairs to serve as our witnesses."

He knew she was ignoring his attempt to establish some sort of intimate conversation, and he didn't blame her. If he were in her shoes, he thought, he might react the same way. Meanwhile, he continued to study her.

His directness bothered Katrina. The speculative way he regarded her made her think about what was to come later. She was about to ask him to stop staring, but he didn't give her a chance.

"My lawyers wanted me to add some clauses to the contract. They think I'm being far too easy on you."

"Funny, I don't see it that way at all." She arched one brow and returned his stare.

"My lawyers think you'll try to get rid of me the minute my money has gotten your oil business straightened out again."

"Our contract pretty well spells it all out, doesn't it?"

"More or less, but I have allowed you to get a little vague with the wording about what happens six months from now."

"If your lawyers are worth their salaries, they've protected you."

He laughed. "It seems they don't trust you, Katrina. They insist you're going to try and dump me."

"What would you do if you were in my position?"

"You and I are so different, I couldn't say."

"Wait a minute. You're not saying you're backing out of the deal before we sign, are you?" she asked defiantly.

He squared his shoulders. "Are you willing to uphold your part of the agreement? If you are, I'll call down to the desk and ask them to send one of your lawyers up. I brought a witness of my own . . . the lawyer I was telling you about, the one who trusts you the least." He hesitated. "Well, are you willing to comply with my demands or not?"

Blair had tried to conceal his unease with harshness. He'd planned the whole evening so that he would control it, but despite his plans, when Katrina had walked into his suite she'd taken over. Her very presence, he thought, had done it.

"You mean am I willing to go to bed with you?" she answered cautiously.

"Yes."

Her mind swam with a thousand ways to resist, her heart hammered out of control, and she felt herself tense up tighter than a wound coil. But she forced each painful word out one by one. "I'm a real rarity in the oil business, Blair. I belong to the old Texas school where a person's word is her bond. I gave you my word, and my word is good."

He felt her words pierce through him like arrows. He could feel the intensity of her emotions, yet he knew he had to proceed. It was almost over.

Calling the desk, he told the night manager what he wanted. The wait for the two lawyers to arrive seemed endless. When he could no longer stand the silence between them, he spoke up. "Since we're going to sign the contract in a moment, why not break out the champagne now?" He walked over to the table and stood in front of her, peeling away the foil on the bottle.

She found herself silently repeating over and over how immensely important her masquerade was. "Here, let me help," she said in her huskiest voice.

She stood up and reached under his outstretched arms for the two champagne goblets on the tray. When she did, she stood close to him, bending her head so her hair brushed against his shoulder, letting her arms graze his as she took the glasses.

He breathed the fresh smell of her hair and her seductive perfume as she moved around him. He wondered what her raven hair would look like fanned out across his white linen pillow. He was still thinking about it when the lawyers arrived.

Blair told them what he wanted with his usual expediency, put down the complimentary bottle of champagne they'd brought, and looked for a pen. As he moved, Katrina studied him, thinking that the entire episode did not make sense. Blair gave every impression of being an exceptional man, she thought, far too gentle for the despicable deal he'd insisted upon.

"I am very, very pleased with this contract, Katrina," he told her after they'd formally signed it and the lawyers had left. Hastily, he popped the cork off the champagne bottle.

Katrina picked up the goblets and held them toward him. "My money is guaranteed," she said, more to herself than to him as he poured the champagne.

"Let's drink a toast to KLM," he insisted.

She forced a wry smile.

"But first I have something for you," he said, reaching in among the fresh flowers on the coffee table. He pulled out a tiny package wrapped in gold foil. "Open it."

The moment the contract had been signed, Katrina felt an enormous sense of relief, as if the weight of the world had been lifted from her shoulders. But now, knowing they were only minutes away from fulfilling the second part of the agreement, her head hammered with mounting anxiety.

She put down the goblets, took the package and opened it. Inside a suede box she found a simple gold-chained necklace with a piece of hammered gold dangling from it in the shape of an oil well. In the center of the gold well there was a canary-yellow diamond.

She held it in her outstretched fingers and shook her head. "I can't accept this, Blair." She couldn't begin to guess the value of the diamond.

"It's meant to honor our contract. I want you to have it."

"I can't seem to find a great deal of honor in our contract." She couldn't resist the cutting words.

Blair refused to let her scathing comment disturb him. Instead, he took the chain from her fingers and placed it around her neck with a proprietary air.

"And now our toast." He picked up the goblets and held hers out to her. "To the future of KLM. May it be even better than before with the two of us to care for it." He touched his glass to hers and then drank, watching to see what she would do.

Katrina thought she might choke. This overbearing man, she thought, was adding insult to injury. All she wanted now was to be rid of him, but she reminded herself that she was getting what she wanted, that she was merely playing a part. Aware of his watchful gaze, she took a sip and closed her eyes, feeling the bubbles slide down her throat.

"Is something wrong?" Blair studied her, trying to decide how to proceed.

Everything, she wanted to scream. "No, nothing. How about another?" she said, holding her glass up for a refill.

Blair filled her goblet, and his too. They sipped the champagne, cautiously eyeing one another over the rims of the glasses. The tension between them grew until he thought he could hear it.

"Do you mind if I call Andy?" she inquired, already turning toward the telephone.

He reached out and caught her. "And then?"

She felt her hand unexpectedly engulfed by his, and spilled her champagne to the floor. He tilted her hand upright and stepped closer. This wasn't working, she thought, flustered and unsure.

Now she looked at him and realized Blair wasn't a star-struck suitor looking for a night out with one of Houston's most prominent young women. He was a man, a man in complete control of himself. She looked down at the spilled champagne, watching the way it spread across the carpet.

"And then we'll see what develops," she promised huskily, retrieving her hand before he could feel her quiver.

His eyes darted to her face, questioning, confronting. She smiled suggestively at him, hiding how much the situation was hurting her

He let her go, never taking his eyes from her, and listened to her talking on the phone to Andy. As the time grew nearer for him to tell her the truth and end the game he'd established, Blair wondered how to begin his explanation. Katrina's test was almost finished.

When she had assured Andy everything was signed and finalized, Andy laughed raucously and told her he was going to celebrate. Feeling as if she might explode, Katrina slowly hung up the phone, telling herself to get her debt over with as soon as possible so she could go on with the rescue of KLM. She swung around to face Blair.

"And now to finalize all the conditions of the contract," she said, lowering her dark lashes and bringing her hand up to her strapless gown.

Blair had dimmed the lights, their bodies casting elongated shadows as they stepped toward one another. "Katrina, I've wanted this since the first time I laid eyes on you," he said

Katrina began to slide the dress downward with her fingers. She'd rehearsed this scene over and over in her mind for the last twenty-four hours—not because she wanted to, but because she felt she had to. She knew beforehand that her reactions at this moment would be compounded by nervousness. After all, she told herself, she was doing this against her will, sacrificing her body in a way she'd never dreamed possible, stripping herself of a self-respect which meant everything to her. And he was behaving as if this were the natural culmination of their relationship.

Blair reached out and let his open hand slowly begin to caress the curve of her shoulder. His touch brought a shiver to her spine, and she was mortified at how her body was betraying her. From the smile she saw forming on his lips, Katrina knew he had assumed her body's reaction was one of pleasure rather than protest.

He brought his lips down to the base of her throat, sampling the taste of her skin, then let his mouth move across the soft flesh until he reached her shoulders. "Shall I help you?" he murmured as he brought both hands around her back, then moved them down to her waist.

"I'll do it myself," she insisted with a catch in her voice.

As she spoke, his hands moved commandingly to the curve of her hips, and she was aware of a light but steady pressure as he maneuvered her body closer to his. She tried to pull back, struck by the abrupt rise of temperature in the room as well as the hungry way he was staring at her.

Reluctantly, he released her, his hands still hovering next to her hips. He waited to see what she'd do next, his desire for her so fierce he felt on the edge of panic, like a man about to go over an immeasurably high waterfall.

Katrina looked into his eyes and caught the blatant desire that flashed there. He was acting as if he believed she actually wanted to be here with him, she thought, and there was no doubt he intended to get what he wanted from her.

She was mortified at having to put herself on display. Nothing could have prepared her for the shame she now felt, and he was doing nothing to make it less difficult for her. Katrina found herself hating him.

Steeling herself, she was about to lower the gown to her waist. Then she looked in his eyes and stopped. He seemed so pleased with himself, she thought, so smugly self-satisfied that she wanted to scream.

Blair gazed at her delicate breasts, partially exposed above the gown. Their fullness seemed erotic, invitingly taunting him. His body throbbed with a soaring sense of frustration. He wanted her more than he'd ever wanted anything in his life.

Her dark eyes flashed, and Blair realized how painful this was for her. He knew she was only willing to do this to save her company. It was a sacrifice. It made no difference that she pretended to be willing and eager, her eyes told the truth.

He watched as she began to lower her gown even farther. His heart went out to her, and then his hand, to stop her. "Katrina, wait."

She didn't understand. What was wrong?

"You've proven yourself. There's no reason for you to go any further." He held his hand firmly atop hers and began to explain. "I never intended to force you into doing this. You've fulfilled all your obligations to me. We're even now."

Confusion stunned her as she pulled her gown back over her breasts. "I don't—"

"I know." He nodded vigorously. "I know." He took her hand and led her to the sofa.

Katrina followed him, her mind awash with questions, her anger unabated. Yet she followed his lead, fury pounding inside her head.

"How to begin?" he asked, bracing himself to look directly at her, feeling her wrath. "Okay." He sighed, still clasping her hand inside his. "When I let it be known confidentially to a few investor friends of mine in New York that Katrina McAllister was coming to see me with a proposition of some kind, they hit the roof. They warned me repeatedly against getting myself involved with a Texas-style wheeler-dealer who'd take my money and leave me with a dry hole."

Katrina noticed that his eyes didn't waver as he talked. Whatever it was he was leading up to, he was certainly serious about it, she decided. She moved farther away from him, trying at the same time to calm herself and collect her thoughts, but he leaned toward her until their faces were inches apart.

"I wanted to get into the oil business. You knew that." He looked at her as if he expected an answer.

"Everybody wants to be in the oil business." She wasn't about to make anything easy for him.

"But I wanted it like a kid wants a new bicycle, and so I tried to think of a way I could make sure I wasn't fleeced by a big-time operator." He blinked. "My friends were right in trying to protect me. I've never made any deals in my life. I've always left that up to my lawyers."

"You've made your point. You have friends." The idea of being called a wheeler-dealer didn't appeal to her at all.

"You came to me with an offer that I knew from the start was based on false information, and you asked me for millions of dollars. Can't you see why I was leery of you?"

Katrina thought of jumping up and leaving, but his sincere appearance and her burning curiosity restrained her. The calm man was gone, replaced by a demanding, persuasive person speaking with emotional conviction. She gave him a condescending shrug.

"But it didn't take me long to figure out how I could deal with you."

She watched an annoying grin begin at one corner of his mouth. "I realize you're very proud of yourself, but I hope you're not waiting for congratulations from me," she warned.

His grin became a laugh. "I guess not, but I thought it was clever of me, nevertheless."

"Go on with your story," Katrina said, her curiosity piqued.

"I sensed immediately that there were two things which were immensely important to you—two things I could easily identify with. You were ready to fight like hell to keep your family company, and you treasured your own inner core of self-respect."

The impact of his words rocked her. He couldn't have been more right, which made her feel uneasy and vulnerable. She got up from the sofa, and at a lost for anything else to do, went to find her champagne glass. When she brought it back with her, Blair poured more champagne for both of them.

"One thing about me, Katrina, that you have to understand—to appreciate what I'm telling you—I grew up without all the niceties. I never had a new bicycle. I wore my brothers' hand-me-down clothes. My family had no money. We survived on the barter system."

He thought he saw a faint glimmer of pity in her expression as her lips lingered on the champagne glass. "Don't get me wrong. I'm not asking you to feel sorry for me. I had a good childhood, a very good life. But, Katrina, I'm willing to bet that thirty million dollars means a great deal more to me than it does to you."

She felt herself gradually weakening as she listened. This was a totally different man from the one she imagined she'd find tonight, she thought, and continued to sip from her drink, if only to draw her eyes away from his.

"I knew I had to find a way to see how far you'd go, how much all this meant to you. And so, after I had the chance to study you for a little while, take in all that proud arrogance of yours, and hear you tell me about your family's company, it all clicked together. I created those two conditions to find out how sincere you really were about saving your company." He lifted his hand to let one finger slide slowly across the curve of her cheek. "And I found out."

CHAPTER EIGHT

Icily, she reached up and took his hand away from her face. "What am I supposed to do now? Thank you?"

She felt like a punching bag with all the air knocked out of it. Anger and humiliation sprung to life in her in a hot fury like a spring forest fire.

"I'm asking you a question. What do you expect from me now?" She couldn't believe this was happening. It still didn't make sense to her, despite his explanation.

"I'm trying to be as honest with you as I can," Blair replied. "I want you to understand what I was doing and why I felt I had to do it. I'm not the ogre you've been thinking I am."

Katrina stood and began pacing the room. "Why me?" she whispered with a shake of her head. "Why did you want to degrade me so?"

Abruptly, she stopped pacing and stood in the middle of the room, her dark eyes focused on him, searching his face for the answer. Her voice stirred him, and he averted his eyes for a moment to gather his thoughts. There had to be a way to make her understand, he told himself.

"Don't you see?" he finally answered, walking over to Katrina, who looked forlorn. "I had to do it."

"No, I sure as hell don't see," she replied hotly.

He raised his arms as if he might embrace her, but seeing her angry look, let his arms fall back. "Give me a chance, won't you? At least agree to listen while I try to explain."

She eyed him uneasily, her body rigid with tension brought on by the situation. All her life she'd made her own rules and constraints, but now she felt so thoroughly shaken that she couldn't make up her mind what to do.

"Katrina, please," he begged, taking her hand and leading her back to the sofa. "Listen, now. I want you to think of what you would have done differently had you been me. Put yourself in my place."

His patience camouflaged his fear. Making her understand was more important to him than anything had ever been.

"If you had been raised all your life without anything, and suddenly years of hard work and persistence pay off and you became the target for every crank nickel-and-dime investor in the country, what would you do? Don't you think you'd be a little leery of people's motives when they approached you with an offer to make you even richer by using millions of your own money?"

He refused to continue until she signaled that she was listening. A few seconds of silence ensued before she gave him a brief nod. Blair cleared his throat to continue, but before he did, he brought one arm around the back of the sofa and let his hand rest near her shoulder. Katrina made no effort to move away.

"And then you're warned repeatedly about someone who is coming to you for a colossal investment, and when that person shows up she fills you with information you know is false . . ." He took a breath. "Now don't give up on me, hear me out," he warned, feeling her start to draw away. "Remember, I'm asking you to pretend you're in my shoes."

As she listened, Katrina felt her distress slowly begin to ebb. If she looked at the situation from his point of view it began to make a little sense. But she couldn't have said whether she could forgive him for having hurt her.

"And then, Katrina, you had the unmitigated gall to ask me to hand over millions of dollars with no collateral, not one solid shred of collateral. Now I ask you to tell me, what would you have done?"

She sat quietly for what seemed hours, staring down at the glass in her hand, slowly twisting and turning the stem back and forth across the fabric of her skirt.

"I . . . I think that I would have told you to go straight to hell." She let out a deep sigh of relief. There, she'd said it. She'd told the truth. "Looking at it from your vantage point, I think that's what I would have done."

As immense relief came over him, his eyes swept across her face. He longed to hold her then, but he knew he had to exercise restraint. They had broken new and precarious ground. Instead of reaching out to embrace her, he put his fingertips to her shoulder and let them lightly rest there.

"I'm asking for your forgiveness." His voice came thick and unsteady, surprising both of them. "I'll do anything I can to mend things between us. Give me a chance to prove I'm really not so bad."

If she faced things from his point of view, Katrina realized, it was clear he was as aggressive as she was, willing to risk his fortune to get what he wanted. The full impact of the situation began to sink in—how he'd challenged her, pushed her to the outer limits in order to judge whether she wanted to save her business badly enough, and then stopped when he knew he'd succeeded.

The fact that he'd stopped when he did meant a great deal to Katrina. A lesser man would have taken full advantage of the situation, she thought.

The longer she thought about it, the more she admired him for the way he'd handled himself. Blair Warren could prove to be a true asset to KLM, she decided. He was precisely the sort of man she could use.

Katrina felt her rage begin to float away to be replaced by a triumphant feeling. She knew she was now getting exactly what she wanted from the situation, and more.

She put down her glass and extended her hand toward him. "Shake."

Blair immediately responded, his white teeth flashing in a smile. "Thank you."

"For what?" she asked, aware of how he held her hand after the handshake was finished. She pulled it awkwardly away.

"For opening yourself up. For being able to look at things from my perspective. It takes a certain kind of person to be able to do that, and I'll always admire you for it."

She was amazed. Despite all the pain he'd caused her, there was something fascinating about his ability to focus his entire being upon her, making her feel as if she were the most important person in all the world. His microscopic attentiveness stimulated feelings she didn't want to admit having.

"Now let's drink a sincere toast to KLM and the two of us. Will you?" He leaned across to the coffee table and picked up the champagne bottle.

She watched him carefully, wondering how a person could reverse himself so suddenly, and found herself wishing they'd only just met.

A shock of sandy hair had fallen across his forehead. When he raised his head to hand her the champagne glass, Katrina resisted a powerful urge to push it back. Instead, she lowered her eyes to the glass. Ridiculous, she thought. This was the man she'd sworn vengeance on only hours ago.

"To KLM and to us," Blair toasted. "I hope you're able to drink with better feelings toward our union than you were earlier tonight."

The warmth of his smile made her respond in kind. "Indeed I am." She sipped from her glass again, letting the tension drain away from her.

There was a long silence between them, but it was relaxed and easy.

"I'm thinking of my father," she said dreamily, interrupting his thoughts. "The more I think about it, the more I think my father would have admired your style too."

Raising an eyebrow in open disbelief, Blair laughed. "I hardly think so. I've heard about those Texas men, and if Andy's any example, I think your father would have had me shot before you and I ever had time to negotiate."

Her mind raced back to when her father had been alive. "You're right. He would have. All right, I'll put it another way. The fact that you did this to me—that I was a victim—I won't pretend to appreciate. But I admire your strategy, and he would have also."

Blair's expression turned serious. "What about Andy? Did you tell him about . . . about my proposition?"

Concern was written all over him, and Katrina decided it would be kind to quickly alleviate it. "No, I didn't."

"I'm very grateful," he said, his concerned look evaporating. "I would have hated to . . . well, let's just leave it at that. On to the positive." His voice rose enthusiastically.

"The positive is saving KLM," Katrina declared. "It's the most important thing we'll be involved in for the next six months of our lives."

"If you should find yourself able to forgive me, it might not be."

As her mind absorbed the meaning of his words, she found herself wanting to flirt with Blair with all the abandon of a lovestruck teenager. Blair gave off an aura of expectation, she thought, that made it seem that something was always on the brink of happening. Katrina didn't know whether she felt as she did out of sheer admiration for the way he'd handled himself, or because from the very beginning she'd found herself physically attracted to him.

"What else do you have in mind?" Her voice sounded

too breathless, too light and airy for her, but it suddenly seemed she was beyond help. She whirled her champagne glass between her delicate fingers.

"Let's play it by ear, shall we?"

Her formidable demeanor had softened, and Blair wondered if she was caught up in the vibrations humming around and between them. He let himself imagine the dynamics the two of them could awaken in one another.

"I don't know how to do that," she answered. "I never have been very good at letting nature take its course, playing it by ear, or rolling with the punches," she stated dramatically.

Blair collapsed against the sofa, his legs and arms sprawling outward as wave after wave of laughter rolled through him. His eyes were watering as he glanced over at her and saw the dumbfounded look on her face. Her expression made it seem even funnier, rekindling his laughter.

"You're absolutely right," he said between outbursts. "I'd bet a million dollars on the truth of your statement, Katrina. I'd bet there's not much that escapes your control."

She found herself grinning at his hyenalike antics. Maybe he was right, she thought, but on the positive side, she did have a knack for handling things. Settling her head back against the sofa, she thoughtfully watched him.

It struck her that for the first time in her life she'd met her match. He flustered her, he was unnerving to a fault, he drove her mad with his far-ranging reactions and his ability to arouse emotions within her she'd never felt before.

Here was a man who wasn't the least bit intimidated by her, she thought. If anything, his actions had proven that *he* was the intimidator—an absorbing man whose character seemed strong and commanding.

Briefly, Katrina closed her eyes. It felt good to relax, after having been so tightly wired with anxiety earlier in the evening.

"Very well," he said, "since you don't want to let anything evolve naturally, I'll tell you what I have in mind."

"Good." She opened her eyes and sat up straight.

"I have a vision . . . about the two of us. I'm attracted to you. I'm hoping you've been struck with the same thought."

He stared at her point-blank, and she was reminded of how she'd first thought his eyes could see the truth inside her. Uneasily, she shifted on the sofa. "Well, that's certainly what I'd call laying your cards on the table," she admitted.

"I thought you wanted me to."

"I thought so too."

"And now?"

"Now I'm not so sure. Too much has happened between us tonight."

"With any other woman I could believe that, but not you. You have enormous capabilities, Katrina. You can handle it."

She looked around the room. It seemed as if she was caught in a distorted Alice in Wonderland role. Remembering the softness of his mouth when he'd kissed her in the back of the limousine in New York, she found herself wondering what it would be like to feel his lips on hers again.

"The two of us are like highly charged combustibles," Blair went on. "I don't know why. I'm normally easygoing. It's only when I'm around you that things start to go haywire."

A thousand warning lights were going off in her head. She felt him edge closer to her, and thought she might not be able to breathe. The room was suddenly too warm, too small.

"I find that hard to believe."

"Would you like references?"

She shook her head, even though she knew from his tone of voice that he was teasing. "Then maybe it would be safer if we remained business acquaintances," she said.

"Probably," he agreed. "But when did you ever look for the safe side of things?"

"Never," she admitted.

"Then why start now?"

He began to toy with her new necklace, first tracing the form of the oil well with his index finger, then running his finger along the chain's length, toward the back of her neck. She shivered.

"Tell me, why should we look for safety?"

Katrina pulled back to escape his disturbing touch. After a second he reached out to touch her in the same place, his eyes never leaving hers.

She moved again. "Odd, don't you think?"

"What? Us or the situation?"

She laughed, twisting her neck away, but he merely followed. "Both," she replied.

"Scientists have always found the combination of different chemicals which cause fires and explosions exceedingly interesting—odd and interesting at the same time."

A strange feeling came over Katrina. It seemed she was floating toward the ceiling and looking down at herself on the couch. She told herself she had to get out of his hotel suite—now, before it was too late.

"Well, on that note I think it's time for me to go, Blair. It's been a long night." She started to stand. "Don't get up."

Ignoring her, he stood and walked closely beside her. At the door she turned back and gave him a friendly kiss on the cheek. "Good night. I'm glad things worked out the way they did for us."

"Are you?"

The look on his face communicated tenderness and yearning. She felt numb. "Very," she answered softly.

"Are we going to be able to start over? Put the past behind us?"

She watched the way the subdued light in the entryway fell on his eyes, making them shine, and she felt she couldn't deny him her forgiveness. No man had ever stirred her so. "I think we have started over, Blair," she said.

"Then before you go I have one confession to make. It will be brief, but since you've been willing to put up with me thus far, give me a chance to get this off my chest."

He enveloped her hand with his and led her back to the sofa, dimming the lights further with a flick of the wall switch. She started to sit down but he pulled her up and began to walk toward the window.

"What are you doing?" She laughed nervously.

"I want to be looking at you when I say this. It's important."

"What on earth?"

"I'm not the suavest of men, I know," he apologized, "but here goes." He cleared his throat and smiled crookedly. "When I made all those conditions that night in New York, it wasn't strictly from a business angle. I'd like to have let you believe it was, but I wouldn't be admitting the truth."

He paused, and she watched the way his eyes wandered across her face. She could tell that he was as uncomfortable with what he was about to say as she had been when she'd entered the hotel suite earlier.

"I wanted to have you, Katrina. In the back of my mind I kept thinking that you were a unique happening." He lowered his voice. "I can honestly say I've never wanted a woman so desperately in my life."

Her eyes took in this man who stood before her—warm, handsome, intriguing, totally different from anyone she'd ever known. She longed to reach out to him.

"Often I've thought that if I could just capture your spirit and touch it with mine, I'd have something no other man in the world could possess. If it sounds crazy to you, then think of how crazy it sounds to logical me. But it's the truth."

Katrina was enchanted with his capacity to make her feel desirable, and found herself smiling. "Did you say you weren't suave, Mr. Warren? I'd have to disagree.

148

What woman do you know who could be angered by a man's confession that he found her so captivating?"

"I haven't changed," he replied, his voice thick with passion.

She did not resist when he gently took her into his arms. When he bent to kiss her, she slowly opened her mouth to receive him, and when his tongue began to roam her mouth, she lifted her arms to embrace him as her own desire sparked to life.

The kiss went on and on until both of them were breathless, yet neither would pull away. Katrina could feel her heart rocketing, and she thought Blair could feel it too. His hand increased its pressure on her back, and he lifted her up until she was stretching tiptoe.

When he did pull his mouth away from hers, he bent his head down to the curve of her throat. Taking a deep, ragged breath, Blair shuddered in reaction to the waves of intense longing breaking over him.

Shocked by the force of her desire, Katrina tried to make light of the situation, knowing that whatever she did to resist her feelings would be in vain because it would only be halfhearted.

"And to think of how this night started off," she awkwardly teased, still breathless. "I'm not promising to forget what you did to me. If you weren't a full-fledged partner I'd probably think about suing you for mental cruelty."

He raised his head and kissed her tentatively, then hungrily. Their tongues met and the kiss felt like liquid heat. She ran her fingers through his sandy hair, absorbed in the feel of him.

"And you'd win," he whispered hoarsely. "But can't you see I'm trying to make it up to you?"

Soft but powerful fingers began to rub against the curve of her shoulder, pulling, releasing, kneading the delicate skin around her neck. Then they moved down to the base of her throat, where his touch became more gentle, like a trace of wind caressing her skin on a hot summer day. A sound echoed inside her head like ocean waves hitting the shore, and she forgot everything except the two of them and the way he made her feel.

Then they faced each other. Blair felt the force of her tremendous will and reached out to her, speaking to her without sound. He eased her trembling body toward him and walked with her in the direction of the open bedroom door. He kissed her head, then brushed his lips against the back of her neck, not giving her time to stop.

With difficulty she found her voice. "No, Blair." Her protest sounded weak, even to herself.

They stood at the bedroom door. He put both arms across her shoulders and looked down at her, his hands moving up and down her sleek back before he pulled away and his eyes searched hers in silence.

Finally he spoke. "It's up to you, Katrina."

She watched him, conscious of how much it would take for him to pull back now, knowing that the two of them craved the same thing. She wasn't prepared for the feelings she had.

If she stopped now, she thought, she'd walk out the door and leave a man who had the ability to make her feel as if she were the only other person in the universe.

She'd walk out on the only man she'd ever met who had all the traits she'd longed to find in a man.

After all she'd gone through in life, she thought—taking chances, struggling, gambling to make her dreams come true—after all that, how could she leave him now for the safety of her own lonely existence? She knew if she did, she'd regret it for the rest of her life.

Nor could Katrina deny the provocativeness of Blair's caress, or his intriguing ability to make her believe there was something greater to be found between them. Struck blind with desire, consumed with the urge to know him more deeply, she reached up and pushed the bedroom door farther open before smiling up at him.

Inside, standing beside the bed, responding to the maddeningly slow removal of her dress, Katrina felt a burning sensation where Blair's soft lips trailed across her flesh. He began where he'd left off, at the base of her throat, then moved back to press his lips against hers, tracing the outline of her mouth with his kiss.

She felt on fire as his hands began to move across her arms and toward the top of her dress. Katrina helped him by shrugging her way out of her dress. With a deliberate kick of each foot, she finished removing it and stood smiling up at him with nothing on except the gold necklace he'd given her.

That she wore no undergarments made her even more intriguing, Blair thought. Her body was as provocatively magnificent as he'd imagined. As he openly studied her, Blair found himself enjoying the way she watched without a hint of embarrassment or shame as his eyes roamed over her body.

He brought his lips down to brush the peaks of each

breast. Taking them one by one into his mouth, he felt her body tense and strain toward him. She lifted her chin and then arched her back, her eyes closed in total absorption with the feel of her body reacting to his hands and mouth. Each new sensation brought her more to life, and she reveled in the feeling.

Telling himself there would be more time later, Blair quickly slipped out of his clothes and took her in his arms. Together they moved onto the bed, their naked contact driving them closer to the brink of mindless passion

"Katrina, this is important," he rasped. "We're destined to have much more between us than just business and conversation." He drew in his breath and made her look at him. "I want you to bring to my bed the same power you've invested in saving your company. Then I'll be happy."

His eyes held hers, and after what seemed to be an eternity, he brought his face down to kiss her soft and inviting mouth. She reached up to embrace him, and as she eagerly ran her hand along the smooth muscles of his back and down to his buttocks, she felt her desire throb and wanted him inside her. She wanted satisfaction. Pulling him onto her, she stretched her body upward to welcome him.

But Blair was different from any other man she'd known, and was proving it now. Slowly, he allowed her body to press against his. She could feel the hard shell of his ribs, the thrust of his manhood, and the curve of his hip as their bodies intertwined. She imagined herself floating high in the air, her body attached to his. And then, with a gasp, she realized he was moving away.

"There's no reason to hurry what we share, Katrina."

He brought his mouth down over her fluted collarbone, then his tongue began to work its way across the hardened peaks of her breasts, teasing with a rhythmic flicker, leaving then returning, until she thought she might scream. When he moved his head lower, she arched her body upward to meet him, driven by a burning intensity. He ran his tongue along the swell of her stomach and down, his hands reaching out to open her legs.

Katrina moaned aloud until her breath was gone and she could make no other sound. She lifted herself until her head was bowed over him, kissing his back, his neck, any place she could find as new sensations hounded her to the brink of madness. And then his lips moved across her legs and she knew she had to have him inside her.

"Blair, please," she half cried, half murmured. "Please."

"Pleasing you is what I intend to do, Katrina," he answered her with a rasping laugh, then moved his lips across her hip.

Katrina was beyond rational thinking. She stretched her arms to pull him to her, urging his body toward hers with a powerful upward thrust of her hips. Then, when he finally entered her, she felt their bodies begin a rhythmic race that sent them spiraling and soaring together.

"Katrina," he cried, "open yourself to me."

Their bodies thrust in mounting intensity as everything around them disappeared and Katrina found herself urging him with her hands cupped below each of his buttocks. When they reached a united climax that drove all thought away, she heard a voice cry out. Only later did she realize it had been her own.

As they lay spent and unwinding, their chests still heaving, Katrina felt him wrap his arms and his body around her, as if absorbing her into the cocoon of his flesh. He brought his mouth to rest against her ear, and they remained softly still for a long time.

Over and over in her mind she replayed the sensations she'd discovered, still basking in the afterglow of passion. For her their union had been the most incredible experience of her life, and she wanted to make it indelible in her memory. Never before had a man aroused her with his words as well as his touch, never had she known a man who was so willing to let her know how much he wanted her, and never had she shared herself like this with anyone else.

CHAPTER NINE

"We almost succeeded," he said with a sigh.

"*Almost* succeeded?" Katrina propped herself up on one arm and glared down at him, annoyed by his words and the fact that he'd disturbed her tranquil state.

"Yeah, we came close," he said matter-of-factly.

"Maybe you're used to something else, something better, but I thought it was pretty damned wonderful."

She was angry, but also curious about what he thought they'd missed. Maybe he hadn't experienced the same feelings she had, she thought.

"Don't you remember, Katrina, when I talked about our spirits touching?" He lifted his hand toward her. "Well, our spirits almost touched."

"I certainly thought there was a lot of touching going on," she replied, as uneasy with the conversation as with the idea that he'd somehow found the experience less than perfect.

"You don't understand what I'm hoping will happen between us, but you will." He smiled up at her and let his fingers run idly through the waves of her hair that fell around her face. "You will," he repeated, pulling her toward him.

She closed her eyes, readying herself for his kiss, wanting to once again experience the sensations she'd had before.

"Now, where are you ticklish?" he asked, at the same time sending his hands and fingers dancing across her bare flesh.

"Ticklish?" Disbelief caused her to open her eyes. After a few seconds of resisting his touch, she moved away.

"Yes, we're going to get to know one another, Katrina. Our first encounter was like the traditional rote love-making of most couples. Our next one won't be."

He pulled her back toward him and buried his face in the valley between her breasts. She could feel his mouth moving back and forth while his hands lightly traced the outline of her hips.

"Rote? You call that rote?" she asked in amazement, already beginning to breathe hard.

"Don't be offended," he said, looking at her. "It's just that I know what the two of us can be together, and I'm a little impatient. What about a massage?"

"No, I don't think so. I really need to go."

"Go?" Now it was his turn to be incredulous. "You can't go."

"Really, I need to . . ." Her voice trailed off as she watched him sit up in the bed and cross his legs Indian-style.

He was shaking his head. "Because we've only begun, Katrina. Now tell me where you're ticklish and then we'll have a picnic. I'm famished."

156

She started to laugh, then brought her hand to her mouth, trying to stifle her giggling "This is crazy," she protested. "You look like some guru."

He smiled and nodded. Then he reached out, pulled her into his arms, and cradled her in his lap. "We're going to have fun together, Katrina."

An expression of satisfaction shone deep in his eyes. Blair was far more than she'd bargained for, she thought. It seemed he wanted to introduce her to a different kind of relationship than she knew about.

She might be the expert when it came to the oil business, she told herself, but Blair made her feel she was a novice in bed. She felt her skin tingle as he lifted her hair and began kissing the back of her neck.

"There's a neck muscle right behind your ear that's very sensitive," she heard him say as if he were speaking from a distance. "Tell me when I've found it."

"Mmm." She tried to speak but couldn't. Her body was responding to his touch, the flames of desire flickering inside her.

"I guess I found it," he murmured, kissing the spot he'd sought. He held her tightly, taking pleasure in her reaction.

Katrina sank weakly against him, feeling a piercing hunger open inside her and demanding to be fed. She twisted her body toward his, greedily pressing herself against him, wanting him to take her.

"Now for the picnic," he said, giving her a chaste kiss and moving off the bed.

Through a haze she watched him quickly wrap one of the loose sheets around his body and look seductively down at her. Still on edge with desire, she remained motionless as he left the room. She heard him whistling. What was he doing? she wondered. Trying to drive her stark raving mad? Why had he aroused her then pulled away and laughed?

Katrina found herself wanting him more and more with each passing moment, and while she knew she craved physical satisfaction, she also knew she wanted the deep emotional pleasure in being with him. Recognizing a strange peacefulness within herself, she waited quietly on the empty bed, curious.

"Caviar and more champagne," he said when he returned. "That's all I could find, but at least it was on a tray."

Blair handed her the tray. "Hold this for a moment." He stepped up on the bed and seated himself in the middle, his sheet still draped casually around him.

Taking the tray out of her hand, he set it down between them. "The glasses aren't chilled, but it's the best I could do on short notice." He poured bubbling champagne for two, then handed one of the goblets to her. "To us," he said, smiling crookedly.

She returned his familiar smile and sipped the champagne, pulling the bedspread around herself.

"I wish you wouldn't do that," he said while spreading caviar on two crackers. "I like looking at you."

Her expression changed, a streak of red staining her cheeks. She tightened her fingers on the spread.

"I didn't mean to embarrass you. It's true that I like to look at you, that's all." He offered her a cracker, ate his in one bite, then made himself another. "One of my fantasies has always been to have a woman undress me. What about you?"

"Me?" she sputtered. "Are you asking me to undress you?" Her eyes were bulging.

"No." He laughed softly. "I'm asking you about your fantasies."

She shook her head. "My fantasies are secret."

"Too bad," he said, taking another sip of his drink before zeroing in on her again. "I've heard you described as everything from a quiet domestic cat who treasures her independence to a crazed tigress from the jungle. Which is it, Kat?"

"Please don't call me that. Only a few of my old friends call me that and I hate it."

"And your enemies?"

"They probably don't use anything quite that civil," she said, laughing.

Blair eyed her for a moment. "Seriously, Katrina, what is it about you that won't let anyone get close?"

He was ruining the entire evening with his questions, she thought, making her feel oddly off-balance. "And what is it about you," she shot back, "that you're not content to let the situation be? We've had a good time together, don't push it." She added, "Besides, I'm not some little old lady who needs to be escorted across the street."

She glanced at the sheet draped across his lap. "And you don't look like any Boy Scout to me."

He smiled knowingly. "That's your way of keeping your distance from people, isn't it? A sharp, clever tongue puts people in their place. Add it to the power of your money and your looks and whammo—you've got the toughest woman in Texas."

"And what about yourself?" she asked coolly.

He ignored her question. "I think you enjoy it all, but you're smart enough to know something's missing. I think you're looking for someone to love."

"And I think you don't know what you're talking about. I also think you'd do better analyzing yourself— like why you'd pick such an improper time to start a conversation like this."

"I don't think it's such bad timing. I'm just interested in you. Maybe I'm thinking I might be the man to make some changes in your life."

"And what if I said I had no desire to change," she asked defensively. "What if I said I was perfectly content with my life?"

He looked at her for a long time, Katrina eventually turning away from his hard gaze. Finally, he said, "Then I'd say I didn't believe you."

"Then you'd be wrong."

As he'd talked, anxiety had enveloped Katrina like the spread she'd gripped tightly to her. Now, awash in a swirling current of emotions, she started to lift herself off the bed.

"No, Katrina." Blair reached for her arm and pulled her back, then put the tray down on the floor.

"We're going to talk," he said, easing her down beside him on the bed, pushing aside the sheet he wore as well as the spread she'd used to cover herself. He smoothed away a crease in the pillow cover and eased her head back with the gentle touch of his hand, ignoring her resistance.

"I've got to go, Blair. It's past three in the morning and I think enough has happened for one night."

Yet she let him continue to run his fingers through

her hair and along her throat. Feeling his lips touch her ear, her response was immediate. A ball of burning heat arose in the pit of her stomach and stayed there, making her immobile.

"Oh, no you don't. We're going to talk until we agree there'll be no more games between the two of us, Katrina."

She looked up at him, entranced by his seductive whisper. But along with the seductiveness was a hint of steel. She tried to make herself think rationally while still responding to the emotions he'd previously stirred up.

"Let's talk, Katrina."

She shook her head back and forth across the pillow, feeling the soft give of the goose-down feathers, noticing how her mind was filled with these new sensations of touch and feel. It would be best for her to get away, she thought, because she couldn't possibly hope to outthink or outwit him. Not right now when she was so vulnerable.

"What could be so urgent that we need to talk about it right away?" she asked. "I really must go."

"About us—in bed. I want to know your likes, your dislikes, how I can best please you."

She raised herself on both elbows and glared belligerently at him. "Are you kidding?" she said.

Nodding sagely, Blair replied, "You must have been with mind readers in the past." He stared at her. "Did they bring their crystal ball when they came to your bed?"

She was thrown by his talking about her past in an intimate, knowing way.

"Look, Blair, you're—" With quick slicing movements of her hand she chopped the air. "I have no wish to discuss any of this with you!" She swept back a thick swatch of her dark hair. "Come to think of it, I wouldn't want to talk about this sort of thing to anyone. This entire discussion borders on the idiotic."

He put his hand on her arm and reached over to kiss her bare shoulder. "What kind of life have you led that you've missed all the fun and laughter involved in making love?"

Angrily, she pulled her shoulder back. "I haven't spent my evenings with anyone from Comedy Capers, but I don't think I've missed much." Still smarting, she kept talking. "I also think you've got a tremendous ego if you're thinking you're so great, Mr. Warren."

"Not great, Katrina, caring." He made a swipe at her shoulder again and laughed when she pulled back. "To top it all off," he went on tenderly, "I don't think you've been with a man who cared enough to find out exactly how to please you."

"Oh, come now," she argued.

The conversation frightened her. Her heart seemed to swim inside her rib cage, and she wanted to gasp aloud for breath. He was far too intimate, she thought. It made her feel defensive and uncomfortable.

"Why the resistance?" he said. "Why resist a man whose only interest right now is in making you happy?" He pulled her toward him. "Bring me that power, Katrina. Share it with me."

His hands came up to cup her cheeks, and she looked deeply into his eyes. Slowly he settled her across the bed. As she felt herself give in to the gentle touch of his lips, Katrina wondered what magical spell this man weaved to make her give in so easily to his demands.

A moan issued from his throat as his tongue began to rove inside her mouth. Katrina let her eyes float shut as she surrendered to desire. His breath came quick and uneven as he began to slowly brush his body against hers.

The ball of fire in her abdomen flared up and seemed to course through every vein, every nerve in her body as she felt herself quicken with passion.

When he bent to take one nipple into his voracious mouth, she missed having his lips pressed to hers, but she gasped with a primitive urge as his tongue flicked against each nipple. Then his mouth sucked and squeezed, hardening them until they ached with a heated swelling. Slowly, he began to move his hand up the inside of her leg, over the curve of her calves, into the interior of her thighs.

Her hands caressed him, moving up and down his back, intent upon feeling each hard contour of his body. Her excitement built to the breaking point as she touched him and as his hand brushed against her. She let her hands roam to his chest, where they sank into the brittle curl of his chest hair before plunging down to the curve of his waist.

His breath came fiercely, hot against each breast, and she ached with need. She moved against him, digging her nails into the curve of his back, gripped by a shivering wave of passion.

"Tell me how to please you, Katrina," he said, his voice breaking through to her.

In answer, she moved against him and met his lips

163

with hers. He was an expert, and she was weak with the potent arousal he'd introduced her to.

"You are pleasing me, Blair," she replied, sighing.

"Kiss me again," he said, and she willingly obliged, sending a passionate message with each stabbing dart of her tongue.

Katrina arched herself toward him, and Blair quickly slipped his hands beneath her. When he entered her, she tried to pull away, the throbbing inside her driving her to exquisite pain and pleasure. But he held her to him so that their bodies could move together, each thrust growing more and more powerful, like the eye of a spiraling tropical hurricane.

She gasped for air as she felt him swell inside her. Together they responded to the tremors of each other's body. When she felt she would burst with the pressure of her own passion, her mind and body seemed to explode into a million sparkling colored lights.

She rode volley after volley as though she were in the eye of the hurricane, her body charged to a quivering explosiveness. This time when she cried out, Katrina held nothing back.

"That's more like it," Blair said finally when their sweat-dampened bodies lay sealed in a numb embrace, exhaustion having settled over them. "We're getting closer all the time. Oh, Katrina, you are some kind of woman."

She'd received compliments from both expert and beginner, but none had made her feel so womanly as his. Lying inside the curve of his arm, she still marveled at his way of making her feel her own identity so overwhelmingly. A small smile crossed her face, and she twisted her head toward the inside of his arm and kissed him there.

"Don't leave me now," he whispered hoarsely. "Let me hold you."

Forgetting everything but each other, they drifted into a sleep of complete contentment.

Hours later, Katrina was awakened by a persistent knocking sound. It was muffled, coming from the outer door of the hotel suite. She felt Blair begin to move, then watched him rise with half-opened eyes, throw on a robe he found in his closet, and groggily move to answer the door.

Suddenly, a hot rush of fear grabbed at her, clutching at her insides. When she heard the messenger's voice it dawned on her. The letter! She'd forgotten all about the letter!

Pulling the sheet from the bed, the same sheet Blair had worn a few short hours ago, Katrina hastily wrapped it around her like a wrinkled toga. She raced into the living area, wanting to stop him before he read the letter she'd written so vengefully.

When she'd written the hateful words to him, it had been because she thought he was intent upon harming her. She still harbored some doubts about him, but knew she'd made too many snap judgments. The letter would only serve to reinforce his negative opinion of her, she thought, and the Alice in Wonderland evening would end in bitter acrimony. He mustn't read it, she told herself—not here, not now, not ever!

Katrina opened the bedroom door and saw him reading it. Seeing the changing expression on his face, she remembered the night they'd just shared. He'd been a tender yet amusingly gentle lover who'd been able to light a fire inside her that still burned. Blair had made her laugh, she thought, and treated her as an equal, signifying his respect in everything he did.

Katrina's heart sank when she saw the black look of rage on Blair's face. He crumpled the letter in his hand and threw it at her.

"Blair," she shouted, "if you'll give me a minute, it's my turn to explain."

She bent down and picked up the crumpled letter. Feeling the tension from across the room, she walked toward him, her pulse racing.

"Get out." His voice rang out with contempt, leaving her breathless. His rage was more powerful than any she'd ever encountered, and she felt helpless.

"Try to be fair. I was—"

In two long strides he was standing over her, his mouth white around the edges, his eyes wild. "You don't know the meaning of the word! Now get out!"

He was too hurt and humiliated to listen to her. "Beginning here and now," he said, "we're strictly business. It looks like you got what you wanted and I got what I wanted." He thrust out his jaw in bitter accusation. "Isn't that the way you'd sum it all up, Katrina Longoria McAllister?"

A dizzying pain engulfed her as she listened to the caustic way he spat out his words. She dropped the letter to the floor and slowly walked back to the bedroom to gather her clothes.

"I thought it was going to be different between you and me, especially after the night we shared, but you couldn't let it be, could you?" he shouted as he doggedly followed her into the bedroom.

She ignored him and went into the bathroom to dress in her clothes from the evening before. She emerged with a defiant lift in her shoulders. Unhurriedly, she went to the telephone and dialed her home, asking that James be sent to pick her up. Then she turned and spoke in her huskiest voice.

"For a man who was so intent upon getting me to see his point of view last night, you've certainly done an about-face." She picked up the crumpled letter again, this time holding it out in front of her. "I wrote this when I thought you were about to strip me of my self-respect. Can't you see that?"

Blair shook his head. "I almost feel sorry for us."

It was as though he hadn't listened to a word she'd said, but his words twisted through her, driving her to respond the only way she know how. "Stop that! I don't want to ever hear you say that again. Nobody feels sorry for me! Do you hear? Nobody!"

He stormed over to her, and his voice shook when he answered. "I dared because I didn't want to begin a relationship with you that was false or shallow in any way. I wanted us to start out right. I thought we had something special." He stared at her.

Hurt and bewildered, she blurted, "You're no different from any other man, Blair Warren, and I've had more than enough of your philosophy. Save the rest of it for someone who needs it."

A rush of warmth filled his throat. "That's too bad, Katrina, because I disagree. I do think you need it. You sell yourself short. You're desperate to save your

167

company, and you're distrustful because you spend time around the scum of the earth and then you think everyone's like that. The life you lead must be miserable."

Haughtily, she gave him one final look, her glare meant to hide any vulnerability from him. Then she swung around and walked to the door, stopping once to pick up the signed contract. Her steps were defiantly measured and imposing, and she never looked back.

She'd gotten what she wanted, she thought, and that should be enough. There was absolutely no reason for her to feel the disappointment that blurred her thinking, she told herself. Absolutely no reason.

CHAPTER TEN

By Monday morning Katrina was trying to do everything she could to expel all thoughts of Blair from her mind and to wipe away memories of their night together. As she dressed she told herself that satisfaction would soon be hers, and the fact that he'd turned her personal life into a shambles would not interfere with the professional triumphs she anticipated.

She had spent Sunday with Andy and her lawyers, revising the financial statements so they reflected the new assets of KLM Oil. Katrina intended to enter the judge's chambers today with all the pomp and circumstance she could muster. Rubbing her step-uncle Albert's nose in her updated financial statement would be marvelous, she thought, having no intention of behaving in the least bit humble.

Katrina decided to wear a new Bill Blass spring suit with a sunshine-yellow woven silk-and-linen jacket, a dotted silk camisole, and a slender black skirt. She completed her outfit with a shiny black straw hat that went well with her upswept hairstyle, earrings that were clusters of yellow and black jade, and a handbag to match her hat. When she stepped into her limousine for the drive to the courthouse, she felt as if she were embarking upon the second part of her plan to rescue KLM. Except for the nagging disturbance Blair's actions had created, she was totally self-assured

Andy was waiting for her on the courthouse steps. "Your uncle and his people are already inside. Our gang too. Another minute and you'd be late," he scolded.

"My step-uncle, you mean, and he'll wait, I'm sure," she retorted.

Andy took her arm and the two of them proceeded toward the judge's chambers. "Albert will wait all right, missy, but the judge won't. If you're late with no good reason, that judge can slap you with a contempt of court charge faster than you can spin sideways. He don't know you've gone and crowned yourself the Queen of Sheba again." Andy kept his eyes on her.

Katrina sped up, stretching her legs as far as her straight skirt would permit. She'd allow nothing to diminish her thrill at beating her step-uncle in his own game, she thought.

"The day you quit trying to wish me back to a six-year-old in pigtails is the day I'll know you've lost your mind, Andy."

His laugh sounded more like a cackle. It bounced around them and echoed in the high-ceilinged building. "You look mighty pretty, and you look like you know it too."

"A woman always likes to hear compliments, even when she's aware of how she looks."

"Old Albert's going to know as soon as you step into

170

the chambers that you've got him. He won't know how till he sees that report, but he'll know he's been had when you walk through the door." Andy started to wheeze. The pace was catching up with him.

"Here we are," Katrina said as they stood in front of the wood-and-glass door leading to the judicial chambers. "And you are a very bright man." She smiled oddly as she turned her full attention to her companion. "I want dear step-uncle Albert to be miserable, waiting to find out what's happened to KLM. I intend to scare him off, and now I've got the clout to do it." Her smile widened. "I told you I was going to make him wish he'd left me alone, Andy. Shall we go?"

Katrina waited for him to open the door for her, then made herself hesitate a few seconds before striding commandingly into the judge's chambers, aware of the impression she made on everyone in the room. "Judge Newcombe, I hope I'm not late. Those courthouse steps weren't made for ladies, were they?" She walked over to the judge's desk, aware of her femininity as she leaned across to shake his hand.

The elderly judge's eyes lit up. Instantly, he found himself agreeing with her, coming around from behind his massive desk in his black robe to help Katrina to her seat. "Now then, Miss McAllister, I hope you understand, this is a formality of the court," he said, talking to her like an adoring grandfather. "I must see your financial statement, and your step-uncle Albert and his representatives are here to see that your statement is filed within the time limit imposed. I trust it wasn't inconvenient for you. I tried to be overly fair in allowing you a few weeks to gather your information." He smiled

171

down at her as he returned to his high-backed leather chair.

For the first time since she'd entered the book-lined room Katrina glanced in the direction of her step-uncle. Wedged between his two lawyers, he sat in a wooden court chair and glared over at her, his heavy arms folded across his chest. Katrina gave him her boldest smile and watched as his eyes clouded and his arms went slack.

"Judge Newcombe, I have no complaints whatsoever. You've been more than generous." Katrina motioned for her head lawyer to hand her the necessary documents, and then she passed them to the judge.

Katrina waited, her smile never changing, while the judge went over the documents. When she saw the judge nod affirmatively she looked arrogantly at Albert Barnes. His heavy, jowled face turned red.

Born four years after Katrina's father Karl, when Karl's mother had divorced and remarried, Albert was nothing like his step-brother. But Karl had never spoken negatively about Albert, at least not in front of Katrina, and she grew up thinking of her step-uncle as a distant relative who preferred to live a private life. It wasn't until her parents were dead and she'd involved her step-uncle in her business, that she discovered why her father hadn't seen much of Albert. After Andy had recovered from his heart attack, he'd told her the full story. Albert Barnes was more leech than human, Andy had said, and he took advantage of any opportunity that came his way.

"These documents seem to be in order, Miss McAllister. Are you prepared to sign a statement declaring them accurate and all-inclusive?" The judge peered over his half-moon glasses at her, his expression full of kindness.

"Indeed." She nodded.

"Your honor, will we be allowed to see these documents?" one of her step-uncle's attorneys asked.

"No," the judge said with finality.

"But, your honor, I respectfully cite the case of—"

"Mr. Barnes," the judge said, ignoring the lawyer and speaking directly to Katrina's uncle. "I have bent over backwards by letting you and your representatives sit in on this session in the first place. You seemed to think your niece wasn't going to file the proper statements, and I told you that I'd allow you to sit in chambers as an observer because the courtroom was being used. Now, didn't I remind you that I would entertain no motions in my chambers?"

"Yes, you did," Albert Barnes answered, his face growing a deeper red in color.

"Miss McAllister has filed the proper affidavits. That's all I am interested in at this time." Sternly, Judge Newcombe addressed Barnes: "Get your people out of here right now."

Katrina thanked the judge, started toward the door then hesitated, turning back to address him, "Judge Newcombe, I was hoping you could answer one other silly question for me."

"I'd be delighted."

She glanced once again in Barnes's direction, thinking about his pending suit. "If it could be proven that an individual coerced a person into a false testimony, could they be sent to prison?" Her smile was innocent and polite.

"They certainly could. Our laws can be very strict about those kinds of things, Miss McAllister."

She nodded. "That's good to know."

Waiting for Andy out by her limousine, Katrina couldn't help but laugh aloud. Her day was going even better than she'd hoped. "I did it, Andy. I could tell by the expression on my scheming step-uncle's face."

Andy shook hands with James and waited for Katrina to continue. She was watching her step-uncle and his attorneys gloomily enter their cars.

"He knows I've got him, but he's still not certain how. I think he'll ease up on me now, especially when he finds out that KLM can't go under. If he's smart, he'll drop the suit now."

"You're hell on wheels, missy, hell on wheels." Andy laughed and patted James on the back. "James, don't ever go against Miss McAllister here. She's hell on wheels."

James grinned and bobbed his head up and down. "I wouldn't ever do that anyway."

"Now, let's get over to the office and begin straightening things out, Andy." Katrina got into the backseat of the limo.

"I think I'll go out to the ranch. They've got the part for Old Baldy, and I want to make sure those men are breaking their backs to get her pumping again."

"Okay. Do you want James to drive you?"

"Nope. I can drive myself. What's the matter? You think I'm getting too old to drive myself?"

Katrina leaned back toward the open door and wrinkled her nose playfully. "I told you, you old rascal, you'll never get old. See you tomorrow."

She settled in, shifting thoughts of how she'd managed to upstage her uncle to thinking about KLM Oil. As the car drew closer to her office, she told herself to concentrate *only* on business.

The last several days of tense upheaval had been like a bad dream, she thought, telling herself she could explain away her out-of-character reactions to Blair as part of that crazy nightmare. But now that she'd managed to get what she wanted, Katrina couldn't escape the feeling that she was still in the grip of conflicting emotions. Her fists clenched. She abhorred any recollection of the night they'd spent together. It made her wonder how she could have been so out of control to confuse lust with something much more important, and she wondered why she felt so defeated.

By the time they reached the KLM offices, Katrina had promised herself for the final time that the only thing of importance right now was saving her business. Each step she took through the lobby and toward the elevator reinforced her feeling. Keeping all of this was what was important, she thought.

"Hello, Maggie," she greeted her secretary. "I bet you've had a wonderful few days without me around."

"Not at all. It's been too quiet." The middle-aged woman spoke with a trace of irony in her voice.

"Andy gave me a lecture on the way to New York the other day. He told me I'd been too cranky at the office. I'm going to try to do better. Pass the word. The ogre's back but she's happy." Katrina grinned, walking steadily toward her private office door.

Maggie gave her a weak smile. Having been with her young boss for over five years, Maggie felt at ease with Katrina, using her own quick wit and efficient nature to make herself indispensable.

"Don't make any promises you can't keep," Maggie said with a roll of her eyes.

Katrina stopped at the door. "Are you saying I'm permanently ill-humored?"

"I predict you're going to have a fit within the next ten minutes. I want to warn you—"

"Thank you for your vote of confidence," Katrina interrupted, frowning at her secretary. "Remind me not to give you a raise anytime soon." She flounced into her office, slamming the door behind her, mumbling about the conditions of finding good help these days.

In less than ten seconds Katrina came roaring back through the door. "What in the hell is going on here?" she shouted.

Maggie looked down at her watch. "That's what I was trying to tell you. A stranger has moved into your office. He instructed the maintenance crew to put his new desk right next to yours."

"Well, why on earth did you allow this, Maggie? Did he hold a gun to your head?"

"The man introduced himself as your new partner, Blair Warren. The word had already come down to us that the man was going to work with KLM and you were in court—"

"Where is he now?"

Maggie rolled her eyes again, a habit Katrina had come to know well. "He said something about a computer and then he went with Willie from maintenance to show him what kind of electrical cable he wanted installed in your office."

Katrina yanked her black straw hat from her head and began to take off her jacket. "Call back downstairs to maintenance," she demanded. "Tell them to get up here on the double and remove this desk from my office."

"Should I tell them what you said earlier?" Maggie kept a straight face.

"What I said?" Katrina was still fuming, unable to concentrate on Maggie's question because of her own ferocious anger toward Blair.

"Yeah. Do you want me to tell them the ogre's back but she's happy?"

Katrina glared at her, then stalked back into her offfice. "Tell them they have less than five minutes to remove this monstrous piece of wood from my office," she shouted. "Tell them that."

Katrina could hear Maggie's giggle and wanted to go back to the reception room and tell her to be quiet, but she didn't. Instead, she dropped her jacket and hat on her desk and began to shove the obtrusive desk away from her own.

She heard him before she saw him. He was in the reception area, talking to someone about a cable. The nearer he came, the angrier she became. By the time he walked into her office, her legs felt watery from pushing the heavy desk across the thick lambskin carpet.

Still reeling from the powerful effect Blair had had on her when they'd shared his bed, Katrina felt an ache in her throat. If only he'd gone back to New York, she thought. If only they didn't have to come face to face again. If only she could stop remembering the intense way he'd fired her to life . . .

"Get this damned thing out of here right now!" she screamed at him. Her face flushed with her anger, and a few strands of hair fell down around her ears.

Blair wore a wide-lapeled kelly-green linen blazer, and pale cream-colored slacks. His shirt matched the slacks, and his tie had alternating stripes of the two colors. She noticed all this because the way his clothes fit made him look taller than she'd remembered, almost overwhelming. In her anger she felt her vision blur.

He stared calmly at her, then turned back to the two maintenance men who stood behind him, each holding lengths of cable in their arms. "Why don't you two take a short coffee break and then come back. We'll finish the job then."

"Sure thing, Mr. Warren," one of the men said, watching Katrina. The two men backed out of the room, almost stepping on one another in their haste to get away.

Blair stepped back and gently closed the door of the office so that they were alone. It was the first time they'd seen each other since Saturday night, and he'd rehearsed an attitude of abject indifference. "I don't think it's necessary to have everyone in the building privy to this scene, do you?" He leaned back against the door.

"How dare you," she gasped. The way he spoke made her feel like a fool. "You have the audacity to come in here and set yourself up in *my* office? This scene, as you call it, is all your making."

"I guess I'll have to remind you, Katrina. I'm not the

one screaming." His eyes strayed from her face to the desk. "You'll get a hernia pushing that desk like that. It probably outweighs you." He kept his voice low, aware of the tension gripping the two of them.

After Katrina had left his hotel room early that morning, he'd spent the remainder of the weekend trying to make up his mind about what to do. Finally, he'd decided that no matter how much it hurt, he was going to be involved with KLM Oil exactly as he'd planned. He looked at her now—the glowing cheeks, the fiery eyes—and caustically reminded himself that there was only one thing he'd forgotten. The reason for his initial attraction to her was still there. Nothing had changed as far as her appeal was concerned. She was indeed special.

"I'm going to tell you one more time. Take this desk out of my office."

"This is the best office on the entire floor. I know because I've looked at all the others. It's also the largest." He eyed the dimensions of the exquisitely furnished room.

She hardly listened. Instead, she was wondering why she was able to create a situation to her liking when it came to her step-uncle Albert, and then dismally fall apart as soon as she had to deal with Blair. It was as if she were two entirely different people.

"I'll be installing my computer in a few minutes. That's why the maintenance men are up here. We're going to have to run a cable under the carpet."

"You're not going to run a cable under my lambskin carpet. You're not going to have your office in here at all." Wildly, she looked around at the careful balance she'd created in her office between the casual ambiance of two white damask facing sofas and her ornate Louis XIV desk and tapestry chair. Merely having this maddening man in the room, she thought, knocked everything off-balance.

"I have a contract, Katrina. That contract guarantees me a fifty-fifty partnership and involvement in every aspect of KLM. You have your thirty million dollars." His stare was bold and declarative. "Let's stop arguing and get on with saving KLM. To do that efficiently, you need to make sure I have as much information as I can get. We're together in this one thing and we're going to work together until we get this company back on its feet. That's all I expect from you." He hesitated, then added, "That's all I want from you."

Fuming, she watched him easily rearrange the desk so that it butted up against hers. As he moved the furniture, Katrina watched his muscles ripple beneath the green blazer. There was no calling time back, she thought. The thrill of the morning was dead, her intimidating victory over Albert pale in comparison to the choking sense of defeat she felt now.

Katrina shrugged her shoulders dramatically, as if she were suddenly indifferent to having him around. "If I have to, I can do anything, but there's no reason for you and I to coexist in my office. I'll have Maggie set you up in the office down the hall." Her words sounded bitter but controlled.

"No, I don't think so," Blair replied. "I want to be involved in every aspect of this business and there's only one way to do it. I intend to be right next to the woman who runs it."

He made his statement sound logical and simple. In response, Katrina could only glare at him.

The seconds ticked away as they glared at one another. His mind made up, Blair intended to have things his way now. To him, her vengeful letter stood between them like an impenetrable wall of steel. It was the reason he intended to be unwavering now. She'd hurt him and hurt him badly, and he wouldn't allow himself to forget it.

"Is this your way of getting back at me?" she demanded.

"Are you kidding?" Blair's eyes filled with disbelief. "No."

He moved closer to her. She could see the curved line of his jaw as he spoke, as well as the firmness of his mouth. She held her breath.

"Your statement absolutely proves the difference between the two of us."

What did that mean? Katrina wondered, and asked, "How?"

"You're the kind of woman who dwells on revenge. It never crossed my mind."

"How pure of you."

He shook his head. "No, not really. It's just that you never understood what was happening between us in the first place." His voice rose in anger.

"And you do?" she snapped

"Did. I thought I did. Now I'm wondering myself."

His bleak tone sent a shiver of apprehension down her spine. She couldn't put it into words, but she knew exactly what he meant. She'd felt it, too, but that was before the letter.

Carefully, Katrina stepped back and walked behind her desk, wanting to put distance between them. She'd begun to feel her hands grow icy, and the tension in the stifling room was almost palpable.

"Enough about our personal battles," she said, bracing her hands on the desk. "Let's get back to our business differences."

"Can you separate them?" Blair lowered his head, put his hands in his slacks pockets, then slowly raised his eyes to look steadily at her

His charged directness made her want to retreat farther. She knew he had no compunction about saying precisely what he thought. Andy was the only other man she'd met who was as direct, but in Blair it was unnerving.

"Of course I can separate business from personal differences," she replied. She raised her chin defiantly, to remind him of who she was and what she stood for because he seemed to be doubting her independence.

"Congratulations," he said.

The sound of voices, both male and female, came from outside the office. Time was running out for Blair, who pushed for a commitment from her. To get the immense job done, he thought, they were going to have to declare a truce.

"Katrina, let's get this settled before the men come back. I don't intend to have a shouting match with you in front of the employees."

Since he made it obvious he wasn't about to give an inch, Katrina said, "We'll try it for a few days."

"A few days." He gave a firm nod of his head. "Only don't start thinking you'll get rid of me in a few days."

Blair walked to where she was standing and looked down at her. "Your letter said I should go back to New York." A muscle tightened along his jawline. "I'm looking for a condominium here in Houston. I've already sent for some of my things, including a few computers."

"We don't need computers," she argued.

"We're going to use them. I'll show your people how." He went to the office door and opened it. "Now then, partner, haven't you had enough bickering for one day?"

"I'm not—"

"Maggie," he called to the secretary, "Miss McAllister would like you to call a meeting of the employees for two o'clock this afternoon. She's anxious to properly introduce her new partner to all of you."

CHAPTER ELEVEN

Katrina met with over twenty of her KLM employees in the formal boardroom of her penthouse offices at two o'clock that afternoon in order to introduce her new partner. But not without misgivings. She was still upset at his settling himself into her private office.

The next morning she made certain she was in her office before her customary nine o'clock arrival. Besides the fact that she'd been away too long, trying to raise money, she was expecting a detailed report on oil production per well, and had asked one of her geologists to come in to discuss a potential drill site he'd found near McAllen.

Entering her office, she was startled to see Blair already sitting behind his desk, his blue suit jacket slung over the back of his chair, one hand working the computer keyboard and the other holding a steaming cup of coffee. The sight of him triggered a memory: she saw him as he lay across the hotel bed, sheets flung to the floor.

Abruptly, she swung the door shut behind her. Her

movement broke his concentration, and he turned as she approached her desk.

"Dressed for combat?" His eyes ran up and down her body with deliberateness before he turned back to his computer screen.

"What does that mean?" she asked.

He didn't look at her. Instead, he turned one shoulder her way and waved his arm up and down at her, as if to say "See for yourself."

Reading his signals, Katrina looked down at her clothes and immediately knew what he'd meant. She wore a military-style khaki Vartey shirtwaist with a three-inch wide handworked leather belt wrapped twice around her waist.

More self-conscious than she wanted to admit, she grinned. "I guess I do look a little like a soldier."

"A combatant."

He sipped his coffee without so much as a glance her way. On the green screen she saw column after column of figures.

"In the interest of starting off my morning right, I'll act as if I didn't hear that remark. Are those the figures you called me about last night?"

"Yes."

"Who did the computer work for you? Surely no one in this office knows how to work that machine yet." She leaned over the left side of her desk, staring at the screen.

"I did the work. In another few hours I'll have a twelve-month production report on the well you call Old Baldy, and maybe a few more of your wells."

Katrina was astonished when she thought about the

time he must have spent setting up the columns of figures she saw on the screen. "How late did you stay here last night?"

"Two thirty or so."

"Where did you get this month's reports? I haven't even seen them yet."

"Maybe you should come into your office a little earlier." Blair whirled his chair around and his eyes focused on the red curve of her lips. Then, aware of how easily she could distract him, he went on with his story. "I met with your chief accountant Jake Ortega over breakfast this morning and he gave me the report he said you'd been wanting. It's on your desk."

"He went over it with you?" Her voice rang with disbelief.

"Is something wrong with that?"

The challenge hung between them as pain throbbed in her eyes. She said nothing

It was hell, she thought, being around him, watching him, trying to blot the desire for him that was always grating on her.

"The geologist will be here at ten this morning. I hope he's a patient man. I'll have lots of questions to ask him." Blair caught her quizzical expression. "I took the liberty of reading the note on your desk."

When his words finally registered, Katrina began grappling with the handle of her desk drawers. When she had every drawer pulled wide open, she snapped angrily, "Here, make yourself at home."

"I don't think so. If there was anything of real importance in any one of those drawers you wouldn't have been so quick to open them." He gave her a tight grin and propped his feet up on his desk. "No, I don't think so, but I *would* be interested in looking at some of your files."

Her mouth fell open. "Oh, you would, huh?"

Blair leaned back in his chair, casually stretching his arms over his head. He gave her a short nod. "Yes, I would. Let's start with the two land maps and current information on the areas the geologist is coming to talk to you about this morning." He popped his chair and body forward. "Correction." He smiled. "Us. He's coming to talk to us."

Katrina clamped her jaws down tightly and ground her teeth together. She couldn't stand much more of this, she thought. The idea of his being there was enough to set her on edge. For good reason, she told herself. Blair was an intruder disrupting her management style, and her thoughts as well.

"When is Andy coming to work? I thought he helped you run this business of yours." Blair looked down at his watch and stood up to put his Dior suit jacket back on. Katrina had taken his attention away from his computer and he wanted to get back to it. Maybe it would help take his mind off her, he thought.

Katrina's hands flew to her hips, and she stood there glaring defiantly at him. In spite of her stance, his pleasant expression never changed. Finally, she began slamming each of her desk drawers shut.

"Nobody," she replied icily, "has ever run this business but me. Andy is a dear friend and advisor. He owns a part of Old Baldy." She didn't try to hide how affronted she was by his question.

But Blair acted as if she were joking. "And now

somebody," he said in a melodramatic voice, "has had the audacity to come into your secret little place." He sat down again and turned back to his computer. "And that somebody is going to help you run this business. You just hate it, don't you?"

That he made fun of her infuriated her even more. His words, his actions, everything about him, she thought, seemed to rub salt in a fresh wound.

Katrina slammed the last drawer shut and the hard thud resounded through the lavishly decorated office. She perched one hip up on her desk and folded her arms across her chest, ready to give him a piece of her mind.

"I almost forgot," Blair said as he began to type a command on the computer keyboard. "Besides land maps, I assume you have a written file on the land the geologist's coming in to discuss. I'd like a chance to look it over. Can you get it or would you rather call Maggie?"

"Since you're so proud of the fact that you're a fifty-fifty partner, why don't you just call her yourself!" Katrina exclaimed, then stalked across the room.

She slammed the door behind her, giving Maggie a stormy look as she walked through the reception area. Her inclination was to leave and not return, but she knew she couldn't—the geologist would be there within the hour.

As Katrina breezed by, she heard Maggie casually comment, "We're going to have to do something about that door. It must be off balance or something, the way it keeps slamming closed."

"Oh, shut up," Katrina groaned.

She stood in the hallway a moment before heading for an office she knew had a private phone. Still furious, she forced herself to wait a few moments before dialing, not wanting to sound upset when she talked to Andy.

"Andy," she said when he came on the line, "when are you coming back to Houston?"

"Well now, missy, why don't you ask about Old Baldy first?" he countered

"How is it? Do you have it going yet?" She'd been so absorbed in the melodrama going on in her office, she'd forgotten about her most important well.

"Now that you ask, yes. The boys started her back up about six this morning."

"That's good news."

"Yep. If nothing else goes wrong, she'll be pumping again just like clockwork."

"When are you coming back?"

"I'll be back in Houston before dark. I promised your new partner when he called me early this morning that I'd meet him for dinner. He's got a bag full of questions." Andy laughed. "I swear he already asked me about two million of them while we were on the phone."

She felt as if the top of her head might blow off. Quickly, she asked, "How did he know where you were? What kinds of questions did he ask?"

"Whooah, missy, slow down. What are you so fired up about?"

"Never mind, just tell me."

"I don't know," Andy drawled. "He said something about Maggie helping him out last night. Maybe she told him. And don't knock the boy for asking questions. He's just trying to find out about KLM." He coughed into the phone. "Sounds pretty smart to me," he added.

Katrina said a fast good-bye, so the fury she was

feeling wouldn't show, and hung up. She put her hand on her forehead and held it there with her eyes tightly shut, trying to will away the painful throbbing in her skull.

Just as he had the night he'd made love to her, she knew that Blair was making all the right moves. Seeing him in action made it easy to understand how he'd gained his reputation as a computer wizard. Grudgingly, she admitted to herself that she had to give him credit for his clever calculation, and that again she'd underestimated him.

Katrina spent the rest of the day, and the day after, scrutinizing his every move. Watching him work with the geologist, Maggie, and the office staff, she concluded that Blair had the natural instincts to be successful in any business he took an interest in.

For his part, Blair was at odds with himself. Miserable whenever he was near her, as well as when he wasn't, he nevertheless realized he loved the oil business. It was the challenge he'd been longing for, and he immersed himself into it with all his energy.

Hoping to find a release for his frustrations as well, he wore himself out studying everything he could about KLM during the day. Eventually, being around Katrina while studying the company, he began to see evidence of her insulated way of life. As much as he didn't like it, he found himself growing more understanding of her behavior.

On Friday morning he sat at his computer terminal working on what he thought was the last stage of his well-analysis plan. When she came into the office, looking small but imposing in a tiger-print dress with black slashes of color running across it, he started to tell her about his work. They hadn't been alone together in days, which had been as much his fault as hers. He was holding a tight grip on his emotions, but being near her made his grip seem fragile.

"Good morning," he said, standing up to greet her.

She saw his soft smile and immediately felt a swell of irritability engulf her. Having to see Blair on a daily basis was getting no better. "Good morning," she said, nodding briskly.

"I've been working on something I'd like to show you," he ventured.

Her eyes flashed with annoyance. "Something on that damned machine of yours? It ought to be good for something, anyway. You've managed to tear up my office with all your gadgets." She motioned to the additional equipment he'd set up on the floor around his desk.

"It's a bigger job than I thought. Takes more equipment." He followed her eyes.

"I don't have time—"

"Sorry to interrupt, Katrina." Maggie stood inside the doorway. "But your social calendar is in desperate need of work. There's a mile-high stack of invitations and phone messages on my desk that need answering. When will you have time for me?"

Blair studied Katrina's face. He'd seen so much in the past few days that he wondered how she managed to accomplish any work at all, what with the constant interruptions.

"Shall I bring you your coffee and work on this now?"

"Sure." Katrina nodded, noting the relief on Maggie's

face. She looked over at Blair. "Let's talk about whatever this is as soon as I finish here. She's been waiting for days."

"Sure." Blair returned to his computer work, certain that she was trying to show him who was in charge. Maybe it was better if they didn't talk this morning, he thought. About four o'clock in the morning he'd assured himself that he was ready to deal with her professionally without getting hung up in his emotional noose, but now he doubted he was as prepared as he'd thought: anytime she was around, he found himself unable to think straight.

When Maggie returned with a tray, she handed Katrina a cup of coffee and brought the pot to refresh his. Maggie sat down in one of the gold-edged French chairs and asked, "Where do you want to start?"

"Just hit the high points," Katrina replied. "The geologist is coming in at eleven."

"Okay, the high spots." Maggie chewed absentmindedly on the end of her pen. "Mr. Trumbull's secretary from Miami called and complained that you've not responded to his invitation to a five-day island cruise for the first week in May. He says he can't do any planning until he hears from you."

Katrina opened her drawer, took out a paper clip, and began bending it back and forth. She was uncomfortable with Blair in the same room. It made him privy to all her personal as well as her professional business, leaving her stripped of all privacy.

"No," she told Maggie. "Tell him no."

"Okay, next. Miss Kellogg herself called three times

in the last week. She says you agreed to help her with the antique benefit show the end of this month."

"Tell her I'd love to, but I have pressing business. I think we'll be getting started on that offshore well by then."

"What about a dinner party at the Roosevelts' in Laredo next Friday night?"

"Tell them I'll be there. I haven't seen Bernice and Ernie in a long time."

"Your friend Linda called and said she's having cocktails on Sunday evening and wants you to bring your new partner." Maggie looked over at Blair and smiled when he looked up from his work.

"This Sunday? Tell her I'll call her back." Katrina turned sideways in her chair. Seeing Maggie becoming so friendly with Blair was one more abrupt reminder of how he'd charmed everyone in the office. She scowled. "What's next?"

"I can go on and on."

"Maggie, do you have everything arranged for my Los Angeles trip?"

"Yes. Mr. Gene called and wants you ready for a fitting next Thursday. He says you must promise him all your time that day if he's to have the dress ready for Saturday. Also, Ken Waldrip called and asked if you were taking the plane. I think he's looking for a ride."

"Yes, but don't call him back yet. Maybe I'll get lucky and he'll find a ride with someone else."

Blair heard every word as they went on talking. The social life Katrina led sounded overwhelming in itself, and he was in awe at the way she seemed able to handle it.

He stared at the computer screen, listening to her husky, authoritative voice, feeling her powerful vibrations. If he had any sense at all, he thought, he'd get out of Houston.

But when the geologist arrived later that morning, Blair found something to be angry about and used it like a weapon against her. It was a different geologist than the one he'd met on Monday, and Blair instantly disliked him because he seemed too crafty.

"Miss McAllister," the geologist said, looking over three maps he'd unfurled across the coffee table, "I think I've got something you're going to like. It's down in San Saba County."

Blair sat on the sofa across from them, studying the presentation. He still had a head full of questions, but he didn't want to ask the geologist because he didn't think he'd trust his answers.

"San Saba County? I didn't remember having anything much down there except a couple of wells my father capped off years ago."

"Yeah, well, I met a young kid who's just been hired as a landman for a fella by the name of Ferguson. He's got several wells around San Saba and Laredo. Anyway, I bought this kid a few drinks one night and he slipped up and told me that Ferguson's drilled an oil well right in the middle of the county and it's bringing in a hundred steady barrels a day."

"Sounds good." Katrina glanced over at Blair and wondered if he was doing his mental arithmetic, figuring out how much money that would be. She already had.

"Yeah, well, you'll like this better. I went to the courthouse the next day and looked up where the kid

194

said the well was. Then I looked up where your land is, started doing some figuring, and took it upon myself to strike up a deal with a rancher whose place is next to Ferguson's drill site. The rancher remembered your father."

"Why would you do that?" Blair interjected. He didn't understand why the geologist would take it upon himself to strike a land deal.

"There wasn't any time to wait for one of your men to come down, Miss McAllister," the man answered, looking straight at Katrina. "I knew you'd understand when I told you. We can slant pump right below that Ferguson's well. Guaranteed oil."

Katrina glanced over at Blair, then began to study the map. After a few minutes she declared, "You're right."

Blair couldn't stand the suspense any longer. "How about explaining this to me?"

"Well, this is the deal," the geologist said. "Ferguson's got a good pumping well that's come in, but the way the land formation runs downhill, we could put in a well right below his and slant pump it so that we're taking from the same deposit."

"Is that legal?" Blair asked, his eyes intently set on Katrina."

"With all the stiff, ridiculous regulations in the oil business, Blair," she replied, "hardly anything's legal."

He stood up. "I asked you if that's legal."

"No," she answered in a hard, small voice. "It is not entirely legal."

Blair reached down for the maps and spoke to the geologist. "Was there anything else you wanted to say?"

"Well, uh, no, I guess not. Just wanted to know what you wanted to do about all of this." He looked perplexed.

Without giving Katrina a chance to reply, Blair began to roll up the maps. He handed them to the geologist. "We'll let you know."

"But—" the man started to say.

"We'll let you know." Blair took three long strides and opened the office door, then looked pointedly back at the geologist.

When he left, Katrina said, "I can't believe you. We need to act on this right away."

"We're not doing anything illegal. If you've been operating that way in the past, today it stops. Do you hear me?"

"Yes!" she shouted. "I hear you! But I can't believe you know what you're saying! This entire business is run on the edge. There isn't anybody who has anything to do with oil who follows the exact letter of the law as laid down by the state railroad commission."

"Then we'll be the first."

"And lose our shirts!"

"No, we won't."

"Then you're the most naive man I've ever met. You don't know the first thing about this damned oil business."

"Maybe so, but we're going to run it honestly."

"I'm putting in that well."

"We are not!" he said, slamming his fist down hard on her desk.

"Oh, no?"

"No. We're going to make history, remember? When we do, I want it made honestly."

"You'll ruin us yet." She edged toward the door, so

full of blind anger that she knew she couldn't bear to stay in the same room with him any longer.

"I don't think so, Katrina." He watched her, knowing she'd soon leave. "When someone ruins something it's usually something good that's lost." He stared at her. "I promise you, I won't be the one who ruins anything."

She left, unable to deal with her rage and frustration. She stayed away from the office over the weekend, hoping that not seeing him would help. At the same time, she tried to hold onto her gloomy feelings, thinking that once and for all she could block out the ambivalence being near him always revived.

But by the end of the next week Katrina realized she was at her wit's end. There was no escaping his presence, whether it was working next to him at the office every day, answering his business phone calls at night, or thinking about him at home, all alone in the black hole of the midnight hours with her doubts, fears, and longings keeping her awake.

Meanwhile, Blair's treatment of her was civil. Sometimes she thought him cool, other times his conversation seemed to border on taunting her. But most often he acted as if she were just another person in the office, which she found the most maddening of all.

Over and over again Katrina wondered what would have happened between them if she hadn't sent that letter. Trying to forget the delightfully glorious intimacies they'd shared was an impossibility. She brooded over it, remembering, distilling, magnifying.

For his part, Blair seemed to have shut himself away from her, and she couldn't understand how it was possible. Surely if the night they'd shared had meant as much to him as it had to her, she thought, he'd be reacting differently to her. Instead, he couldn't have made it any more clear than if he carried a banner and a portable neon sign that he wanted nothing to do with her if it didn't have to do with oil. It saddened her to think there was no chance for them on a personal level. None whatsoever, she'd concluded.

Andy called her on Saturday morning. "Katrina, what are you doing tonight?"

"Nothing," she answered, wondering what he was up to.

"Miracles, miracles. I can't believe it." He paused. "What's the matter, no parties to go to?"

"I'm not up to it, Andy." And I'm not up to your teasing today either, she wanted to tell him, but didn't.

"Good, because I want you to call Blair and invite him over to dinner tonight."

"I will not," she replied crossly.

"Now, missy, you haven't been very kind to the man, and he's doing one hell of a job for us. I'm not saying you should invite him over alone. I was thinking all three of us could have dinner and talk a little business, or better yet, you could invite some of your society friends over to meet him."

"Why?" she asked.

"I've got two things on my mind," Andy began to explain. "One is that you need to be seen around with your new partner. Your step-uncle Albert is telling people at his country club that you're trying to chase this new partner of yours off. That gives Albert some high hopes, let me tell you, hoping you'll lose your financing that way. Two, this computer wizard of ours has what he calls a management plan. He wants to go to every one of your wells, look them over, and do some sort of analysis on his computer. . . ." Andy started sputtering. "Hell fire, I don't know how to explain it, but it sounds good. Let him tell you tonight. Besides, we're hurting. Old Baldy's broken down again."

Katrina frowned. She'd thought it would do her good to be away from Blair for two days, and now Andy wanted her to invite him over. It seemed the complications she'd thought she would be rid of had merely changed faces.

"I don't want to," she declared. There was absolute silence on the phone. "Oh, all right, Andy, I will if you say so, but nobody else. Just you and Blair and myself."

"Good girl. I'll be there at six. Nothing fancy, either. Tell the cook to fix us some good old regular food." His tone grew light. "I think I'll spend the night too. Is that all right with you?"

"I can't believe I'm hearing you say that, Andy, after all these years. When have you ever had to ask me about spending the night?" He'd hurt her feelings.

"Missy, I just wasn't wanting to upset you. The last week you haven't been yourself."

Her voice became vague. He was right. "I know, but don't ever ask again, hear?"

"All right, it's a deal."

"We'll have sirloin, country fries, lemon meringue pie. How does that sound?"

"Bourbon. Let's have lots of bourbon too. Good-bye, missy."

She hung up and went to find the cook, but by the

time she reached the kitchen, a maid was calling her to the telephone again. "Hello."

"One more thing, missy," Andy's familiar gravelly voice rasped. "Try to be nice to the computer wizard. I like him. You should too."

Katrina nervously dressed, choosing flowing wide-legged white silk pajamas and an ornate black onyx-and-ivory beaded necklace and earrings. She still had forty-five minutes before they were expected, and spent the whole time sipping from a single glass of wine and pacing through the house like a captive tigress. Over and over again she mentally rehearsed how to act, what to say, what to do, changing her mind so many times she didn't know if she'd be able to babble out her name by the time they arrived.

Despite the tense encounters, the undercurrents between the two of them—or perhaps because of those undercurrents—Katrina had found it impossible to extinguish her memories of Blair. She had begun to focus on the openness of his attitude that night, the caring way he'd behaved with her, the infinite possibilities he'd offered. All these thoughts surfaced when she was least prepared, when he was talking to her, when she was working alone, and sometimes when she awoke during the night. Nothing she'd done so far could extinguish those thoughts.

Each day seemed more unbearable to her than the day before. It was a hell of a thing to admit, she thought, that she felt exactly like a small child who harbored a secret, painful pocket of fear deep inside, fear she couldn't do anything about. Except it wasn't fear, it was something else entirely, something she didn't want to name.

When the doorbell rang and Andy's voice bellowed out in the entryway, Katrina put on a gracious hostess smile and went to greet them, still holding her wine goblet tightly in her hand. She wanted to give the impression that having Blair to her home meant nothing whatsoever to her. If only the overhead lighting in the hallway wasn't so bright, she thought.

"Here she is," Andy exclaimed, and gave her a big bear hug.

Katrina put out her hand to Blair. "Hello."

"Your home is beautiful, Katrina. Thank you for inviting me here."

She gave him a formal nod and a tight smile.

"What the hell are we doing standing here?" Andy boomed again. "Come on in, Blair, and I'll introduce you to my dearest old friend."

Katrina followed the two of them into the library, Andy leading the way. Blair wore a pair of khaki twill slacks and a maroon gold-button blazer over a matching open-necked striped shirt. He was dressed more casually than she'd ever seen him, and it seemed she was the only one who was uneasy.

"Here he is, Blair. I want you to meet Karl McAllister, Katrina's father and my dearest friend. May he rest in peace." Andy pointed toward the painting over the fireplace.

Blair stood with his hands inside his pockets, his feet slightly apart, the picture of calmness as he silently studied the painting for a few seconds. He turned to look at Katrina, then looked back at the picture once again.

"There's quite a resemblance," he said softly.

Andy started to laugh. "In more ways than one."

"They have the same proud stance. That's the first thing, and then the mouth."

Andy nodded as he listened to Blair, but he was bursting to interrupt. "They're alike in thousands of ways. Both stubborn as hell." He laughed again, then added in a more subdued tone, "But Katrina looks an awful lot like her mother too."

"Do you have a picture of your mother?" Blair asked her.

"Yes, but it's upstairs in my bedroom."

"Katrina always says she represents her sweeter side." Andy chuckled. "Let's have a drink, Katrina. I'm fixing." Andy started over to the bar. "How about us sitting by the pool?"

As Andy talked, Katrina suddenly caught Blair's eye. For the briefest moment she imagined she saw his eyes soften, but when he looked her way she couldn't be absolutely sure. To her, the situation seemed too explosive, too dramatic—his talking about her resemblance to her father, his being here in her home. These were some of the things she had daydreamed in the past few weeks, but the actuality was so strange and awkward it didn't seem the same at all.

"A pool?" Blair dragged his attention back to Andy, thinking that he shouldn't have accepted the invitation to come. He'd thought he could handle it, but it was turning out to be just like every other time he was around her. While watching Andy fix him a drink, Blair wondered about the possibility of making some excuse and leaving. He'd do anything, he thought, to get out of this room that was overflowing with the atmosphere of Katrina McAllister. "I'd like to see the pool," he stated, still trying to decide whether to go or stay.

"Why don't you two go for a swim? Katrina usually swims every day. She likes to swim and then eat out on the patio. I like to swig a drink or two while I watch her. Makes me feel like I've taken part in her exercising." Andy laughed at himself, seemingly aware of how uncomfortable the two of them were.

And so Katrina put things into motion, showing Blair the dressing room with its variety of bathing suits to choose from, arranging for their drinks and dinner to be served out on the terrace, busily trying to avoid the feelings clinging to her like cotton candy. More than ever she felt she shouldn't have let Andy talk her into this. Having Blair here, she thought, was the worst thing she could have done.

But it was too late to undo it. The three of them met around the pool, Andy settling himself into a comfortable chaise longue near the tea cart stocked with an abundance of wine and bourbon, Katrina and Blair changing into their bathing suits.

This was the first time Katrina had seen so much of Blair's body since the night they'd been together. His face was tense as he stood on the pool's edge, poised to dive.

Katrina noted his full shoulders and well-knit body. His skin was pale, as if he needed sun. It struck her then that he was working too hard. As difficult as it was for her to admit it, she knew that he was keeping his promise to help KLM.

She cooled her sympathies and her too intense observation of his body by diving into the Olympic-size pool first. The water enveloped her with a lover's embrace and she stayed under until her lungs felt like they would burst.

When Katrina rose to the surface, Blair dove in and began a series of long, steadily stroked laps. She swam to the far edge of the pool and watched his agile strokes, admiring his swimming.

"Very good," she told him when he'd stopped and stretched out on the water, floating peacefully toward her.

"I love to swim." Blair flipped over, reached out, and gripped the coping edge of the pool.

When he settled himself his hand was only inches from hers. He kept only his eyes and nose up out of the water. She faced him, swinging her legs in a light scissors motion just below the surface of the water.

"Hey, you two, want me to bring your drinks over?" Andy raised up from his seat.

"Not for me, thanks."

"Me, either," Blair called out.

She could feel the vibrations of his words as they bounced along the surface of the water. There was something basically sensual about being in a pool of warm, still water with the underwater lights shining like dreamlike beacons, Katrina thought, feeling the nearness of his body and the movement of his legs near her own.

Heart racing, she looked away from Blair, watching Andy walk over to the tea cart and fix himself another drink. Meanwhile, she wondered what she could say to Blair. Being so close to him had caused her to recognize a fact lurking at the edge of her mind for weeks: it was vitally important to her entire future that she try to resolve their differences. She realized that this might be her only chance.

The right words wouldn't come. Instead, she said, "I wish Andy wouldn't drink more than one cocktail before dinner. I don't think it's good for him." She was watching Andy pour the bourbon.

"You really care about Andy, don't you?" His question was more a statement of fact.

"Very, very much," she answered.

"You are probably one of the most complicated women I have ever met." Before the words were out he was sorry he'd said them. Intimate conversation was precisely what he'd wanted to avoid. He began to swim toward the ladder.

Swallowing an enormous amount of pride, Katrina swam after him. "Is that all you wanted to say?"

"That much was too much." He kept his eyes averted.

"Blair, tell me something."

He put a hand out to hold on to the ladder and watched her follow suit. "If I can."

"Do you think we're ever going to be able to work together? I guess I'm trying to say that our being in the same office doesn't seem to be working." She thought she saw a flash of disappointment on his face and knew she hadn't said what he'd expected.

"Under the circumstances I don't think it's too bad." He let out a surprised laugh. "Not good, mind you, but not unbearable."

Katrina moved one leg in and out of the water. Her

throat was tight with tension and she felt queasy with anxiety. She'd never done this before.

"Let me try this again." She moved closer, turning toward him, forcing him to look at her. "I, uh—I owe you an apology for that night, Blair." She held her eyes squarely on him, willing him to see that she indeed meant what she said. "The letter was vicious, cruel, and inexcusable."

"You've got that right." His mouth turned into a hard line and his eyes became as cold as ice.

She swallowed. "All right, I understand, but I also think you owe it to me to think about my position that night. You've virtually said it yourself. You had me down—about to strip me of my self-respect, something I couldn't bear to have happen."

He bent his head forward and flung himself back into the water. Katrina started to get out of the pool, thinking herself an absolute, certifiable dope. Then, as abruptly as he'd left, Blair surfaced right next to her, sending whirls of water to each side of her body.

His fingertips brushed against the curve of her hand and she felt the shock of it vibrate through her. He moved beside her, his arm gliding in the same spot, so that their touch was unchanged.

"I appreciate what you're saying to me. I'm just not ready to accept your apology yet." He let his eyes wash over her, then let his feelings spill out: "When someone exposes a little bit of themselves by reaching out to another person, and they get their guts ripped out, forgiving isn't all that easy."

She blinked and looked up at the darkening sky, pretending to count the stars she saw, both wishing she'd never said a word to him and terribly relieved she had.

"Let's leave it at that, okay?" he said.

Katrina realized that was all he intended to say. But having swallowed a little pride, she decided she could swallow a little more. "Are you at all interested in our being friends?"

Blair was surprised. "I said before that I wasn't going to involve myself in any way with you again except for the business. Being friends doesn't exactly fit in. Don't you agree?"

She gave him a watery shrug. "At this point I don't know what I think anymore."

"Then that puts us on equal footing." He vigorously shook his head back and forth. "I'm wondering if we've let this go too far." He looked at her, his eyes coldly analytical.

"Hey, Andy, I'm ready for that drink now," he yelled, and started up the pool ladder. After what he'd just done Blair made up his mind he'd have two strong drinks: Resisting her overture had been the second most difficult thing he'd done in their shaky relationship, but he'd felt he had to do it.

She watched him pull his lean frame out and shrug his way into a towel. It was amazing, she thought. With anybody else she would be furious: he'd rebuffed her. Yet she knew something unspoken had been communicated between them. It was almost as if they were reaching out for some common ground—a way to begin anew. For the time being she was satisfied.

After dinner the three of them began discussing Blair's proposed management system, one Katrina believed would be promising. They talked business for two hours more before Katrina left to see about having one of the servants prepare a late-night after-dinner drink for the three of them.

As she was returning to where the two men sat, she heard Andy mentioning her name. She stood where she was hidden from view, and strained to hear.

"Don't be too hard on Katrina," Andy was saying. "She grew up like a fairyland princess. Everything she ever wanted, stuff she didn't even dream of, she got. That was the way Karl was. He wanted his princess to have everything. Her mother, Beatrice, knew better. She was a real lady, but as many times as she'd scold old Karl for doing too much for their daughter, Beatrice had the good sense to realize that he couldn't help himself any more than a bird can stop itself from flying. He loved her and he wanted his princess to have the world. He protected her from anything that wasn't pretty. And being brought up that way, see, it was a real shock to Katrina to all of a sudden lose her folks like that, just as she was learning the ropes at KLM, and then me off to the hospital and nobody else around. It would take too long to describe it all to you, boy, but finding out about her step-uncle's double-dealing, and having people you'd trusted trying to take advantage, well, let's just say that it turned the spoiled girl into a tough woman who needs a little softening."

Katrina watched Andy take a sip of watery bourbon. She stood where she was, unwilling to interrupt.

"Yep, she just needs a little softening."

The two men sat quietly for a while, and Katrina felt

her face flush with embarrassment. What she was doing seemed ridiculous, but she didn't move.

"You know much about turtles, Blair?" Andy's gravelly voice started up again.

"No, not much. Why?"

She could see Blair shifting in his chair and then easing back down again. His face looked solemn, intent upon Andy's words.

"I don't know. It's just that when I see Katrina acting all tough and mean, I always think about a turtle. They've got shells hard as rocks, but underneath, inside, they're as soft a meat as you ever saw. She'll lose that shell one of these days. It ain't permanent."

Katrina held her breath. How could Andy talk that way about her?

Blair started talking. "I'm going to help her, you know. That's part of the reason I'm here, besides my purely selfish desire to be involved in oil. I can help her."

"I'm betting you can . . . have been ever since I met you. I'm thinking you've got the right stuff, boy." Andy stood and stretched. "That I'm banking on." He walked around the back of his chair and quaffed the last dregs in his glass. "And I don't mean money, either."

Hurriedly, Katrina stepped out of her hiding place and began walking toward them, just as Andy approached her. He kissed her cheek and said good night, and she was relieved not to be caught eavesdropping.

Blair was standing up when she returned, and began to thank her for the evening. Since their swim and their private conversation, they'd managed to talk more easily together, but he seemed formal and stiff as she walked him to the front door.

After he had said good night and turned to leave, he abruptly spun back around and looked at her somberly. "I might be interested in friendship with a fair-minded, honest woman." His words came slowly as if he'd chosen them with a great deal of thought. "She'd have to prove herself."

For a second there was only charged silence, and then Blair took a step toward her, drawing in his breath with one sharp inhalation, his eyes searching hers. Katrina waited expectantly, a crazed pain swirling through her chest.

Abruptly, he swung back around and quickly walked down the brick steps to his rented MG. Katrina watched until the car's red taillights had passed from sight.

For the first time in memory, Katrina realized, she was caught in a situation she had no control over. The importance of it was only now beginning to crystallize for her: there was no way this man could be shunted out of her life. He was here, she thought, and she was going to have to deal with the realities of the situation, as well as the truth. But so was he, she concluded.

CHAPTER TWELVE

Katrina was learning to live with her miserable condition. Every night she awakened at some point, her body echoing with the memory of the feeling Blair had brought to life for her. Being a woman of intelligence, Katrina put all her reasoning skills to work as the next few weeks stretched into the second month of her partnership with Blair.

She spent her time doing what was necessary to resurrect KLM, and following Andy's suggestion of bringing Blair into a more visible role as her new partner so that all of Houston could get to know him.

She took Blair to lunch at Ma Maison, to cocktail parties, to dinner at La Reserve and to Brennan's for oysters. They were always polite to one another: Blair was a perfect gentleman, Katrina a charming hostess. From time to time they spontaneously let down their guard and had fun—laughing, telling one another interesting anecdotes about themselves, freely relishing the pleasure of being together—but those times were few and far between. Most of the time their conversation

211

revolved around KLM and occasional wooden remarks about the weather.

Yet Katrina had surprised herself with her patience. She still clung to the idea that the night he'd come to her house they'd communicated a silent agreement that something might evolve. And day by day she was discovering how much she treasured that shred of hope.

One morning when they arrived at the office at the same time, Katrina told him, "I want you to be the first to know that I've called Ferguson down in San Saba County and told him if he wanted the land lease next to his well he could have it for what I paid for it."

Blair had never considered himself anything but logical. The fact that he'd made a fortune in the computer field and was now embarking on a costly venture in a business that was known for its instability, was something he couldn't quite figure out about himself. When friends suggested that he had a secret yearning to be an adventurer, he'd merely laughed. But now, when he found himself trying to decide how to deal with Katrina, he discovered logic was absolutely useless. His emotions were overriding his brain.

Every day when he went into the office, he swore he wouldn't let himself be overwhelmed by her, yet day after day he failed. Now, in response to her admission that she'd been wrong about Ferguson's well, he gave her a perfunctory nod and reached over to switch on his computer, something he did every morning as soon as he came into the office.

Katrina was hard-pressed to hide her irritation. "Well, don't you have anything to say about it?"

"What do you want me to say?" he asked, making a

point of his indifference. "That you've done a good thing?"

She was unable to answer and stood gaping at him for a minute before storming over to her desk and throwing her Vuitton handbag down noisily. "It wouldn't hurt you to be nice about it. I thought you'd like to know, that's all."

"Okay, you want to hear what I'm really thinking?" He swung his chair around to face her. "I'm thinking you did the right thing."

"Oh, thanks," she bit back sarcastically.

Blair could tell by the expression on her face she still wasn't comprehending his message. "Notice, I didn't say *nice*—I said *right*. You never should have encouraged the idea of slant drilling out of his oil deposit in the first place."

The look on their faces mirrored one another's. It made her mad that she'd even bothered telling him what she'd done, and she thought his criticism uncalled for. Why should he be mad? she wondered.

She was the one who'd relented and let him come into her company as her partner, she mused. She was the one who was making all the sacrifices, all the changes. And he still harbored the most naive attitude about the oil business she'd ever encountered.

Still seething, she took a deep, uneasy breath. "Look, there's something you don't understand." She leaned toward him. "This . . . this is not the Boy Scouts of America. I keep telling you this business is different, and what I do is no different from what everyone else does. That's the way you make money. You can't go around being Mr. Nice Guy all the time."

"Hey, wait a minute," Blair exclaimed, feeling bound to make her see his point. "I'm just asking for some of the time."

"Okay, Mr. Perfect. I'm getting tired of you judging me without understanding anything. You want to see what it's all really like? I'm going to Lubbock to spend a night or two out by well thirteen. I'm staying as long as it takes to find out what's going wrong out there."

"Are you inviting me to go along? If you are, the answer's yes."

"It won't be fun. We'll probably have to spend the night out there in the Jeep."

"You just say when." He lowered his voice. "I'll be ready."

"Are you sure you want to go? I'm telling you, it's going to be hot and uncomfortable."

He couldn't stop himself. He knew he was going to make her mad, but he started to laugh. "Katrina, I'm not the one who has to have two people to make my bed and two more to dress me. I'll be fine."

She began to flush. "Tomorrow morning," she said between clenched teeth. "Nine o'clock, at your hotel."

"I can't wait." He turned back to his computer, fighting back his feeling of regret over the battles they continually waged.

This time her eyes had looked almost sad before she let the anger take over, he reflected, and wondered if she, too, wished things were different between them. It was taking a great toll on him, but he was too proud to admit it to her.

* * *

214

"This is the Jeep, huh?" Blair asked the next morning as he threw a blue canvas bag into the backseat of Katrina's new four-door Jeep Wagoneer Limited. He made a point of toying with the automatic door and window locks when he got in. "Crazy me. I thought you really meant we were going to be roughing it. I brought my pillow. Didn't have a sleeping bag." He grinned as he threw his pillow on top of his bag then ran his hand across the soft leather seats.

"And good morning to you," Katrina replied, noticing his faded jeans and plaid sport shirt. "Where'd you get those boots?"

Blair looked down at his feet. He had on pointed ostrich-skin boots. "Andy took me to buy them. Told me if I like them well enough I should have my next pair handmade." He slammed the door and Katrina drove off. "When I found out how much a good pair cost I decided these would be just fine."

"You can't wear out a good pair of boots, though. They'll last you a lifetime." She wove the Jeep in and out of heavy traffic with a deft hand.

He nodded. "That's just what Andy said." Blair watched her drive, one hand on the wheel, the other arm propped up on the armrest. Even in a Jeep she looked like a princess, he thought, glancing down at her red leather boots with the letters KLM stitched down the sides. She wore jeans, a creamy silk blouse, and a hand-tooled leather belt which matched the boots.

"Why did you make me promise not to tell Andy we were going?" Blair asked her after they'd left the city limits.

"Because he would have had a fit. He thinks what

215

we're doing is dangerous." She glanced at him and then back at the road, finding herself extremely interested in the way he looked in his jeans and shirt.

"Is it?"

For an answer she reached down under her side of the seat and brought out a gun. "It could be."

"What in the hell is that for?" His eyes were wide open, staring at the menacing-looking instrument.

"Listen, Blair, if we get lucky and happen up on the people I think are stealing my oil, we'll need this."

"Lucky? You call that lucky?" He shook his head and let out a low-pitched whistle. "Do you know how to use that thing?"

She grinned and put the gun back under the seat. "I wouldn't carry it if I didn't."

His look of utter surprise made her relax, and suddenly she felt as if all her problems were light-years away. She began to tell him what she suspected, and Blair's interest was evident.

"I think that my step-uncle Albert has somebody working for him near Lubbock, somebody who's going out to my well and stealing the oil from it after it's been pumped up out of the ground and before it's sold to the refinery." She explained how the oil and water from underground had to be separated before the oil could be placed in the reserve tanks. "I think they're pumping it out of what they call the gun barrel before it goes into my tanks. They're clever too. They haven't been caught though Andy's put several men on this well to watch it."

"Then how do you think you're going to catch them when the people you've hired haven't been able to do it?" He peered over at her, trying to make up his mind whether to try to contact Andy or not. The entire thing sounded like a bad late-night movie.

"I'm gambling, just like they are." Exasperated, she shook her head. "I've been trying to tell you what a crooked business this is. Anything could be happening. These men could be paid off by my step-uncle, or the driver of the tanker truck could be smarter than they are. My guess is there's a scout who rides by the well in a pickup and looks things over before the tanker drives up. Somehow he's managed to spot the people whom we've sent out here."

"I still don't understand how you think you're going to catch them." He put one arm across the back of the seat and his fingers accidentally grazed against her shoulder, but he left them there.

She felt his touch through her blouse and it sent a current of warm sensation through her entire arm. Self-consciously, she adjusted her shoulder. "I'm hoping we're going to get lucky. Plus we're going to sit out there on the ground where nobody can see us. I'll park the Jeep way out of sight."

"And the fellow's just going to drive up and give himself over to us?" he asked incredulously.

Katrina grinned. "I've checked your computer records and there hasn't been any oil removed lately from thirteen so I know he's due to show up there soon, and, of course, I always have my trusty friend." She reached down and patted the seat under which the gun was concealed.

He stared at her for a while, then decided she wasn't kidding. "I wish I'd watched more cowboy movies. It might have helped." Still shocked, he began to look at the passing scenery outside the window, mulling over all she'd told him.

From time to time Katrina glanced over at him. He rode with his eyes closed, and from where she sat she thought he looked far more tired than before. She wanted to ask him how he liked the pace they were keeping. The offshore oil rig would start production in less than six weeks time. The only problems now were Old Baldy, which was still acting up, and the Lubbock wells.

Still, there remained a high degree of tension between them. As she drove, Katrina wondered why she—a grown, sophisticated woman who could have any number of suitors—was letting herself become so wrapped up in this man. He was dominating too much of her time and her thoughts, she mused. If you aren't careful, Katrina, she thought, you're going to think you're in love.

If he became interested in her again, she tried to tell herself, the attraction would dissolve as quickly as it began. Every time he looked over at her during the several-hour drive, she tried her best to make herself remember her own words.

When they started into the west Texas countryside, Blair began questioning her, asking about every wildflower, every rock formation and piece of property along the way. They had a pleasant conversation, and began to talk about whatever came to mind.

But nothing ever went very smoothly between them for long. This time Blair instigated the tension. "You know, I've been thinking about something and I might as well tell it to you now," he said when they'd stopped for gas at a station in La Mesa. "I found out how much the tickets cost to the Joffrey Ballet in Los Angeles, and I also did a little investigating into how much it would cost to fly your plane to Los Angeles. I don't think that's something KLM should spend its money on. If you want to go, I think it would be best for you to pay for it yourself."

"Are you kidding me?"

"No, I'm not. How about my driving for a while? You can give me directions."

She slapped the keys into his hand, grumbling as she walked around the Jeep. "I've already had a dress designed for the event. You can't really be serious."

He got behind the wheel and pulled away from the gas station with a lurch. "Indeed I can. You keep forgetting we're partners, and the sooner you get that through your head the better we'll be. It's an unnecessary expense, flying that gas-guzzling plane out there. In fact, I think it's an unwarranted expense. Right now we're trying to get KLM back on its feet."

She stayed silent for a while, pouting at first, then thinking about his rationale. When they'd gone another fifty miles, she began talking. "I hate like hellfire to admit it, but I see your point." He didn't answer her, and she giggled. "Except my dress cost more than it would cost to fly the plane."

He started to laugh, too, shaking his head with disbelief. "I guess I shouldn't talk about you and your indulgences. I just sold my New York condominium and the price I got for it was ridiculous. I had no idea one person could live in such an expensive place."

Good, she thought, at least they were on common ground, both laughing at themselves.

"Why did you sell it?" She took a drink of the diet Coke she'd bought at the gas station and made a face. It was hot and the fizz was gone.

"I'm moving to Houston. There was no need to keep a place in New York, not as expensive as that one, anyway."

"You're really going to move to Houston?" The overwhelming sense of gladness she felt came as a complete surprise. Two months before, she would have been enraged.

"My life is centered in Houston now, and that's where I want to be. I've been looking at a town house in Montrose." He drove as capably as she had, keeping the cruise control on a steady sixty-five.

"Montrose?" she exclaimed and then broke into peals of laughter. For Katrina, Montrose was a once-beautiful piece of Houston gone to seed.

He listened to her laugh, thinking about the distinct differences between them. She was like a gigantic magnet that drew smaller, less powerful ones to her. No one crossed her, everyone catered to her most minor whims, and her personal life was like something out of a fairy tale.

No wonder she was so indulged, he thought. Only Andy brought any normality to her life, and now, perhaps he did too. Blair wanted her to see what life was like on the outside. He wanted to break through her insulated, very rich, very artificial ways. With each passing day he understood more about why Katrina was unable to recognize her own feelings.

"Tell me why you don't like Montrose," he said softly.

Her laughter was only now beginning to abate. "Because it's a weird place, Blair. Houston's full of wonderful places to live. I'd be afraid to even be out on the streets there at night."

"Well, that's because you don't know anything about it. They're revitalizing the area, but it's still a neighborhood. You can walk down the street and talk to people, and you can live next door to anybody from a belly dancer to an astronaut. It's exciting, like a daily adventure."

He pulled over onto the shoulder of the road. "You drive and I'll tell you about it." He could tell he had her interest, and he wasn't going to stop now.

When she had them back on the road, he leaned his head back against the seat and told her everything he'd discovered about the area, finally promising to take her to a neighborhood café where they served the best homemade pasta he'd ever eaten. And when the late afternoon shadows fell across the dry, dusty country of west Texas, Blair began humming softly to himself. In another minute he was singing, loud and off-key.

Again Katrina started to laugh.

"I've never once been able to carry a tune, but I love to sing," he explained.

"I know what you mean." Her laughter slowed to a smile. "Sing something I know."

For the next two hours they sang, both of them at the top of their lungs, the car full of his deep off-key croaking and her low, vibrant pitch as they sang everything from Christmas tunes to old church hymns.

Finally, voices hoarse, they stopped for gas and a late

dinner. When they were ready to start up again, he drove, but when they were almost there Katrina took the wheel, explaining it was easier to drive the side roads herself than give him directions. For both of them it was a warmhearted, magical time.

The highways turned into gravel roads, and when they'd crossed a cattle guard, Blair said, "Are you sure you know where we're going?"

"Yeah, we're coming up on the back side of the oil well. This road is never used."

The headlights caught only dry hard-packed ground and mesquite bushes. "A fellow could choke from the dust," he commented as she wheeled the Jeep in behind an especially large mesquite tree. "Now what?"

She turned off the motor and started to get out. "Now we walk," she answered, reaching down to put her finger over the light switch so that the car remained dark. "How about reaching into the toolbox back there and getting out a flashlight." She looked up at the moonlit night. "We'll try not to use it."

Blair crawled over the seat and gave a low whistle. "You didn't tell me we had a full picnic basket." He brought back the flashlight and they began walking down the dirt road.

"It's liable to be a long night, Blair. You may get hungry before this is over." They walked for about a mile before they saw the oil well, an awkward, gangling piece of metal silhouetted in the night. "Let's check it out first."

Katrina knew something was wrong when they approached and the well wasn't pumping. She'd checked the specifics on it before leaving Houston and knew it should be. A hasty inspection told her there was a loose bolt on the arm of the well.

"We're going to have to go back to the Jeep, get a wrench, and see if we can twist this bolt back on there," she told Blair. "If the well isn't pumping there sure won't be anybody stopping tonight."

Wordlessly, Blair went over to study the loose bolt and then followed her back to the Jeep. Taking charge, he found the right wrench, and together they worked to twist it back. Ten minutes later the well was pumping again.

"Thanks," she said as she wiped an offending spot of grease off her hands. She was surprised at their mutually cooperative efforts, but after the pleasant day they'd spent together, she told herself she shouldn't be.

"What now?" he asked, and reached down to wipe a streak of grease from her cheek. He frowned and turned her face toward the moonlight and began wiping again, as if it were the most ordinary thing in the world to do.

"Now . . ." She couldn't get her breath. The feel of his finger bearing down on her cheek was something she wasn't prepared for. She drew back.

"Am I too rough?"

She looked into his face and was struck by his disarmingly crooked smile. If she knew him a hundred years, she mused, would she ever get used to seeing it? "No, not really," she answered.

"Then let me get it off. If we're going to have a shoot-out I want to be with a woman whose face won't be distracting me every time I look at her."

Katrina tilted her head up and he took her face in his left hand, gripping her gently at the upper curve of each side of her jaw. With his other hand he ran two long fingers across the offending spot.

When he finished he held her there and studied her face for a moment, his burning eyes holding her still. "It's going to be a long night," he whispered.

"Uh . . . let's put the wrench back and get the gun." She took a partial step back, moving her face from the vee of his hand. She'd started to shake, an involuntary response to his touch, but she didn't want him to know it. Was it just her imagination, she wondered, or had she felt him react too?

"Yeah, let's get the gun." He sighed and began to walk faster back to the Jeep. When she caught up with him, he said, "Now what? Are we going to sit out there by the well or what?"

"I thought we'd go in shifts. One of us could take the gun and hide by one of those mesquite trees while the other one sleeps in the Jeep."

"Katrina, this is your party and all, but if we rolled down the windows of the Jeep don't you think we could hear that tanker drive up? There's nothing around here for miles. We'll hear it coming."

He was making sense, she realized. "Nothing out here but jackrabbits and rattlers and us. I guess you're right."

"What's in that picnic basket? Got any wine?" He delved in the back of the Jeep and in a minute he came back with a bottle of chilled champagne and two glasses. "Yeah, you really believe in roughing it, don't you? There's enough smoked turkey and cheese back there in that wicker basket to last the two of us a week."

She accepted the champagne and got into the front

seat of the Jeep, leaving the door open so they could get more of the night air, while carefully keeping the interior light turned off. After they'd finished one glassful, he poured another. "This is all I'm having," she said. "I've got to stay alert."

"I still don't see why you didn't hire somebody to do this. You really amaze me. If I hadn't seen it for myself I wouldn't believe you were really out here." He stared at her. She had tugged off one of her boots and had one heel braced on the seat, her thin fingers laced around her ankle, knee sharply bent.

"I don't know why you'd say that," she replied. "I can do just about anything I put my mind to."

"Oh, grow up, Katrina. Your life is like an old movie where everyone grovels at the feet of the princess."

"Why do you insist upon fighting?"

"Because I want you to see the world as it really is." The two of them had twisted around to face one another as their voices grew loud.

She threw her glass out into the night, as far as it would go, and started to yank her boot back on. "Do you honestly think I wanted all of this to happen to me?" she cried. "Do you believe I wanted to be caught up in some wild-assed cat-and-mouse game trying to hold off a step-uncle who's going for my jugular?"

After she put her boot back on she reached under the seat and grabbed her gun. "At thirty-two I should be able to grow, to have the time to get in touch with myself—finding out more about the real me I want to be. Do you think I want to be a game player all my life?" She slammed the Jeep door shut and stormed off toward the well. "If you think that," she yelled back, "then maybe you're the one who needs to grow up."

He sat where he was, his mind reeling with her accusation, then he jumped out and began to follow her. When she heard him coming, she began to run.

"Don't run with that damned gun, Katrina," he cried and then caught up with her, flinging both arms around her in an embrace meant to hold her completely still.

They were both breathing hard. Katrina was so angry she thought she might explode, but the touch of his body against hers sent an erotic thrill racing through her. Slowly, he bent down toward her, his breath fluttering uneasily against her face.

She felt the pressure of his mouth on hers and a glow suffused her. Both their heartbeats pounded together in a wild staccato beat. His mouth moved until it met gently with every curve of her own and she could feel her own lips, moist and pliant, responding to him.

Her mouth parted easily to allow his tongue entrance. For a long moment he explored the deep recesses hidden inside, then let his arms begin to move, to envelop her within his embrace. While the passion of their kisses intensified, Katrina savored the memory of that Saturday night so long ago, when Blair had shown her something very special. He'd shown her, Katrina Longoria McAllister, the disbeliever, that she could experience an easy, romantic, sexually exciting, laughing kind of love. The possibilities made her return his kiss with even greater desire than before.

He pulled away, letting his eyes travel to her lips, then he pressed her to him again, this time with barely controlled intensity. His hands moved, making her feel every part of his body from his rock-hard chest to the suggestive power of his thighs as he held her closer and closer.

For a split second Katrina had a vision of the two of them locked in a provocative embrace. As much as she knew she wanted it, she didn't know if she could handle it. From Blair, she now realized, she wanted everything—not just passion, but love. Without fanfare of any thought of regret, she let her emotional defenses begin to drift soundlessly away.

"Let's go back to the Jeep," he said, and she nodded.

But when they got back, Blair said, "I'll stand first watch," took the gun from her, quickly spun around, and left.

Angrily, she got into the Jeep. When she'd calmed down, she tried to sleep, reminding herself that Blair Warren was as complicated a man as she was a woman. But his kiss had told her that he could no more control his emotions than she could. He was fighting his passion, but he was losing the battle.

She slept, and in the stillness of the purple-and-blue-tinted early morning, awoke stiff. At the base of her skull she felt the beginning tingles of soreness where her head had rested too long against the armrest of the door.

"Are you awake?" Blair asked, looking in at her through the window.

Instantly alert, she nodded.

"Come on, then. I heard something coming down the road." He helped her out and led her behind low mesquite bushes two hundred feet from the oil well.

Now she could hear the sound herself. It was coming closer.

"Katrina, about last night," he said, his mouth so close to her ear she winced. "I was wrong."

227

She said nothing, but looked straight ahead and waited for the vehicle to approach.

During the silent, unfamiliar night Blair had had time to think about what she'd said. The fact that she'd hurt him, that he hadn't liked the way she did business—all the things he'd detested—seemed inconsequential when he was with her like this. He also realized that she was gradually changing, and told himself he couldn't make demands on her overnight. It was too soon.

"Look, Blair. There it is." They watched as a pickup drove slowly by, followed ten minutes later by a vacuum truck. "They've got a vacuum truck to suck the oil out of the gun barrel, and two-way radios in their vehicles." She watched Blair patiently write down the license number. "Take a good look at their faces."

"Let's follow them if we can, Katrina." They waited until the vacuum truck had removed the oil, then started up their Jeep before the truck moved. "By the way, where was your night watchman?"

Katrina drove the Jeep slowly down the road a long way behind the truck, trying not to stir up any dust. "I was given information about my old night watchman sleeping on the job, so he was fired. This new one obviously works for whoever owns that truck, and they probably lied about the old night watchman."

When the trucks drove up to a small refinery on the outskirts of Lubbock, Blair took down the name and address of the refiner. Within a few hours they found that the refinery was leased to her step-uncle and the truck and pickup were owned by the refinery. Blair called Andy and told him the story.

By the time they arrived back in Houston later that

evening, Andy promised he'd hire a team of investigators to follow up on the information. They planned to trace the relationship between the thefts and Katrina's step-uncle Albert. When they reported their findings to the railroad commission or the police, Katrina thought, victory would be hers.

Elated with their discovery and buoyed by what had happened between the two of them, Katrina had decided on the way home that it was time to pursue her relationship with Blair. She planned to wait until she and Blair got back to Houston and then confront him about his feelings for her.

Never before had she felt the need to try and please anyone, nor had she worried about another person's reaction to her, but now these things were paramount. The time she'd shared alone with him had cemented the feelings she'd been fighting since the one night of love they'd shared.

Buoyed by her discovery, Katrina felt as if the world were hers again. But hours later, when they stepped inside her cool, quiet mansion, she was unexpectedly struck by a twisted bolt of fear so severe that she was speechless. The importance of trying to win him over was enough to take the words away from her, because now she realized she couldn't bear to lose him.

She decided to stall for time. "Blair," she said, "I'll have one of the maids bring you a drink and I'll be right back down. I've just got to get some of the dust off." She led him into the study. "If the phone rings, you can answer it. It'll probably be Andy."

"Okay, I want to talk to him anyway."

Katrina dashed up the stairs, and told the maid to

prepare a rum and tonic for Mr. Warren and to tell the other servants to take the night off. Quickly, she got into the shower, trying to regain her confidence as she washed away the dust.

When she'd finished, she impulsively wrapped a long blue towel around her damp body and went downstairs, intent upon saying what was on her mind.

She opened the library doors and went in, not caring how she looked, only sure that having regained her nerve, she had to let him know how she felt. Yet the words refused to come out as she wanted. "Look, we've gotten off on the wrong foot and I regret that, I really do," she blurted out, too sharply. "I'd like to make amends. Come to my ranch this weekend, Blair, and we'll try again. Just the two of us. It's important that we—"

He stared at her, tight-mouthed, and she could sense that he wasn't with her at all. It was as if he had pulled away to some distant spot, some cold far-off place where she wasn't wanted.

Her heart shifted inside her chest and she became painfully aware of how ridiculous she looked—standing there dripping water on the Oriental rug. His eyes were full of a fierce intensity she didn't know he'd had as he looked her up and down before twisting his mouth into a sneer.

"Are you kidding?" he spat out. "Do I really look that stupid to you? I just helped you discover who'd been stealing you blind out of that refinery of yours, and you still think I'm dumb?"

He gave his head a violent twist and she could feel a rage welling all around them. Something had happened between them and the fury with which he looked at her made her afraid. In the past she'd had an idea of how she mishandled situations between them, but this time she didn't know what she'd done, only that something was desperately wrong. An unfamiliar dread tightened her stomach with cold, hard fear.

"Well, I've got news for you, your highness. You only get to kick me in the teeth once. I just answered your phone for you." He swung his head back toward the phone on the desk. "You never should have told me to answer it. It was your friend from Venezuela. He says he's sorry he couldn't accommodate you earlier, but he thinks he's found a man now. I guess he thought I was Andy." Blair's voice became increasingly harsh with each sentence he spat out. "I didn't tell him I wasn't. Didn't have time, actually. He was too busy telling me how he could help you out of your predicament."

"Blair, I—" she started to explain, but he spun around and knocked everything off the top of her desk except the telephone. It seemed to make the offending instrument grow larger.

"Why did you go behind my back? Trying to get a better deal? I'm a fast learner, Katrina, and I swear before all of Texas you've had your last shot at me." He grabbed up the receiver and shook it in his hand. His face was dark red and she could see the tendons in his neck standing out as he shouted. "When did you talk to him? Before we left for Lubbock?" He threw the receiver down hard on the desk. "Go find yourself another fool!"

Katrina was so stunned she couldn't move, but when he stalked out the door she ran after him. "Blair, wait!"

she cried. "Please, please let me explain!" But he kept walking as if he had not heard even her.

She ran out the front door and onto the steps, watching him as he got into her Jeep. "The games are over!" she screamed. "I love you, Blair Warren, and this time you're wrong! Give me the chance to explain!"

It didn't make the least bit of difference to Katrina that she was standing in the middle of exclusive River Oaks with only a towel draped around her naked body, shouting aloud to all the world her love for a man who was leaving her in a blur of dust. For once her pride had disappeared.

"I'm not going to lose you, Blair. I love you," she cried, knowing he couldn't hear her as he drove off. She prayed she'd have another chance to tell him.

"I love you, I love you," she cried out again. Katrina knew now that she wasn't going to lose him without giving it everything she had and already she was building up her courage. She raised one clenched fist toward the sky. "I love you."

In the still of the evening she promised herself she could face anything now, anything but losing him, and she vowed that would not happen. After all, she told herself with a feeling of strength in her heart, winning was her game.

CHAPTER THIRTEEN

As Blair floated in the hotel pool the next morning, he thought about his life. It had been over three months now since he'd come to Houston. He'd given up the management of his computer business and his close friends, and departed for a strange new life.

By now his vengeful rage had cooled somewhat and he was trying to look at the situation with Katrina more realistically. But realism was a slippery illusion when it came to dealing with a woman like her, he thought. She didn't fit any pattern. And as hurt and angry as he was, he still was unable to free himself from her haunting memory.

Feeling waterlogged, he turned over in the water and swam to the side of the pool. After spending the night pacing in his room, it was clear he couldn't spend the day floating in the swimming pool. Throwing his towel around his shoulders, he went back to his room and picked up the telephone.

"Andy," he said when the connection was made, "it's

Blair. I was wondering how you'd feel about having a weekend guest?"

Three hours later he stood beside his rented MG, breathing in the sweet smell of newly cut hay. "Thanks for having me," he yelled when Andy rode up on the noisiest tractor Blair had ever heard.

"You're always welcome here, boy. You've got a standing invitation." Andy turned off the engine and took off his straw hat before wiping a red bandanna across his forehead. "Of course, there's always work to be done too. This ain't anything like the McAllister place."

Blair looked out over the field of hay. "I hope you're right about that."

Eyeing him carefully, Andy stuck his bandanna into his jeans pocket and thrust his hat back on his head. "As bad as all that, huh, boy?"

Blair was leaning against the side of his car. He absentmindedly stood up and kicked the tires on the tractor. "Yeah," he said softly.

"Well, you've come to the right place." Andy spoke with a trace of mischievousness. "Strangers have been known to call this Uncle Andy's Ranch for Lost Boys. What you need is for me to give you enough work so your tongue will be hanging out of your mouth when suppertime comes, then a good home-cooked meal with real stick-to-your-ribs food and a little bourbon to make it all go down easy." He looked up from beneath his craggy brows. "I guarantee it works every time."

"How many times have you had to use this remedy on the men Katrina's mauled?" Blair found his sense of humor beginning to return and he hoisted himself up beside Andy on the tractor. "Give me a ride?"

"Ride, hell. I'm going to have you running this thing in another five minutes. We've got to bail all this hay before dark." He started up the tractor's noisy engine again. "In answer to your first question, my friend, the answer is none. As far as I know you're the first ever got this close. The first one who counts, anyway."

"I don't know whether I want to be counted or not," Blair called out over the chugging engine. "I feel like that rodeo cowboy you told me about who had all his bones broken trying to tame Brahma bulls."

Andy leaned his head back and let out a peal of loud laughter. "Just hold on, boy. You've almost got your ride won."

Blair merely stared out at the acres of hay swaying in the warm Texas wind. "We'll see," he replied unhappily. "Meanwhile, teach me how to drive a tractor."

By midnight Blair decided Andy's prescription was working. He'd taken over the tractor operation and they'd finished cutting and bailing the hay, then Andy's cook had fixed a huge platter of chicken-fried steak, mashed potatoes, gravy, and homemade biscuits. They'd been sipping bourbon all night long. After the first strong drink Blair had told Andy everything that had happened between himself and Katrina. He spared neither himself nor her, telling the entire story from beginning to end.

When he'd finished, the old man took a long drag on his cigar. They were sitting on Andy's back porch, each of them in an old creaking oak rocker with soft cushioned seats.

"I bet you've never hunted bobcats, have you?" Andy asked.

Blair laughed. "Never have." He took a drag on a cigar Andy had given him earlier, and sipped from his glass of bourbon.

"We used to have bobcats all over the state. Don't see many of them anymore. Not like we used to." Andy slowed his rocking chair down. "We'd go on hunts and track them down. If you've never seen one cornered maybe this won't mean much to you, but I'm here to tell you that those little rascals would try to chew through rock. Their freedom meant everything to them and they'd just about go crazy trying to get free." Andy lifted a crooked finger toward Blair. "Am I reaching you, boy? Am I telling you anything?"

Blair watched the man's eyes. "I think so," he finally answered.

"It bears thinking about." Andy stubbed out his cigar in an old chiseled shell he used for an ashtray. "Enough said. I'm going to bed. Breakfast is at six o'clock sharp." He started across the porch. "If you're interested in staying around KLM, I've got an idea I'll tell you about in the morning. Night."

Blair remained where he was, listening to the sounds of the occasional whippoorwill mix with the other unfamiliar ranch sounds. After reflection he realized that Katrina's desperation to save her oil company could have led her to do almost anything. Watching the way Andy had accepted what she'd done, even though he seemed surprised at some of the revelations, was enough to give Blair second thoughts. Andy loved Katrina and nothing she could do would ever change that. He loved her enough not to judge her.

Blair couldn't stop himself from recounting over and

over in his mind the times she'd disappointed him, as well as the times she'd hurt him deeply. His problem was that he was afraid, he thought. When it came right down to it, he was afraid of trusting her again. He didn't know if he wanted to hear her explanations. If he did, he thought, if he really let himself open up to her again and she flaunted her rejection of him in his face, he didn't know how he'd handle it.

But he was certain that he loved her. That was an absolute fact which was never going away, he told himself, no matter how much he tried to avoid dealing with it. Hand in hand with his love was the solid conviction that he could bring a new dimension to her life. Only his confusion and his fear stood in his way, he decided. The heartbreaking complexities of his life made him want to howl out loud with sheer frustration. He fell asleep in the rocker, the whippoorwill still calling out to him in the night.

The next morning Andy woke him up and told him breakfast was ready. He made no mention of the fact that Blair had never gone to bed. He just gave him a long look, laced with understanding. Over breakfast Andy asked, "Have you decided yet, boy? Is it going to be stay or go?"

Blair pushed away the plate of fried eggs and bacon. "I'm staying," he said.

"Then eat your breakfast and listen to my plan." Andy reached across the table and pushed Blair's plate back toward him. "You'll need nourishment."

In less time than it took Blair to finish his meal, Andy told him what he wanted to do. Katrina had wells spread out all over the state of Texas, and Andy had decided that if Blair was to be a partner in KLM, he should see every one of them. Andy was offering to go with him and show him what he knew about the oil business.

"You're on," Blair snapped before Andy was finished. "I'd like nothing better."

"We'd be gone about a week. Have to be back next Saturday night because Katrina says we're all invited to a big party her step-uncle's giving at his place. It's a command performance." Andy was pouring more coffee for both of them.

"What will Katrina say when we tell her we're going?"

"She won't say anything, boy. You two need a breather, anyway." Andy began to stack up the dirty dishes. "She's hoping that those private investigators we hired will have plenty of information for us by next Saturday. She wants to confront old Albert at his own party." Andy chuckled. "Isn't that just like her?"

Blair answered with a heavy sigh. "Yeah. The woman definitely has her own distinct style." Then he began to laugh. "You know, we could use Katrina's new Jeep for our trip. She said it belonged to the company and it's still sitting outside my hotel."

"The one you drove off in when you got so mad?" The thought seemed to amuse Andy. "Okay. Let's leave today, then. The first stop will be Corpus Christi. I want you to see what an offshore well site looks like."

Andy's enthusiasm was contagious. Blair was already planning ahead. "No, the first stop has to be back in Houston at my hotel. I have a portable computer I want

238

to take along with us. That way I can work on a few things as we go."

Blair stood up and stretched. Andy's plan was going to be a lifesaver. Now, Blair thought, he would have some time and distance away from Katrina, and Andy would be around to keep the clouds of depression from settling over him permanently.

For Katrina the week proved to be more difficult than she would have thought possible. The office staff had quickly become accustomed to consulting with Blair and using the information from his computer for everything from well production to reports due in to the state railroad commission. Now her office seemed oddly empty, not only because Blair was away, but because the hustle and bustle of the employees coming in and out stopped as soon as they were told he was gone. Already he'd trained two of the office staff to run identical computers, and so Katrina found herself going into their offices.

On Wednesday morning she couldn't stand it any longer. She swept into the office announcing to all within hearing distance that she wanted to learn how to operate the computer. Eager employees volunteered to teach her, and for two days and late nights Katrina stayed at the keyboard, finally admitting she was fascinated with what Blair had been able to do for the KLM operation.

Seeing their boss like this, having the chance to get to know her, the staff became more talkative. Before the week was out, it seemed that the entire mood of the office had changed. The formality was officially broken, and Katrina vowed she'd never let it return. She was enjoying these people for the first time.

But that was the only pleasure she could find, and that knowledge alone was like being on some solitary ocean voyage in a rowboat.

She had regained what she'd always professed was the only thing she cared about: daily reports coming into the office showed that KLM was back on its feet. Even Old Baldy was finally back producing oil, and making money in record time. All her adult life she'd sworn that a successful business was all she wanted, all she needed, but now the victory seemed hollow and lifeless. She'd been blind, she thought, in thinking only success could bring happiness. And she knew now that if she lost Blair, real happiness would always elude her.

By the time Saturday came Katrina was doubly nervous. She still hadn't heard from the private investigators, and while Andy had called her several times to tell her where they were, Blair had sent her no message. The only consolation she had was the fact that he was still in Texas.

But at five thirty on Saturday afternoon the private investigation team rang her doorbell, and within the hour she was clapping her hands with joy. She had her step-uncle right where she wanted him, and knew that soon she'd let him know it.

When Andy arrived at her house dressed in a white shirt and black tuxedo he claimed made him look like an ancient penguin, Katrina looked behind him, expecting Blair to be with him. But Andy saw her disappointed look and reassured her. "He didn't say he

wasn't coming. That's all I know. Right now he's probably meeting with the other investigators he hired after
we got to talking one night on our trip." A wry smile
crossed his lips. "Our computer wizard is learning fast,
Katrina. After hearing you and me talk about the decep-
tive practices of our fellow oilmen, he decided two
separate teams of investigators might come up with
twice as much information and at the same time be able
to check up on one another. I sure couldn't argue.
Anyway, he'll show up soon."

Forty-five minutes later, Katrina was furious and crest-
fallen at the same time. Blair hadn't shown up and she
was terribly afraid it was because he couldn't stand to
see her again. All the way to Albert's party Katrina
tried to reconcile herself to what she thought was
happening: Blair intended to be her business partner
but he'd decided to have nothing to do with her
personally, not even to be with her when she faced her
step-uncle.

When Katrina entered her step-uncle's home, she
stood inside the foyer, aware of the many stares she was
receiving. She took heart from it, reminding herself
that she'd stood alone for a very long time.

She brought her shoulders back and her head higher
and smiled at all those who studied her entrance. She
wore a tight-fitting black sheath of imported French
taffeta with one voluminous ruffle running along the
curve of her left shoulder and ending at the hem of the
gown in the back, the other shoulder bare. She also
wore a Bulgari collar necklace of diamonds and gold,
her hair pulled high atop her head in a cluster of
cascading raven curls, and carried a black beaded bag. No

one could have guessed that she'd dressed for a man who wasn't present—a man who obviously couldn't bear being near her, she thought.

When she let Andy lead her into the ballroom, the first people she saw were P.J. and Eileen Johnson. Out of the corner of her eye she saw her step-uncle coming toward her, and to avoid him she walked over to the couple. P. J. Johnson was known all over the world as the richest oilman in Texas, and he had a way about him which reminded her a little of her father.

"P.J., Eileen, it's good to see both of you. How have you been?" Katrina began to ask P.J.'s opinion of Exxon's giving up an oil venture in Japan, still aware of her step-uncle Albert hovering nearby like a hungry vulture about to attack.

She felt herself rising to the occasion, and was looking forward to taking Albert on. He was the one responsible for all the grief she'd suffered over the past two years, she thought, intending to repay him in full.

He came toward her. "Katrina, my dear niece, how beautiful you look tonight."

She could tell by the taunting way he looked down at her that he wasn't at all happy to see her. "Thank you," she said coolly. It struck her that since Blair wasn't coming, she might as well do what she came for. "I'd like to see you alone. Shall we say in your study in five minutes?" Giving him no time to respond, she abruptly turned and walked away.

Andy caught up with her. "I'm going to be there when you talk to Albert." He gave his starched white collar a quick tug.

"No, Andy, you're not. You've been with me through

thick and thin, but I won't have you go through this. It's too stressful." She took a glass of champagne from a passing waiter, and when she caught him staring admiringly at her, gave him a partial smile.

"Stressful, my butt. Don't you be telling me what's stressful for me." Andy shot one hand out and took two of the champagne glasses. "You're the one who's always giving me stress, missy." He gulped down and emptied both glasses. "That stuff tastes awful."

Katrina watched him, feeling a wave of love so strong it hurt deep inside her chest. She finished her drink and handed him the glass, waiting to see if he could balance all three glasses. "I said no, Andy, and I mean no."

She left Andy standing there, watching her go. One thing about Andy, she thought—he'd always respected her wishes. This time she hoped he stayed as predictable as in the past. When she came to the closed door of her step-uncle's study, she patted her beaded handbag and opened the door with a wide smile on her face, anxious to put him in his place.

"Dear Albert," she said when she saw him sitting behind his desk, waiting for her. The room was poorly lighted and his face was shadowed. "What's the matter? Don't you want anyone to know we're in here?" she asked coolly.

"What do you want, Katrina? Or have you forgotten I'm hosting a party." He gave her a brutal stare, then poured himself a shot of brandy.

"Yes, thank you. I'd like some too." She was mocking him and enjoying it.

"Serve yourself." His stare drilled into her.

"Very well." She poured a little brandy into a snifter from the crystal decanter on his desk. "My, my, you certainly have an impressive guest list tonight."

"What is it, Katrina? I haven't much time." His voice started out defiant and then slowed to almost a whine.

Katrina could tell that he was feeling more and more uncomfortable. After that day in the judge's chambers, she knew he wasn't as cocky as he'd once been. "I think you'll be interested in what I have to show you," she answered. Her face was full of strength, shining with the sheer joy of watching him begin to squirm.

"I doubt if you will have anything to show me that I'll find interesting." Albert's face was beginning to show the tension.

"Let's see, how about these first. You may have to put your glasses on to get a good look, dear Albert. I wanted to have the pictures blown up for you but they wouldn't fit inside my handbag." Katrina opened her purse and pulled out two pictures which she threw down on the desk in front of him.

Albert sat forward, his mouth slack. Then he recovered. "What are you showing me? A picture of a tanker and a pickup?"

"Your tanker and your pickup truck leaving my well site after stealing oil from my gun barrel. Don't worry, you can keep these. There are a lot more pictures detailing exactly what's been happening. Here's a good one of your hired help connecting the hose to the tanker. Can you see the name on my well clearly enough?" She gave him a brittle grin as he snapped the desk drawer open and took out a magnifying glass.

One by one she dropped pictures down upon the desk, until the top was covered with prints. She took her time, sipping the brandy, commenting on each picture as she went.

"Here's one of your son. He's standing inside your refinery gate waiting for the tanker to bring all the stolen oil to him. I didn't know he was following in his father's footsteps."

Katrina felt all the hate begin to drain out of her. Nothing could make up for what the man sitting in front of her had done to her, she realized. He'd brought something vile into her life and because of that she'd changed from a decent woman into a creature more like him. She only hoped it could be reversed, and now she realized that the only one who could reverse it was herself.

Suddenly, she wanted to tell him what she knew and then run as far away as possible. She'd had enough of the games and treachery to last a lifetime. "Okay. The railroad commission and the Lubbock sheriff's department have this same information. I might as well tell you the rest of it," she said resignedly. "I have—"

The study door was quietly opened and shut behind her. She turned to see Blair's stern face.

He walked toward her and stopped when he was standing beside her, their arms almost touching. "I'm Blair Warren, Katrina's partner. We haven't met." He kept his eyes on Albert Barnes.

Out of habit Albert started to stand and extend his hand. Katrina watched his face change when Blair impatiently waved him away, Albert's astonishment even more obvious than her own.

"Never mind. Where's your tape recorder?" The authority in Blair's voice chilled the room.

Nervously, Albert pointed to a cabinet door. Blair took something out of his tuxedo jacket pocket and threw it skidding across the desk.

"There's been a terrible mistake here," Albert stammered. "I don't know—"

"Save it. Play the tape whenever you want. It's a recording of a telephone conversation of the man you say witnessed Katrina's signing that agreement to share KLM with you." Blair put both arms stiffly down on the desk and leaned ominously toward a frightened Albert. "He's laughing about his deception. He's even telling someone how much you paid him. You picked a guy with a big mouth—too big."

"I can explain—" Albert tried to say, then stopped himself in mid-sentence. He lowered his head.

"If you don't drop your suit against Katrina by ten o'clock tomorrow morning, we will file a countersuit against you for whatever assets you have left when you get out of jail."

Blair took Katrina by the arm and they started to walk away. "One last thing," he said over his shoulder. "The sheriff's office is also looking into the disappearance of one of the night watchmen on that well. Now they're beginning to suspect foul play." He shrugged. "I'll let them tell you all about it." He led Katrina out the door of the study and into the crowded ballroom.

"Thanks," she said in a broken whisper.

Her mind burned with the memory of her first impression of Blair—an honest, honorable man. She looked up at him, her mouth curving into an unconscious

246

smile. He walked with her out onto the dance floor and took her into his arms.

"It was the least I could do. With your temper I was afraid you might kill him." He increased the pressure of his arm against the small of her back, bringing her up against his chest as he moved her around the room.

At first her mind was awhirl with a thousand thoughts, but the feel of his body touching hers was an electric shock that stilled everything else. Grateful she'd worn high heels, Katrina brought her forehead up to nestle against Blair's chest. "I'm not the only one with a temper. I've had the opportunity to see yours more than once."

He was light-footed, leading her with such fluid movements as they circled the dance floor that she felt others in the ballroom begin to watch them. Hoping the music would never end, she told herself to treasure his nearness, aware that only a few minutes before she'd thought the whole thing impossible. She refused to question it now, being right where she wanted to be.

"While you've been off on a tour of the state," she said, "I've been learning how to use the computer. You'll be surprised when you see how capable I've become. I can turn it on and off without any calamities," she teased.

The song ended but the band immediately began another slow dance tune. Smiling to herself, Katrina searched her mind for a way to make the moment last.

Blair stepped back and twirled her around in time with the music, his steps precise and skilled. As he moved her away and then back again, he studied her. "Aren't you going to argue with me about suing your step-uncle? I figured you'd want to countersue right away instead of giving him the chance I offered him."

She clenched her eyes shut. Blair must think her as nasty and cruel as Albert, she thought. "No, there's no need to kick a man when he's down."

Blair decided he'd say no more about Albert Barnes. "I like your dress," he whispered, lowering his head so that the top of her forehead rested against the hollow of his neck. They dipped and swayed with the music.

When he spoke, Katrina laughed and pulled her face away to look up into his eyes. He had the capacity to reduce her to girlish behavior that ordinarily would have made her cringe, she thought, but now she found she loved it. "This is the dress I was going to wear to the Joffrey Ballet, before you stopped me from going."

He gave her his crooked smile. "You could have gone if you'd been willing to fly commercial, and if you'd wanted to pay for the trip yourself."

Hastily, she moved her head back below his chin, enjoying the warmth and strength she found there. "Are you willing now to listen to my explanation about that phone call?"

Blair wanted to make some casually clever comment, but a knot rose up in his throat. What she'd have to say would be entirely too important for humor, he thought.

"The man you talked to was a dear friend of mine," Katrina began. She raised her head up and looked him squarely in the eye. "This is the truth." They stopped dancing. "When I came back from New York after you'd given me the conditions under which you'd loan me the thirty million dollars, I was desperate. I couldn't bear the thought of giving my soul away for money, and the way you defined the conditions it seemed that's exactly what I'd be doing, so I called Miguel."

Blair held her hand tightly. He was staring intently into her eyes, wanting to believe what he was hearing.

"Blair, I flew to Mexico City to meet Miguel and beg him to help me find someone to loan me the money. I told no one about my going, not even Andy." Her voice cracked, sounding even lower than before. "I didn't know what else to do. At the time he couldn't help me, but he promised to keep looking, then you came to Houston and . . . and things happened and it completely slipped my mind. I never gave Miguel another thought."

"Let's get out of this place. We can't talk here." Still holding her hand tightly, Blair started toward the door.

"Hello, Katrina." Lindee Bradley was standing inside the doorway.

Katrina gave Blair's hand a tug and stopped to greet her friend. If it had been anyone else she would have said hello and followed Blair's lead, but Lindee was with Brooks Griffin, the two of them with glowing smiles that were warm and secretive at the same time.

"Lindee, you look radiant." Katrina gave her a welcoming hug. "And Brooks, it's wonderful to see you again."

Brooks Griffin bent down and kissed Katrina on the cheek. He was still as dashing to look at as she remembered from a night long ago when they'd danced together at Lindee's party.

"Are congratulations in order?"

"For me, at least," Brooks joked. "I'm not so sure that

Lindee's gotten a good deal, but I have." He put his arm around his wife and looked adoringly at her.

Katrina gave them a dazzling smile and unconsciously ran her thumb along the top of Blair's hand. "I'm so happy for both of you. It must be wonderful." She glanced up at Blair. "I want you both to meet my partner, Blair Warren. And Blair, this is Lindee Bradley Griffin . . . is that what you're going to call yourself?"

Lindee nodded and Katrina went on: "And this is her husband, Brooks Griffin."

Brooks and Blair shook hands. Lindee said, "Your partner, Katrina?"

Katrina nodded. "KLM Oil is now jointly owned by Blair and myself."

"Does that mean—" Lindee started to ask.

"It means that Blair and I are involved in making KLM the biggest independently owned oil company in the world," she answered with a trace of nervousness and a laugh.

Katrina saw the look of excitement in Lindee's eyes and guessed what she was about to ask: Lindee knew how much KLM meant to Katrina and assumed Katrina would only take in a partner because of marriage. Not wanting Lindee to say as much, Katrina quickly turned to Blair. "By the way, I don't think I mentioned this to you but Lindee is the freshest face we've seen in Texas politics in a long time, and her husband has been offered a job with CBS News. When Lindee runs again, I'm definitely contributing to her campaign."

Blair smiled at Lindee, and Katrina watched him as if from a distance. He had, it seemed, an enormous capacity for caring. Never had she seen him treat anyone with indifference. People seemed drawn to him. Katrina squeezed his hand. She never wanted to let him go again.

"Well, I've told CBS that they'll have to wait awhile." Brooks spoke up. "I'm going to be Lindee's campaign manager this next time, and we're going to start our campaign late this month."

"It's so good to see you two again. We'll have a chance to be together later this week, won't we? Uli Carra called from New York and said she's dying to have one more photography session with the two of us."

Katrina wanted to talk to Lindee, but wanting to be alone with Blair, she said her good-byes and turned to him, ready for whatever came next.

"Shall I take you home?" he asked, unwilling to let the night end.

"Yes," she replied, taking his hand as they walked toward his car.

Blair watched how the moonlight fell across her face. Her features were arranged with such excellence, he thought, she was breathtaking. With her golden complexion and the deepest, dark round eyes he'd ever seen, Blair couldn't resist the surge of pride that he'd felt when they'd danced. It seemed to him that everyone's eyes had been on the two of them, but only because of Katrina.

Silently, they rode to her home in River Oaks. As they drew nearer, Katrina's heart began to race. How could she keep him here? she wondered. What could she say that would make a difference?

They stood outside the front door, heads bowed. After a long, painful silence, Blair asked, "Tell me,

Katrina, do you think that sometimes a business can do better for itself by having two collaborators instead of one?"

"Yes, I do," she answered, and for a second she was surprised at her own words. Before he'd come into her life, she'd never have believed it.

"I hear you rehired the old night watchman who was caught sleeping on the job a few months ago."

"Word travels fast, huh?"

"Well, I've talked to Maggie. She says things are changing around KLM. The grapevine also tells me you've promoted the informer this week."

"The informer?"

"You remember the cousin who told my secretary the secrets about your problems? You managed to find out who it was, didn't you?"

She broke into a smile. "Yeah, things are looking up for a lot of people," she said.

Blair began to run his finger up and down her arm, keeping his eyes on the line he was tracing. "You know, I never offered you or Andy any help on Old Baldy. I felt that once you got her pumping again you'd want to pay me off and absolve the partnership. It's in the contract, you know."

"I know." She nodded and looked into his eyes, biting down hard on her lip to keep from saying more.

"Katrina, Andy tells me the well's fixed. It's been fixed for a while. On our trip Andy and I figured out that if everything goes as scheduled, you'll be able to scrape forty million dollars together by the end of next month."

"I know," she repeated.

"Why haven't you said anything?" he asked in a half whisper. He let his fingers run along the bend of her hand and then laced his fingers into hers. "Are you going to try and settle up next month and get me out?"

"I never intended to do that." With her other hand she brushed against his tuxedo, wanting to embrace him, holding herself back. She shook her head slowly from side to side. "That's not right. At first I probably did, but not now, not for a very long time."

"Good, because I'm in for the long haul," Blair said, paying close attention to the way her hand ran along the edge of his jacket.

"For the money, you mean, or the excitement?"

He didn't answer her.

She slipped her hand inside his jacket, along his chest, around his ribs and to the curve of his back. "I'm in for the long haul, too, Blair. There's no turning back." She stepped toward him, tilting her face up toward his, her deep brown eyes full of the emotion she would no longer hide.

She felt him bend down and she reached to kiss him, feeling she couldn't and wouldn't hold herself back ever again. She pressed her lips to his with a gentle touch, until they grew warm, then languorously swept her tongue from one corner of his mouth to the other until she felt his body relax against hers. In one sweeping stroke he brought his arms around her and returned her kiss with his own insistent, demanding one. The fusion of their embrace felt like a torch on already hot metal.

Breathlessly, Katrina pulled back, her body quivering out of control. "Do you want to come in?"

"Do you want me to?" he asked, his calmness fading.

"You know what will happen if you do."

"Yes," he said softly.

"I want you to."

"Then invite me, welcome me, Katrina."

"Blair, please come inside. I want you."

CHAPTER FOURTEEN

The mood between them was explosive. His blood surged and whipped through his body until his insides felt like liquid mercury. Their hungry, searching kiss had brought back all the sensually romantic memories of their night together, and he felt a spurt of desire so strong he ached with it.

Trembling, they stepped back from one another. Blair reached down to take her in his arms and kiss her again, the angry words that had passed between them long gone. Now he was only aware of the desire that pulsed between them, pleading, demanding to be recognized.

He bent and kissed her slowly and gently. She closed her eyes, trying to match his gentle kiss with her own, but when his tongue pushed through her lips, she shivered and strained her body up to meet his.

When Katrina thought she might lose all restraint, she turned from Blair to unlock the front door, regarding him tenderly when she turned back.

Blair responded by scooping her up in his arms and carrying her into the house and up the winding staircase.

Caught up in passion, Katrina wound her arms around his shoulders, instinctively curling her body against his and resting her head against his arm.

They were both taking long, ragged breaths. When they reached the top of the stairs, Blair asked, "Which way?"

With her head she motioned to her bedroom. He quickly carried her inside, kicking the door closed with the back of his heel. He put her down, and without thinking, pulled her toward him and crushed his mouth against hers, Katrina responding with all her fervor.

His hands began to roam across her back and down across her hips, then he was driving her hips against his own when a crazy, tingling excitement she had known only once before—with him.

Then they stood breathlessly apart. Blair opened his mouth to speak but Katrina lifted her hand quickly and tenderly placed her fingers to his lips. Her voice was hoarse with pent-up passion. "No talking," she whispered, and with both hands began to remove his tuxedo jacket.

"Why?"

"Because as long as we don't talk, we don't hurt one another. Just for tonight, Blair, let's let ourselves be."

He moved his lips against her hair, her temples, and down across her cheeks to her mouth as she deftly removed his jacket and let it drop to the floor.

In tantalizingly slow motion Katrina undid the buttons of his shirt, Blair surrendering to her ministrations. Each time her fingers grazed his skin, he felt that spot come to life, sending urgent sensations to his brain. He helped her by taking off his shirt, then bit his lower lip down hard as she brought her mouth and tongue against his shoulder and moved it lightly across his chest.

With one hand he raised her chin, kissed her lips fleetingly, and gathered her in his arms. She laughed—a solid sound of pleasure—before easing away and reaching for his belt.

She raised her eyes to meet his and searched his face, wondering if he'd remember the night he'd spoken of his fantasy—he had wanted a woman to undress him. With every part of her being she longed to please him, to show him how much he meant to her, and the longing felt wonderful, filling her soul to bursting.

With an urgent movement Blair reached down to help her unfasten the reluctant button on his waistband, but she brushed his hands away, then bent her head down and began to softly kiss the tender flesh just above the belt line. Gently, she raised herself until his lips were on hers, a sigh breaking between them.

Her hands were tugging at his formal dress slacks, then easing his underwear down over his hips. When she felt him begin to lift his legs to free himself of the clothing, Katrina hurriedly reached down and pushed his shoes off each foot then pushed his socks down and away from him.

Next time, she silently promised, I'll be better, slower, more skilled, my darling.

When she straightened it was to feel his searching mouth reaching out for her, leaving an erotic trail of kisses across her hairline and around the curve of her neck behind her ear. With unsteady fingers he searched through her hair until he found each pin that held her curls clasped to the top of her head. One by one he pulled them easily away, firing her to madness with the heat of his breath against the shell of her ear, and the trace of cool moisture left by his tongue.

Blair brought his hands to both sides of her head and ran strong fingers through her hair, commanding it to fall down around her face, working as if his fingers were large combs, brushing, lifting until the hair was massed around her cheeks. His eyes studied the way it caught what little light there was in the room and reflected it back, the strands glowing as if they were precious. He drew in his breath hard, pushed her hair back so it tumbled down below her shoulders, and watched Katrina tilt her head to let it fall.

He kissed her neck then, finding her pulsebeat and holding his lips there until she felt his hands on her shoulders, exploring, like hot molten gold, as they dipped and turned, searching for a way to reach her.

Katrina's breath was coming in long, deep waves of shameless desire. With a single liberating movement she unfastened her gown at the side and twisted out of it. She wore nothing underneath, the two of them standing before one another, letting their eyes and their bodies speak of the desire burning between them in an unimaginably fierce storm. Even as she looked at him, Katrina felt each spot where his eyes settled on her.

Her nipples had become hard and rigid, and her body ached with desire. If his looking at her could carry her this far into the hypnotic world of sensation, Katrina thought, she could only dream what it would be like to be possessed by him.

"Beautiful Katrina," Blair murmured as he grasped

her small body and hugged her, momentarily forgetting that they would remain silent. He picked her up as if she were as light as air, and smiling gently down at her, carried her to the bed.

He grabbed at the spread and shoved it away, settling her down into an expanse of silver silk sheets. He watched how her body rested on them, like a magnificent jewel set atop sterling.

Katrina felt as if every part of her body was moving in quivering anticipation of fulfillment. He settled over her, bringing his mouth down to intimately explore each swell of her breast, allowing his tongue to dart quickly and purposefully across nipples which were already strained to bursting.

His hands began to roam freely, but the two of them had passed the point of readiness and now were caught up in the swirling vortex of smoldering passion, a place without a name, a no-man's land from which there was no return without satisfaction.

She brought her own shaking hands up to caress his buttocks and bring them toward her as he ran his fingers around the base of her stomach and into the soft inner flesh of her thigh. With one shuddering cry, Katrina grasped his shoulders and pulled him down to her, their hips lifting and swaying in desire. Then they were falling deeper and deeper into the vortex, until they reached release in a multitude of climactic spasms, Katrina's voice rising up and then falling as the last quiver left her body.

They lay side by side, waiting for their breathing to slow, drained but majestically alive, their bodies still singing as every nerve, every muscle reacted. At last

Blair reached over to gently caress her face, wanting to speak, but Katrina shushed him, turning her head toward his to kiss him gently.

When their blissful interlude had ended, Katrina wanted nothing more than to keep him there, but instinctively she sensed there were still resolutions to be worked out between them. Nothing would come easy between a woman like herself and a man like Blair, she thought, but there was no doubt in her mind now that every moment was worth it.

Katrina walked him to the door and watched him turn away from her, his expression a combination of tender thoughtfulness and confusion. It occurred to her that when they'd met Blair had been more confident in their relationship, and now she was the confident one. She knew precisely what she wanted and he was confused. It should have given her a sense of pleasure, she thought, but it didn't.

"Don't give up on me, Blair. I'm worth it," she cried out as he got into his car. "Really I am, and I love you so."

He stood there for a second before turning to look at her. Her head was inclined against one of the wooden porch columns. With her hair fanned to her shoulders and her face softened from the afterglow of their lovemaking, she looked more strikingly beautiful than he'd ever seen her. And vulnerable, he thought.

His heart went out to her, but the lump in his throat silenced him. He drove away watching her through the rearview mirror, the image of her vulnerability imprinted on his mind.

By declaring herself, Katrina had put matters squarely

into Blair's hands. Meanwhile, she vowed to bide her time. No matter how long it took, she told herself, no matter how hard the struggle, she'd find a way to prove her love for him.

Late on Sunday Blair had telephoned her, but the maid had told him Miss McAllister was entertaining a few friends for dinner. When Katrina was told of the call, she tried to reach him, to no avail. And by the time Monday morning rolled around, she was afraid he'd returned to New York. But he showed up at the office late Monday afternoon.

Uli Carra had flown in from New York with her makeup men and her cameras, ready to photograph Katrina and Lindee in their home state. Uli arrived at Katrina's office in a frantic huff, three hours late. She wanted a few shots of the young oil executive at work.

Just as they were setting up the powerful lights, Blair came in to find his computers had been moved out and Katrina's office restored to the same formal look he'd seen the first day he'd entered the office building. Because he'd planned to walk into the office and find her alone, waiting there for him, the activity irritated him.

"Oh, Blair, I want you to meet Uli Carra," Katrina exclaimed when he entered. She was wearing more makeup than usual, and was dressed in a checked wool suit with a cape.

"Aren't you hot?" he asked. It was ninety-eight degrees outside.

"This is a fashion layout for the fall," Katrina explained, looking down at her Christian Doir suit. "Uli, this is Blair Warren, my partner. Why don't you take his picture with me?"

"How do you do, sir." Uli Carra gave him a perfunctory handshake and then screamed at the man arranging the lights. With a burst of expletives, she bounced over to change the lighting herself.

"I'm so glad to see you, Blair," Katrina told him.

He thought he noticed a certain spark in Katrina's eyes as she spoke. "The room looks different without your things," she was saying. "We'll have them replaced in just a little while. Uli wanted it this way for her camera shots." Katrina stood on tiptoes and lightly kissed his cheek. "I have a present for you. It's on top of your computer screen in the other office.

He smiled wanly. "I don't need a present, Katrina."

"Here, here," Uli interrupted. "I need Katrina to move right over here, behind her desk." She eyed Blair. "Maybe I will want you in a moment. I will see how this shot goes first."

He moved aside as Uli posed Katrina behind her desk, capturing a shot of the downtown Houston skyscraper behind her, her head lifted high in a regal-princess pose. Blair watched her as she visibly grew before the cameras, and thought her the most independent, baffling, intriguing woman he'd ever known.

The question ripped through him again, the same one that had been tearing his guts to shreds since she'd said she loved him: Could they possibly make a life together? Could two strong individuals use love to develop a lifetime of sharing, of loving give and take, or would each of them fight to control the other?

"Now then, Mr. Warren," Uli was saying. "Mr. Warren, can you hear me?" Her shrill voice broke through to him. "Miss McAllister wants you to have your photograph taken with her, so will you stand right beside her, please?"

Blair stood stock-still. He wasn't sure he wanted to do it.

"Please, Blair, humor me," Katrina pleaded. "I want a picture of the two of us together."

He walked over to where Uli commanded, unable to deny Katrina what she wanted. When he was standing beside her chair, she reached up and threaded her hand into his.

"Like this, Uli. I want you to take the picture like this."

"No, no, no. I am the photographer," Uli argued with a vehemence Katrina had forgotten she had.

"Now Uli, this is a picture you're taking as a favor to me." She grinned playfully. "Won't you please humor me too?" Katrina started to laugh. "Come on, Uli, look into your lens. I'll bet it'll make a wonderful picture."

Shrugging her shoulders elaborately, Uli gave in. In a moment she looked up at Katrina. "I know now how you got so rich, my dear. Is it possible you can charm anyone?" she asked in her heavy foreign accent.

"I'm not sure, Uli," Katrina answered solemnly, tightening her grip on Blair's fingers. "I'm certainly trying."

His hands felt warm where her small fingers lay meshed with his, and he looked down to see her face turned toward him, her bright red mouth opened in a trusting smile. He smiled back at her.

For thirty-five years, Blair thought, he had remained emotionally untouched by a woman, never feeling that he was truly in love. Now, because of Katrina, he realized he had the capacity to love, and because of it he feared what might happen.

Katrina Longoria McAllister was unlike any other woman he'd known. In his lifetime he'd probably never again meet another woman like her. Because he knew how much he stood to gain or lose, he felt himself in an unexplainable state bordering on insanity. If he and Katrina could settle things between them, he thought, his agitation would go away.

Tied up with the photographer from *Town and Country*, Katrina seemed unaware of his distress. She acted as though their problems would resolve themselves. Only every now and then, when he noticed her glancing at him with a faintly speculative look, did he wonder if she might have some idea of what he was going through. It was a torture unlike anything he'd ever known.

When the picture-taking was finished, Blair was ready to leave. "Be sure you go and see what I left for you," Katrina said, feeling an unexpected air of tension between them.

Silently, Blair left, heading toward the empty office where his computer equipment had been temporarily stored. When he opened the door he saw the package atop his computer terminal. It was a small box wrapped in gold foil paper, and he knew without looking that whatever it was, it would be an expensive gift.

Quickly, he opened the box. There was a fourteen-karat gold Corum watch inside, turned upside down so he wouldn't miss the inscription.

"To Blair," it read. "The man I love."

His hands shook as he took his old watch off and put

264

the new one on his wrist. Meanwhile, he looked nervously around the room, trying to gather his thoughts. The power of her inscription had jumbled his brain. Out of the corner of his eye he noticed that the computer monitor was turned on, and he bent down to read what was written on the screen.

Dear Blair, I wanted you to have this watch so that you'll always know the correct time. Each time you look at it I hope you'll remember how very much I love you. Katrina.

He let his body collapse into the office chair and stared at the terminal. What was he going to do? he wondered. He loved her more than he'd dreamed possible, but he felt that he needed time—time away from her to think. He had to be completely certain they could be happy together. Anything less would be a tragedy he would not accept.

Katrina seemed to be such a majestically powerful woman, so all-consuming, Blair was sure that their lives could blend in harmony. The rock-hard confidence he'd felt when he'd first become infatuated with her had been shaken by what had occurred since, and he found himself shaky right now. She meant too much to him to lose, he thought, yet he was his own man, now and always. That wouldn't change. He didn't want to have them grow to despise one another a few years down the road.

Each of them had been able to create their own world through the power and force of their personalities, and to combine their worlds into one might be an impossibility. He was certain he loved her enough to handle it, but was less sure that she'd thought out all of the consequences a union between them would entail.

Could they redesign their worlds to suit one another? he wondered. He could not bear to hurt her, nor was he willing to commit himself to a relationship in which the two of them were not able to share themselves, their love, and their power. They had the possibility to share a lifetime together which could not be rivaled, but unless they were equally committed, he thought, they might destroy it from within.

He loved her. She loved him. Was that enough for them? he asked himself. He concluded he had to get away to decide.

Reluctantly, Blair turned when he heard her open the door behind him. Her face had lost its glow, and he wondered if she was perceptive enough to have guessed what he was leading up to.

"Katrina," he said softly.

"Yes?"

"Katrina—" he said again, then stopped.

She tried to keep herself under control. She was afraid she might cry and the feeling was so unusual she didn't know if she could manage to suppress it. His mood frightened her, and yet in one corner of her mind she was aware that no one before him had ever made her aware of her feelings like he had.

"I'm going to fly back to New York on the six o'clock plane."

His words hung between them, flat, final.

"Wear your watch," she said at last, her deep, throaty voice strained under the pressure she was feeling.

He nodded and tried to smile, but couldn't.

With a spiritedness she wasn't feeling, Katrina asked, "Do you play poker, Blair?"

"No, why?"

"Because we're playing a big hand, you and I, and I've decided to bet on myself."

She longed to ask him when he'd come back, or if he'd come back, but she held herself in check. Words were useless between them now, she thought. She had to let him go. With one last look of heartfelt longing, Katrina turned and walked out of the room, pulling the door closed behind her. She couldn't bear to have him see the hot, salty tears falling across her cheeks.

CHAPTER FIFTEEN

The plane landed in New York forty-five minutes later than scheduled, a common happening for a city whose skies were becoming as overcrowded as its land. As the airplane circled, Blair thought for the first time about where he would go. His apartment was sold, his furniture scattered—either stored in Houston or sold to the new owners—and he had no place to call his own.

When a cabdriver asked him where he was headed, Blair hesitated and then asked to be taken to the Plaza. If he couldn't get a room there, he knew there were other hotels in the area. He'd keep trying until he found one. It didn't make much difference where he stayed, he thought, only the getting-away mattered.

The drive into the heart of the city took less time than usual because traffic was light. Idly looking out the window, watching the way the city looked at night, Blair couldn't help but think about how much he'd always loved the place. New York was a city where the winners came, he thought, those wanting to be and those who already were. But now that Katrina had introduced him to Houston, he knew there was another city he loved as much, a sprawling city where the humidity was so bad he could cut it with a knife but where there was still a feeling of new horizons to be conquered.

It wasn't until later that night, when he had found a room in the hotel and stood staring out at Central Park, that Blair realized his coming back to New York had been impetuous. No matter how much distance he tried to put between the two of them, Katrina was now a part of him and always would be.

There was nothing he wanted more than to get back on the airplane and rush to her side, the woman made of fire and steel and beauty. But he couldn't yet. He'd declared his need for solitude and he wouldn't go back to her until he was absolutely certain that he could be all she deserved.

"Lindee, I'm glad you and Brooks agreed to ride to the ranch with me. Uli and her crew will be helicopter-ing out in the morning." Katrina and Lindee were in Katrina's Jeep, headed out of Houston toward the KLM ranch and Old Baldy. James was driving the limousine following closely behind them, with Brooks in the backseat making some important phone calls on Katrina's mobile telephone.

"I am, too, Katrina," Lindee replied. "This may be the last chance we have to see each other for a long time. Brooks has our days already plotted out for this next campaign." Lindee looked back over her shoulder at the car behind them. "He's so determined we're going to win this time."

"And you will." Katrina nodded sagely. "You will."

"What about you? What are you going to be doing now? Are you going to meet Blair in New York?"

Katrina's life had become a waiting game. When Blair had left so suddenly, Katrina had explained his absence as a New York business trip. She wasn't ready to talk about what was happening because she wasn't sure herself.

"No, I'm going to stay at the ranch for a few days and then I'll probably go down to Corpus Christi to be near that new offshore well."

"And Blair? When will he be back?"

"I'm not sure of that, either," she answered honestly.

"Katrina, is something wrong between you two? With the business?" Lindee's voice was full of concern.

Tightening her hands on the wheel, Katrina glanced at Lindee and then back to the highway. She admired Lindee more and more each time she saw her, and their friendship was growing, but Katrina wasn't the sort of woman who spoke easily about her personal feelings.

"Why would you think anything's wrong?" she replied, and gave Lindee an odd laugh.

Lindee's answer came readily. "You seem so preoccupied, for one thing."

"It's nothing, really, Katrina replied. "Tell me about yourself. You haven't even told me where you and Brooks are living."

"Okay, if you don't want to talk about Blair, we won't. Believe me, I understand."

"Thanks."

"I understand how it is when you're falling in love."

270

Katrina frowned, uneasy. She didn't say anything.

"I have a feeling you and I are a little bit alike, Katrina. I didn't want to fall in love, either. In the end I didn't have a choice in the matter."

"Did it frighten you?"

Lindee smiled and leaned toward Katrina. "I was scared to death." She laughed. "I'd always been in control before."

Katrina's head bobbed up and down in complete agreement with what Lindee was saying. "Yes," she said softly.

"In a way, though, I think it makes it all better. If you can live through it, that is. I mean, once I recognized the fact that I loved him, I knew that it would be forever, no matter what."

A bounty of memories filled Katrina's mind. Indeed, she could admit she loved Blair. At this point hiding her feelings made no sense.

"Then you know what I'm going through," she said quickly. "I love him, but I'm not so sure that he loves me."

"Well then, go after him," Lindee demanded. "Go after him."

"I wish it were all that simple." She let out a deep, resounding sigh. "He needs time, and I suppose I do too. That's why I want to go to the ranch and think things out." She smiled, then reached out for Lindee's hand, giving it a conspiratorial pat. "Don't worry, Lindee. I'm not a quitter."

"I know," Lindee replied. "Neither one of us is."

*   *   *

The streets of New York were overflowing with a parade of color and characters who lived out their fantasies in the open. Blair took to pacing the streets, seeing things, going places he'd never been before. Ready to try anything to keep himself away from the telephone or the airport, he roamed the city for two days.

Once, on the second day of his self-imposed exile, he'd stopped at a phone booth and held the receiver in his hand until he became aware of a derelict watching him from the shadows of an alleyway. Blair didn't know how long he stood, clicked the receiver down, then lifted a hand to dial, only to repeat the cycle again and again, but the curious look the man gave him said it had been too long. Finally, he took his hand off the instrument and hurried away.

His exile was proving more difficult than he'd ever dreamed. Over and over again he talked to himself about Katrina. She was a strong-willed woman with a bounty of talents and gifts to offer a man, he thought. In Katrina he saw excitement and joy, challenge and pleasure.

On the other hand, Katrina lacked the ability to express the gentleness Blair knew existed just below the surface. Andy had alluded to it, and Blair had noticed it the first time he met her. Would she let him bring out that trait in her? he wondered. Would she let him help her to become more complete? If he could somehow reach her, if she would meet him halfway, Blair was certain that between them they could create a lifetime of loving. If she loved him as much as he loved her, he thought, the two of them could enhance one another's strengths. But did she? With all his heart and soul, Blair wished he knew.

Katrina found that the passing days did nothing to ease her pain. After Uli and her camera crew had left and Lindee and Brooks had been driven back to Houston by James, the sprawling ranch house seemed more like a silent tomb than the refuge she'd always known it to be.

Toward the end of the week she called her office. "Hi, Maggie, it's Katrina. How's everything going?"

She knew it was silly, but she couldn't help but hope that Maggie would reply that Blair had returned. When she didn't mention him, Katrina plunged in. "Have you heard from Blair?"

"Sure have," Maggie said. "He called early this morning. You two must be on the same wavelength. He wanted to know where you were."

Katrina's heart began to pound so hard her chest ached. "He did? What did he say?"

Again it struck her how infantile she sounded, but she didn't care. She wanted to know every word he'd spoken to Maggie.

"He said that he's staying at the Plaza in New York if I needed to get in touch with him. He told me where the stats were on the Luling chalk wells. Let's see . . ." Maggie droned on.

"What did he ask about me, Maggie?" Katrina demanded.

"He asked where you were, and I told him."

"Did he ask when I'd be back in town?"

"No, that's all he said about you."

"Did he say anything about when he might return?" Katrina was begging for any scrap of information.

"No, just told me to call him if I needed him. That's about it."

"Okay, then. Thanks, Maggie. Sorry." She cradled the telephone in her hand for a long time, holding her eyes tightly shut to fight back the tears stinging beneath her lids.

She loved Blair and had made up her mind to fight for him, yet she didn't know how. The irony of her indecisiveness didn't escape her. Here she was, normally the most decisive of women, completely uncertain as to what she should do next.

Unfortunately, Katrina now knew a fear greater than any she'd experienced before—the fear that she might not be able to have the only thing she wanted. Hindsight told her she'd spent too much time learning how to play games when she should have spent it learning the rules of love.

She picked up the telephone again and called Western Union. Her message was short, but she prayed it would be effective. For the rest of the day she rode her horse over the ranch and around Old Baldy, watching the rhythmic pumping of the well, racking her brain to determine some sort of course which she could follow to win the man she loved.

After having a late lunch at a sidewalk café in Greenwich Village with the new president of his computer company, Blair returned to his hotel. When the desk clerk handed him the telegram, Blair walked over to the window and with shaky fingers opened it. He read slowly then leaned his head against the cool glass, unmindful of the odd stares he was getting inside the plush hotel. He read it again, and then again, and finally began to laugh aloud. He hurried toward the elevators still chuckling to himself.

Upstairs in his hotel room Blair read the telegram once more while he waited for the airlines to confirm his reservation. "I'm worth it," the telegram read. "Never will you find another women who will love you like I do. Katrina."

Her bold message provided the final condensation of all his thoughts. It crystallized them, made them solid. He was now certain that they had something to give each other. Together they were special. The parts could never be as great as the whole.

Life with any other woman would become a daily existence characterized by an unrelenting sameness, Blair thought. For him, the idea was repellent. But with Katrina his life would be one of almost unimaginable excitement. She would breathe new energy into each day, each moment. No two hours would be the same.

More than anything else in the world, he wanted the kind of life she could show him. More than anything else, he wanted her.

Yet in order for a relationship to bring lifelong happiness, it would have to be an equal one between them. They were two distinct individuals who could not sustain the deep kind of love he knew they were capable of without equality. Theirs could never be a union in which one of them loved the other more.

On the plane to Houston he was driven by a vision

that had possessed him since they first met—the two of them bound timelessly together. A smile shaped the corners of his mouth. He was going home, he thought, where he belonged, where she wanted him to be.

When they were fastening their seat belts for the descent, an attractive stewardess struck up a conversation with him, but he distractedly abandoned the conversation and closed his eyes. He was heading toward reality, he thought, and it felt good. His reality was Katrina Longoria McAllister, the only woman who could make his life complete, the woman who would turn every moment into an adventure, the only woman he could ever love.

It was almost dark when he finally found her ranch. It seemed he'd driven over the same gravel roads for two hours, stopping for directions at every farmhouse before becoming assured that KLM was just ahead. When he reached it, a strange peacefulness came over him. He sat inside his rental car, looking at the white cross-timber fences which seemed to travel as far as the horizon. Over the gate hung a huge red-and-white sign with the KLM initials spread from one end to the other and on each side of the gate hung two old wagon wheels with a bleached cow skull mounted between them. The road leading to the ranch buildings was smoothly paved and lined with thick-trunked oak trees on either side.

He drove inside, toward the house, mindful of how the setting sun sent a wave of orange streamers spreading across the sky, feeling as if he'd stepped into an altogether different part of the world. Being at Andy's ranch hadn't begun to prepare him for the enormity of the KLM. As he neared the ranch house—a long, low building with a porch running its full length—he forgot about where he was and thought only of being at Katrina's side.

Saddling up her horse for an early evening ride, Katrina heard a car approaching the house. Not until he stepped out did she realize it was Blair. Suddenly, her heart seemed to jam flush against her throat. Holding her breath, she walked to meet him.

For one foolish, silly instant she was sorry she hadn't thought about his coming to her ranch. She pictured herself carefully arranging vases and vases of fresh summer flowers inside the house, choosing her clothing with extreme care, and lavishing attention on herself— her hair, her makeup, her nails. Instead, he'd found her like this—no makeup, hair pulled back and plaited in a dark braid, clothes already sweat-stained from a day's work.

Her hands fluttered to her hair, brushing it back. "Hello, Blair," she said with a confidence she didn't at all feel.

The sound of her huskily warm voice embraced him and he smiled, his eyes focused intently on her, searching for some singular sign of welcome. He reached out for her hand. "Don't touch your hair. Leave it the way it is."

She felt the stray wisps fall back down across her cheek.

"You look more beautiful than I've ever seen you before."

"I'm glad you came."

They stood staring at one another, their hands clasped

tightly together. Katrina was overcome by a preposterous shyness, dropping her eyes to the ground.

Blair cleared his throat. "Where to start?"

"I don't know what you've come to say," Katrina began, her voice shaky with emotion. "But whatever it is, I want you to hear me out first. You're the one who's given me all those speeches about honesty and caring." She laughed softly, still shaking. "And now it's you, Blair. You can't bring yourself to trust me. I can understand why. I don't like it but I understand, and I've been working on making some changes in myself." She paused. "So it seems the dilemma is yours. I'm ready to show you how caring I can be. I'm ready for you to test my honesty." She reached out for his other hand. "I'm ready to take you anyway I can get you. It's up to you to decide what happens next."

He felt a burning in his throat. He hesitated, regarding her quietly for a moment. "I love you. Whatever is said between the two of us from this point on, whatever takes place, I love you. Do you believe me?"

His amber eyes met hers and for what seemed an impossible time they looked at one another. They were so absorbed, neither one was aware of anything but each other as they stood silhouetted against the Texas sky.

"Yes," she answered softly. "I believe you."

A shyness had grown between them and they couldn't break through it. Both of them were struck by an explosion of emotions they'd previously kept locked away from one another.

"I was going riding," Katrina finally said. "Would you like to go with me?" She pointed to her horse.

"I'd love it," he replied, picturing a change in scenery and grateful for it. He was tongue-tied, happy to be near her, but lost in a sea of words that would not come forward.

One of the ranch hands quickly saddled a horse for him, and in a few minutes they were riding out over the land, the sun slowly setting behind their backs. Katrina rode with an ease Blair admired.

"I hope you'll teach me how to ride like you someday," he said.

"Lesson number one is to just pretend you're floating." She laughed. "You see," she said softly, "our someday is already here." She had turned sideways in her saddle, so that she faced him. "Do you want to see Old Baldy, the root of the McAllister fortune?"

Blair nodded, keeping his horse close to hers. Riding out across the ranch, he was reminded of a painting he'd seen in which nature painted its own canvas of perfect white floating clouds in a sky vivid with the bright colors accompanying the fading sun. He sighed softly, feeling as though he'd at last come home.

"Katrina, do you know why I left?" he asked.

"I'm not sure," she answered, patting her horse's neck. "I think I frightened you somehow when I told you I loved you."

He watched her, aware of the penetrating depth of his own emotions. "True, I was afraid, Katrina . . . afraid we might not be able to have a relationship without a struggle for domination. Our marriage would have to be full of give and take, sharing, loving one another so much that we'd vow not to let one personality override the other. I'd rather live without you than have us enter into a marriage where we can't meet halfway. I love you that much." He swallowed. "It wouldn't be easy."

They approached the oil well from the north. He could hear it pumping before he saw it over a low hill. Twenty feet away from the well's base was an ambling creek, surrounded by trees. He thought it looked like a sanctuary.

"I never thought it would be easy, Blair," Katrina replied. "Maybe for two other people it would be, but not for us. Yet don't you see, that's why we're so drawn to one another."

She suddenly longed to feel his arms around her as they talked. It seemed if they held one another close, everything would be all right. Katrina urged her horse into a gallop. "I love you!" she shouted back at him. "Isn't that enough?"

He followed and when he caught up to her at the well site, tied his horse next to hers, next to a stream. "So this is Old Baldy?" he said after dismounting. He turned around, surveying the area, until he'd completed a circle. "This entire place is unbelievable."

"Thank you," she said quickly, immensely pleased to see he loved the place, but brimming over with the desire to settle things between them.

"Did you hear me?" she asked. "I said I love you. Isn't that enough?"

"I heard you, but I'm still not sure it's enough. You're going to have to understand that there'll be no controlling from either one of us." He shook his head, looking around once again, until his gaze came to rest on the oil well. "Katrina, are you willing to share control of all that you have here?"

Keeping her eyes steady she said simply, "Yes."

"We'd have to be equals . . . no domination. . . ."

She walked up to him and put her arm around his waist. "Is that all you're worried about, you big fool? Do you honestly think I haven't thought about all these problems and more?" She laughed, tightening her arm around him. "I love you, Blair Warren, like I've never loved before and never will again, and I'll do anything to keep our love alive. Anything."

He hugged her to him, feeling the warm contours of her body, conscious of how he ached to hold her forever. "Somehow with your vibrancy, you knock away all my logic, all the practicality I've built up over a lifetime."

"That's why we're going to be so wonderful together," she said. "We're a team." She pulled him along with her toward the stream's edge. "Sit here. It's my favorite spot to watch the sun go down."

"For whatever it's worth, I love you, Katrina. I've never known such love in my life."

"What about the barriers, then? I've crossed over them. Can you?" She kept her body close to his. His nearness was more vital to her right now, she thought, than any caress.

"I figured you'd be angry at my leaving," he said. "I think I would have been if I were you."

Her dark brown eyes never flickered as they focused on his face. She brought her hand up to run smooth fingers across his lips. "By the time you left I was committed. One thing about us McAllisters is that we're capable of unbridled allegiances. When I fell in love with you, Blair, I gave you mine."

She felt his lips begin to work their way over the rim of her fingertips, taking them inside his mouth. Instantly, her breathing became erratic.

She turned her body toward his. "Once I make up my mind, I'm a very headstrong woman. I wasn't about to give up on you. I never will." Her eyes caught and held him, enchanting him. "I'm just happy you came back to me."

"Oh, God, you make me so happy I'm crazy." Blair laughed resoundingly, and shook his head. "I'm love-struck," he went on, fighting back a burning sensation that tore at his eyes. He wrapped his arms around her. "I love you, Katrina Longoria McAllister. I'm going to make you happy for the rest of your life."

Her fingers still rested near his mouth. He reached up for her hand and brought his lips down to kiss her trembling palm. "What would it be like if we lived together?" she asked.

"If? You mean when," he said, drawing away only to hug her close to him again. "Hellfire and skyrockets. Is that what you mean?"

She nodded, tilting her head to kiss the line of his chin. "Yes. It sounds wonderful, doesn't it?"

"It will be wonderful when we're married—with all the hellfire, all the skyrockets, all the love the two of us can give to one another, with nothing to stand in our way."

He held her in his arms, a peaceful quiet enveloping them. It was as if all his life had led to this moment, he thought, as if he'd found his purpose for being. He settled his chin against the crown of her head, breathing in the rich fragrance of her hair.

The moon rose over Old Baldy, and the sound of the well pumping kept up a steady, squeaking beat. Every now and then one of the horses would move, tapping out an additional melody as metal horseshoes met rocks.

His voice washed over her, filled with a longing her body responded to immediately. "I want to make love to the woman who's going to be my wife and make the cover of *Town and Country* magazine all in the same month." His voice quickened. "That part I want right now."

Katrina turned toward him, her eyes full of the love and adoration she felt she would spend a lifetime nurturing. They shared one long, hungry kiss, then he bent his head and brought his lips to the softest spots along her chest and neck.

She gently shrugged out of his embrace and began to undress, and Blair followed her example. "Andy's right, you know," she told him as they stepped out of their clothes.

"About what?" He leaned over and tenderly brushed his lips across hers, his passion intermingled with his happiness.

"About Old Baldy. My father should have named it Aces High."

They turned to look at the well standing imperviously alone in the reflected light of a pale round moon. Taking her in his arms, Blair leaned his head down and brushed his lips back and forth across hers with the gentlest of caresses before finally sweeping her, weightless, into his arms.

Knowing she never again intended to be away from this man, Katrina held his face with her hand and raised her head so that her mouth was once more touching his in eager anticipation. A warmth spread through her, an overwhelming sense of security and peace as together they prepared to greet their loving future.

CANDLELIGHT Ecstasy Supreme